D0120354

Also by Paul Pickering

Wild About Harry
Perfect English
The Blue Gate of Babylon
Charlie Peace
The Leopard's Wife

Over the Rainbow

PAUL PICKERING

SIMON &
SCHUSTER

London · New York · Sydney · Toronto · New Delhi

A CBS COMPANY

First published in Great Britain by Simon & Schuster UK Ltd, 2012
A CBS Company

1 3 5 7 9 10 8 6 4 2

Simon & Schuster UK Ltd
1st Floor
222 Gray's Inn Road
London WC1X 8HB

www.simonandschuster.co.uk

Simon & Schuster Australia, Sydney

Simon & Schuster India, New Delhi

A CIP catalogue record for this book is available from the British Library

Hardback ISBN 978-1-84737-829-3
Trade Paperback ISBN 978-0-85720-591-9

Typeset by Hewer Text UK Ltd, Edinburgh
Printed and bound by CPI Group (UK) Ltd, Croydon CRO 4YY

Over the Rainbow

ACKNOWLEDGEMENTS

I would like to thank my donkey man and my donkey, for being very cheerful and steady under fire, but who wish to remain anonymous; the Taliban, for letting us go; Andrew Kidd, for his peerless understanding of this and all novels; David and Angharad James, Mike Jones, Sally Riley, Imogen Pelham, Lesley Thorne, Leah Middleton, Mary Tomlinson, Clare Hey, Sue Stephens; Rory Stewart MP for his brilliant advice on staying alive; Will Beharrell, Shoshana Coburn, Shireen Pasha and everyone at Turquoise Mountain; Ralph Humphrey and Bob Schaus in Afghanistan; Zia, Unver, 'The Doc', Omar and Clare Shafikhan in Karachi and London, and the excellent Sindh Club; Paul Ross of the IMF in Islamabad; Nadja and Jelena Poderegin, Sarah Hochman, David Rosenthal, George Thwaites, Peter Wright, Anthony Levene, Tim Page, Kathleen Wyatt; The Royal Geographical Society; Persephone and Alice Pickering; and the magnificent people of Afghanistan, who showed me hospitality and kindness at my every step.

Nothing is as real as nothing.
Beckett, *Malone Dies*

For Alice and Persephone

ONE

And so it is written.

'I'm afraid you cannot buy a drink, Monsieur . . . I'm afraid you cannot buy a drink in this club unless you're dead. That's the rule. That's the rule, and we keep to the rules. Where is a club without rules? This is Afghanistan, Monsieur!'

'I've come about a goose,' said Malone standing at the outdoor bar. Through the open French doors of a white colonial villa, billiard balls snapped together like breaking bones under the slow ceiling fans and walls hung with hunting trophies.

The barman, who was polishing a glass, shrugged, sighed and leaned forward. 'I don't care the fuck what you do for work or pleasure, Monsieur. But you cannot buy a drink here unless you are dead. I think perhaps you do not belong? *C'est vrai?*'

'I'm here to see a woman called Fatima Hamza. My name is Malone.'

'You still cannot buy a drink here. Unless you are dead.'

The barman did not even smile. Part of Malone had always dreamed of being a bird and flying away and he wanted to right now. He saw his own reflection in a mirrored shelf. He had a patch of oil on his white T-shirt and another in his curly blond hair from stripping down a Cessna undercarriage at the airfield. In his grey-blue eyes there was a hint of panic.

'Do you know where you are, sonny?' demanded a man staring at his empty glass at a nearby table.

'I was given this address.'

'But do you know where you are?'

Malone swallowed hard.

Near by there was the sound of police sirens intermingling with the call to prayer. 'There's still time to leave, Monsieur,' said the barman, his thick eyebrows raised.

Malone was about to speak when a broad-shouldered man wandered over, past the drinker with the empty glass.

'You don't, do you? You don't know where you are. This is the Dead Officers' Club.' His voice was educated and American.

'Dead, dead, dead . . .' said the man.

As if to reinforce the point an explosion to the south echoed and re-echoed around Kabul's ochre hills and a flock of pigeons took to the air. Malone felt the percussive shock through the thin soles of his old boots but no one looked up from the tables. On a bar stool a marmalade cat stretched out its long legs and began to purr. Another cat paraded, tail up, around a wall which enclosed a fire pit, not needed yet in the baking heat at the end of August. The city was waiting for the historic first elections to be announced, although everyone knew that President Hamid Karzai had already fixed them in the interests of peace and security. A calendar behind the bar said *2009, Year of Hope! Year of Obama! Year of Afghan Democracy!* The country was tensed for everything to get worse, for the whirlwind, and there had even been talk at work, at the small aid airline Malone flew for, about everyone getting out.

'The Dead Officers' Club?'

'Correct!'

'So you can only buy a drink if you are dead,' repeated the tired barman, polishing another glass. 'Perhaps you want L'Atmos? But beware. They get their Béarnaise sauce from the packet. We make it ourselves. The chef he grow the French tarragon, not the Russian tarragon. There's no taste to the Russian tarragon. You may as well use hashish. But we get what we choose. Remember that, Monsieur.'

Malone thought for a moment that he might be joking but could tell from his eyes that he was not.

High walls surrounded the compound and on a springboard a very white girl in a yellow bikini shouted in French before she did a perfect swan dive into the pool. Trees shaded the tables and the sprinklers on the hibiscus hedges added to the impression of affluence, while through doors at the other side of the fire pit, waiters in black bow ties and crisp white shirts were already serving up early brunch.

'The Dead Officers' Club?' said Malone. 'I'm sorry but I . . .?'

'Don't worry about it, soldiers are meant to die,' said the broad-shouldered man, who had a cognac bottle in one large hand and two glasses in the other. 'Families understand. It's a surprisingly easy thing to die for one's country . . . *Dulce et decorum est, pro patria mori.*'

Malone felt lost. 'Look, I was told to come here by a friend. I'm supposed to meet someone. Her name is Fatima Hamza . . .'

Then there was a giddying outburst of laughter behind him. 'And Fatima Hamza shall buy Malone a drink . . . Bring me another of these delicious gin and tonics! Bombay Sapphire, if you please. Come and sit by me, Malone. Come and see Toto, the goose you so kindly rescued.'

Malone swung round but the owner of the voice was mysteriously protected from view by a wall of flowering hibiscus, scented jasmine, a small frangipani tree and other greenery. The voice sounded innocent and sweet and had that cut-glass, musical quality of the English upper classes mixed with the ever-so-slight lilt of the subcontinent.

'I suppose then, Monsieur, that you can go over now,' said the barman coldly. 'I will get your drink.'

Malone walked around the bushes. A girl with the most perfect face was sitting at a marble table with a goose on a lead. She had blue-green eyes and a smile that undermined the silent menace of the club. A black-and-white-checked Afghan scarf was draped around her delicate shoulders, and she immediately stood up and kissed him on both cheeks, greeting him with a warmth he was not prepared for.

'You've come to help me, Malone! I prayed my guardian angel might come to my rescue and here you are! *Inshallah*, darling!'

Two

'I'm so sorry about this jolly creepy club ... I don't think they really approve of me,' Fatima Hamza said. Her eyes were jewelled and piercing: as if party to a great vision, eyes from a fairy tale. Most of all they were Pashtun eyes and Malone felt their electric stare. She had an elfin build and her thick, shoulder-length hair was the colour of toasted wheat. Under definite but not unpluck- ed eyebrows was a slightly turned-up nose and a delicate jaw. Many Pashtun had dark-blond hair and very light complexions. There was a kindness in her look, a wonder and a freshness, which was totally out of place in the club or in Afghanistan, and it made him terrified for her, just as he had been for the goose when he had found it on the runway. And yet the way she was dressed would not be considered innocent anywhere, let alone on the streets of Kabul. She had extravagantly mimicked Judy Garland's costume in *The Wizard of Oz*. The blue-gingham, lace-fringed minidress was very short and, though two of the silver buttons down the front were undone, strained at her breasts. The heels on the 'ruby slippers' were very high and her lipstick and eye shadow more than slightly over the top. Her mouth was wide and the slight gap between her two front teeth gave her a vital, aboriginal air. There was mischief in her eyes and the crook of her smile.

'My father insists I stay here. At this club. So I said *inshallah*, darling. It was the only way he'd allow me to come to Afghanistan. I hope you like your gin and tonics quite strong. I learned to make them for my father with a pinch of green snuff . . . I shouldn't really drink in Ramadan, should I? But I'm sure that Allah doesn't mind . . . And thank you so much for my Toto. He's such a dear. I was told by your friend up at the big American base that you knew all about these geese? Your chum was going to help me make a small *Wizard of Oz* film . . . Silly me. That's why I'm dressed like this . . .'

Without him saying a word she began to put ice into the glasses and then pour in the blue-coloured gin the waiter had brought over on a tray. She dropped in the lime slices and a pinch of the green powder before topping it up with foaming tonic. She then lifted one of the glasses to Malone's lips with two hands and he took a deep sip.

'Chin, chin,' she said, handing him his glass and then clinking her own against his. 'Your very good health, Malone.'

It was by far the nicest gin and tonic Malone had ever tasted.

At that moment the goose stuck its head out from under the table and nibbled at Malone's jeans. The bird was mainly grey with bright-yellow feet and two pronounced black bars on the back of its head. It turned its head on one side and blinked at him in a sort of blissful recognition. There was a red-silk ribbon fastened to a little collar around its neck but the goose seemed a very willing captive.

'You know what kind of goose it is . . .?'

Malone nodded. When he had first picked the creature off the runway of the American airbase at Bagram, he did not think it was going to make it. The friend at the airbase who had said he could find the goose a home had persuaded him to come along to tell its new owner more about the bird. This friend was meant to be here too, now, and had not mentioned anything about a video. Malone wondered if he were being set up. But then Fatima smiled, and her smile was infectious.

'Yes . . . Your goose is my all-time favourite,' said Malone. 'A bar-headed goose. *Anser indicus* . . . *Anser indicus*. Order: Anseriformes. Family: *Anatidae* . . . They fly from the high Pamirs over the Himalayas and have been spotted at thirty thousand feet by airline passengers. I'm not kidding. It's minus sixty up there and there's no oxygen but using the jet stream they're all the way to India in a day. They're so bulky it's a wonder they can fly. The Pashtun even call them flying pigs in one fairy tale. Yet these pigs have been seen skidding along the ice clouds over Everest. They're optimists. Jesus, his feet are so yellow. I cannot get over his feet being that yellow . . .'

She was staring into his eyes. 'And why do they do this crazy thing, this flying so high with the planes?'

Malone was into his stride now. 'They have been doing this since before the Himalayas pushed themselves up. The bar-head is a behavioural fossil. They're too stubborn to change their route, which is kind of Afghan . . . I admire that. The Hindu word for the geese is the same as for free spirit. And they do this impossible journey every year to find a mate. It's a journey of love . . .'

There was a wistful furrow in Fatima's lovely brow. 'These geese are sacred to all lovers, you know?' she said. 'They are called Paramahamsa, which means supreme goose. It's the word for one who is truly enlightened. They say these geese can separate milk from water as a true master can tell truth from falsehood. I mean, they, they . . .'

Then Malone was rendered speechless.

Fatima had tears coming down her face. Rivulets among the fake freckles she had drawn either side of her nose. She began to sob and he had the distinct fear that one of the buttoned-down military men might come over and silently kill him.

'I'm so sorry. It's just all the trouble in my family . . . It's . . .'

He handed her a napkin and she took a drink of her gin and tonic and a deep breath.

'So you really know about geese, eh?'

He nodded. 'Yes, I studied them at university . . . And ducks and cranes. I used to have to dress up as a crane to feed the little cranes. They're grand birds. They're reintroducing them in England now . . . On the Somerset Levels, which is a kind of cold swamp . . . And I helped with a small project on the bald eagle . . . We must never forget the bald eagle.'

Malone never knew whether to mention the eagle. He never quite knew how being American went down with Afghans.

She shook her head at him which made him feel even more nervous, as she took a sip of the frosted drink. She dabbed at her eyes.

'Your friend said you're like the birds, that you're a flyer, too.'

He laughed.

'A flyer but not quite in the same league as this guy.' He reached out to stroke Toto. 'I learned on a little plane my dad bought with his brother because they were scared of heights, if that makes sense. They let me fly planes for the NGO air service. I ferry doctors and aid workers around.'

She was laughing now too.

'He said you also do a trade in swimming pool filters and other things the Americans have . . . Are you a smuggler, Malone? It's a tradition hereabouts.' She was teasing him but there was still the trace of a tear on one of her eyelashes.

Malone sighed.

'Oh, you find yourself taking cargo you don't really want from time to time . . . It's hard to avoid, but I try. Here you have to give gifts to get what you need. You shouldn't listen to my friend too much.'

She furrowed her brow.

'I didn't mean to offend you, Malone. I spent most of my life being educated overseas and don't know my way around here any more.'

He shook his head.

'No offence taken. We try not to have too much contact with the military or the people who are here making money . . . It can get you killed. There's a lot of things you have got to avoid.' Malone was feeling the effects of the gin.

'I was educated all over the place too,' he said. 'My father's second-generation Irish American. My mother's English. I suppose that makes me a bit of a mongrel really. But I feel American . . .'

A helicopter thudded overhead and then was gone. She turned until her face was very close to his.

'Your friend from the base was going to come here but I think he has probably got cold feet. Many people don't like to come here. And yet everyone seems perfectly nice . . .'

Malone hesitated.

'Are you sure you want to look after . . . Toto? He'd really do best if he were returned to the wild.'

'I may be going up to the Pamirs . . .'

She was staring at her carmine nail polish. Her hands were long and slender. He did not understand her answer.

'Really? That area can be dangerous.'

Fatima looked at him again with those jewelled eyes.

'I'd never do anything to hurt Toto.'

Malone touched the bird's beak with his finger.

'You love him, don't you?' she said. 'Why did you let your friend bring him to me?'

'I didn't want the goose to die.'

'Die?'

'The new general ordered all the stray dogs at the base shot. He's having a tidy up, his officers said. There was talk of keeping the bird for Thanksgiving.'

Fatima put her hands over where Toto's ears would be. The barman then appeared with more ice cubes and said, 'He's stupid, this general. He's banned the drink. To ban the drink in a country where drink is already forbidden is an act of desperation. And they say he eats snakes.' The barman scowled at Malone and then vanished.

'I like snakes too, don't you, Malone?' said Fatima.

'Yes.'

Malone stroked the goose's head. He didn't want to leave either

10

the goose or Fatima in this club. He noticed a light-blue burqa by her side.

'I can see you've spotted my disguise. I wear it and can post myself across town like a Jiffy bag. In one of those you are quite safe. Come. Let's go up to the pool. I want to show you something, Malone.'

They walked past the outside bar and the barman smiled at Fatima and pressed his lips together as his eyes met Malone's. Fatima paused as one of the cats hissed at Toto, who looked back at it confused. She tickled the bird under its chin and then the goose pattered its yellow feet up the stairs and peered curiously at the light-azure water of the pool. They went over to a pair of sun loungers where an expensive camera rested on a red cushion and, Malone blinked when he saw it, a lion suit was laid out next to thick white towels.

'That's the suit for the Cowardly Lion. I was hoping your friend from the base might play the part. But promise me . . .' She blinked slowly and he thought she was going to get upset again. 'Promise me you'll help me with this. Will you be my Tin Man, Malone?'

'I, well, I . . .' he said, playing with the wedding band on his finger.

'Your friend said you had a wife here. You look so young to be married, Malone. For an American.'

For a moment he did not know what to say.

'She's always pretty busy,' he began.

'So you will help me, won't you, Malone?'

Malone found himself nodding.

She gestured towards the clubhouse. 'This place was built by an Englishman, a hero, Wigram Battye, who was commander of the regiment of Guides and went completely native at times. I love the delicacy of the single-storey design which is completely Indian, you know. He was the one who said all foreigners in Afghanistan are ghosts; pale riders on our dusty plains, soon to vanish.'

Malone laughed.

'So that's why they call it the Dead Officers' Club?'

'No, not exactly . . . Why did you come here, Malone?'

'To the club?'

'No.'

He was gazing at her, not knowing how to answer, and was grateful for the intrusion of the broad-shouldered man with the cognac bottle who had returned but now only with one glass.

The man seemed about to interrupt and then wandered away and Fatima said, 'I have to go down to the south and Kandahar tomorrow and then to Helmand.'

Malone was immediately concerned. She was talking about the official war zones. Even if unofficially the whole country was at war.

'Why do you have to go to those places?'

She sighed.

'I'm doing some research and making a film. My father does not like it, so I am making this little *Wizard of Oz* video for him too. To cheer him up and help him not to worry. It's his favourite movie. The best of the golden years of Hollywood, he says. We used to watch it together when I was a child and sing all the songs and dance around the room.'

Fatima laughed and then danced up and down the side of the pool, singing, ' "We're off to see the Wizard!" ' To Malone's surprise she came back high-kicking and did a very uncontrolled cartwheel.

A couple in the shade of a tamarisk tree laughed and Fatima took a bow.

'Sorry. Mustn't show off. I did a little dance course when I was at Oxford. I shouldn't show off.'

She then sat down hard on one of the loungers and took off her sandals and examined her painted toenails. 'I'm going to tell you a secret, Malone. I think I'm going to end up telling you a lot of secrets. Do you know I never cut my own toenails until I went off to a jolly hockey sticks school in England, aged eight? My father always cut my toenails with me bare-legged on my mother's red-velvet boudoir chair, after a well-meaning servant in Karachi had sliced into my flesh with a pair of kitchen scissors and I had run to him, my feet bloody, my mother fainting and spending days playing Chopin. He always used the same pair of Trumper's silver-plated nail clippers from an art deco gold-and-black-lacquer box that he had stolen from the bathroom of a hurriedly assassinated prime minister, and insisted on checking I had cut them when he came to visit. Snip, snip, snip . . .'

She made scissor movements with the long, graceful middle and index fingers of one hand and then the other, as they passed in front of her face.

'He was devastated when I went to England and decided to stay on for Oxford. Now he has gone into a sulk and is angry with me because I've come to Afghanistan. He's scared for me, poor old thing, after losing my mother.'

Malone nodded. He felt frightened for her too.

'But this is my country, Malone. I cannot hide from it behind my privilege, can I?'

'No, but that does not mean you have to go to Kandahar.'

On the sun lounger was a Big Chief ring notebook and a map on which had been drawn a road in yellow. It was one of the very good Soviet relief maps of Afghanistan. A yellow line ran to the south and then up north and then east, right to the borders of China.

'Look, that's my grand plan. My Yellow Brick Road. I'm retracing the places that were important to Pops . . . It's all for a writing project of his. A secret. So you see, even though he doesn't want me to be here, I am helping him. He's mostly retired now and has started translating *The Dostan of Amir Hamza*, which is the Persian equivalent of *The Thousand and One Nights*, except this tale is faster, more brutal and far more beautiful and central to all bazaar story-telling. Pops says it speaks to him of today and tomorrow, not just the land of several hundred years ago. . . . Amir Hamza was an adventurer and uncle of the Prophet, peace be unto his name, and even in translation the language is exceptional.' She paused and then quoted: ' ". . . The zephyr-paced sojourner, the stylus of fasci-nating accounts of the expert chroniclers, and the flying arrowhead – to wit, the pen that must detail the messages of intelligencers also records the events on Mount Qaf. . ." How Pops loves this book!'

She looked dreamily up at the sky and stretched out her arms.

'He's probably at our house in Islamabad smoking a Havana cigar . . . a Romeo y Julieta Corona from a humidor on the lamp table. He acquired a taste for them fighting the Russians. He will be sitting in his favourite room, in his favourite chair, wearing a green-velvet smoking jacket that, it was said by the unfortunate person he confiscated it from, had once belonged to a British Colonel Hamilton VC of the Guides, who were my pops' old regi-ment, so he has a perfectly good claim on the jacket. He'll be looking down his steel-rimmed glasses perched at the end of his nose, like a revolutionary from the 1930s, or Pakistan's founding father, Mr Jinnah. Pops is not a harsh man most of the time. People say awful things about him but he can be a total sweetie. We have another place at Clifton in Karachi, with big, cool rooms and lots of settees. You'd like my father, Malone.

'He's not big but he can command a room. And when he's at his desk: oh Malone. Picture a not too tall, dapper ex-military man with a clipped moustache on a pale earnest face in very well-preserved middle age with his silver pen poised above the paper and the servants terrified! When he's on one of his writing binges he can stay up for days, working furiously, and then lapse into a kind of trance. Once he shaved off half his moustache by accident. He threw a salad bowl he won playing cricket for Surrey at me before I left. The house in the north is just by the forest and about now, in Ramadan, the hyenas answer the call to prayer first and then so do the monkeys and the jackals from the woods and Pops goes out and feeds them. Most of all he's trying to get back to a story he was writing about the retreat from Kabul by the British which cost sixteen thousand lives and ended on Gandamak Ridge . . . A story he's obsessed with for a most particular reason . . . because he is a foundling who was rescued on a shooting party by my grandfather in his Daimler as a broken-boned infant being pecked at by crows beside a road on the frontier near Gilgit. My God, I am getting carried away! I've always thought being found was very romantic. It is all part of his secret . . . I'll tell you, Malone. I feel I can trust you. But not here, not now.'

Malone was looking at the map. He was trying not to stare at Fatima all the time these words were flooding out of her.

'He sounds quite a man. Your journey though: are you sure it's wise? Some of those places are pretty . . . uncool.'

Fatima took a sip of her gin and tonic.

'Yes, a sightseeing tour for a woman alone is difficult in Afghanistan. But I fully intend to rediscover my country. At present I'm always wearing the burqa of my Western education. I can't see things clearly yet, Malone, even though I have been here a whole month.'

'I'm sure you will. But really, it can be unwise to travel in the east of the country. Especially in Badakhshan,' he said gently.

She nodded and he stared again into those incredible almond-shaped eyes that changed with the light. 'You will trust Toto to me, Malone? I'm already in love with him, and as I'm Dorothy and a Hamza he'll be safe. Excuse me, now. I must leave you. I'm meant to be meeting a dear old friend of my father at the university for some advice on the *Dostan*. Down the hatch, eh, Malone? But I'll see you later, Malone, yes? When you come and help me with my film? I'll call . . . Your friend gave me your number . . .'

She drained her drink, rose to her feet and then, to his utter surprise, leant over and kissed him lightly on the forehead. He stood up too and the smile she had on her face was like another kiss.

He knew instantly that he wanted to see her again. She left him staring at the maps for her insane journey as he finished his drink, watched every moment by the barman.

'Isn't Dorothy a dreamboat?' said the broad-shouldered man, still with the brandy bottle and glass in front of him, as Malone was leaving. 'Isn't she just a dreamboat?'

*   *   *

Out in the street the smell of her perfume was gone along with the jasmine, replaced by the familiar tang of woodsmoke, dust and dung. The city had no drainage system and was one of the few places the toilet-obsessed British had not managed to build one. A dark stream ran under the security post at the front of the club and by it stood a tall, thin Afghan who smiled at him from under a large turban. He had a scar on his forehead.

'*Salaam alaikum,*' called the man. 'Do you need a guide?' he added in Dari.

'No, I know my way around.'

The smile grew larger.

'Do you? Are you sure? I'm certain you'll need one in the near future.' The voice was pleasant and very cultured even though the man was dressed in black rags. The man had something of a raven about him.

'*Tashakor*, but no . . .'

Malone turned and walked quickly away. He passed a ghastly new mosque and the Iranian Embassy, its concrete walls flecked with symmetrical patterns of carefully broken glass, as if the architect was trying to turn the frequent bombings into an art form. He went on to the modern buildings of Chicken Street and then to the river and the market beyond. He was staying in what was called the Prince's Fort, but more commonly the Fort, in a medieval part of town which was now a dormitory for a collection of the more adventurous NGOs. It was very different from the club.

Men in starched black-and-white turbans on small donkeys trotted past market women who yelled they had fresh nan or melons. The garish lights of the restaurants were next, the smell of charcoal and burning meat, and a fish shop with the latest catch fixed to the board with a spike through its eyes, as little boys began to offer him paper packets full of walnuts and dried mulberries which smelt of spice and tasted like the best Christmas cake.

A gritty wind was blowing the dust into small tornados. 'Djinn! Djinn!' shouted the little boys. Malone looked up at the mountains and a bird far away in the sky. He stopped and stared. It was not wrong to stop and stare here; people did it all the time as streams of cars passed honking and swerving into each other's path in a mechanized game of *buzkashi*, the ancestor of polo, played with a dead goat, or better still, the headless body of one's enemy.

Malone had wanted to listen to Fatima all afternoon. The poor girl did not understand where she was, even though her family were Afghan. Here you had to face the unexpected daily: the tribesman who had sworn to kill you because you let your shadow fall on his second wife; the maid who put a headache curse on you because you did not return her affections; the fake aid doctor who pledged eternal friendship and then stole the wheels of your aeroplane. And if you were not ready Afghanistan found you out. There was a quality in the high mountain light in Kabul that got into every secret, yellowed the paper of any master plan. Yet if you conquered all the country's many contradictions, there was an overwhelming freedom. And that was the politicians' greatest problem. How do you bring freedom to people who already have it to spare?

Malone already cared for her. The way he cared for birds when he was growing up. The djinn was out of the bottle.

Cloud moved towards one of the steep-sided hills which formed a backdrop to the city.

A man offered him a sheep and, almost in the next breath, some sticky black opium.

'Thank you, but no,' Malone said in Dari.

Malone wanted to feel more ... for the girl, for the tide of humanity passing him in the street ... He lit a cigarette and walked on. Afghanistan nagged him with questions like America did, but at least it tried, every single day, to get under his skin. To fill him up with sound and fury and intrigue and affection ... Nothing much in his life in the States had done that since his own father had gone; a heart attack, trying to keep cheerful after his mother had walked out for the third time that year, on this occasion with a photographer who worked for *Vanity Fair*. Malone gazed up at the eternal sky. The children's kites danced against the blue. He shaded his eyes as his gaze followed a flock of pigeons. He realized that Fatima had made him feel lighter than he had in a long time; even when he was aloft in his plane, flying. Malone walked back to the Fort with the taste of Bombay gin on his lips. He knew that he was going to go back and help her with her mad film. Where was the harm? Where was the harm in *The Wizard of Oz*?

THREE

An hour later, Malone was making dutiful love to his wife, Kim. She had just finished her shift at the part of the crowded military hospital open to local people. Every time he closed his eyes he saw the face of Fatima and her doelike lashes . . . He opened his eyes again. Kim had her buttocks elevated on a pillow just like the baby book said. Her knees were back around her ears. She had long, muscled American legs conditioned from running after stray calves on a farm in the Midwest. She was a high jumper at school and had been of national standard but had given it all up when she found God and, in her own words, 'didn't need to raise the bar another inch'.

Kim had folded religion neatly into a clearly marked box, as she did everything else, including her dolls and toy rabbit. She was a general surgical intern specializing in trauma and had never, in Malone's eyes, had a moment of helplessness in her life. The baby book, a gift from her quietly spoken mother, said that, if you thought about Jesus as you did it, you had a better child.

And that was so hard for Malone.

To keep one's mind on a kindly, bearded man nailed to a cross.

Kim's golden-blonde hair was spread about the white sheet under the mosquito net. The day was hot and there were beads of perspiration on her upper lip. The bed was a massive four poster and had belonged to the man who once owned the Fort. He had forbidden all air conditioning and the windows were open but the air did not seem to percolate in through the fly screens. Malone felt himself beginning to come.

At that moment the massively amplified Ramadan call to prayer started up from a nearby mosque.

Kim pulled away.

'I wish they wouldn't do that when we're about God's work!'

He smiled and shrugged and eased her towards him. Kim could be so fucking serious these days. She was beautiful and he loved her. He dearly loved her fierce commitment, but . . .

'Well, I suppose they consider they're about God's work too.'

'They're not!' she said, almost falling off the pillow. Malone had noticed she was getting more confrontational with ordinary life in Kabul, and with him, the harder they worked her at the hospital. When there was a big car bomb or an attack on a compound she often did not come back from the hospital at all.

Malone steadied her. 'Let's not argue.'

'No . . .'

He was inside her again but she was gazing up at the white net around the four poster. 'Do you think it's the stress of being here, Malone? I do. I think it's that. I think it's the stress of being here.

That's why I can't have your baby . . .' The last words sounded on the edge of tears.

'It's probably my idiot sperm. They're too Irish. They cannot follow a simple path.'

'Please quit kidding around.'

Malone was twenty-seven and Kim was twenty-five. They had met when he was in a leaky tent in a stormy Yellowstone wondering exactly how hard it was to get struck by lightning if one stood at the top of one of the jagged peaks when the electricity was flashing around them. The girl he was meant to marry had just broken up with him and he was preparing for a grand gesture he did not much feel. He was always preparing for something he did not feel. He had intended to go to Yosemite and stand on a rock he had a clear memory of standing on once with his large, smiling father and see whether it felt right to jump off. However, the memory might have been phoney as his father was scared of heights. But the middle-aged dope-smoking couple who gave him a ride had mixed up the two wilderness parks, even though Yosemite was in California and Yellowstone in Montana, seven hundred miles away, and Yellowstone was where he had ended up. Malone didn't give a damn. He could end it all as easily there. Malone had heard a story somewhere that Kerouac had tried to get struck by lightning and in his present state of mind found it inspiring.

The storm had not been going long when his tent fell down, and as he struggled out Kim was there, her arms outstretched, the rain running down her lovely, wide, high-cheekboned face. There was a flash of lightning and she tripped and tumbled into his arms. A patch of ground was smoking near by. Rain and hail were bouncing up as high as wheat. 'You look a little lost,' she had said. There was another flash, which struck a tree and sent a branch tumbling onto a car. 'We had better go inside,' she said sensibly. 'My family are over there in that trailer.' He looked at the tree and the smoking ground. Kerouac's lightning wasn't going to strike him now, so he went quietly along with the tall, blonde girl.

Kim and Malone had been married three weeks later in the Old Faithful car park by her dad, who now had a chain of Christian hardware stores and loved to go out into the backwoods for the summer, testing his faith against the wilderness. Malone still was not sure if he was really married.

His own father, who was also called Malone, was a second-generation Irish American newspaper man. The younger Malone had grown up in Washington, amid the rows and makings up with Malone's striking and unpredictable English mother, who adored her only child. His mother started to spend more and more time in New York, where she worked in the perfume busi-ness and smoked French cigarettes in ivory holders and wore sunglasses indoors. The house was full of gigantic, sharp-edged perfume bottles, excellent for throwing. His father was left with his foreign-correspondent war stories – from two trips to Afghanistan – and a much better job in Washington, advising an insurance company on press relations, which did not take him anywhere but lunch. His dad had died a year before Malone's university sweetheart walked out. It was then Malone met Kim and decided to come with her to Afghanistan, their flights paid by a Christian group with whom her family had marriage and hardware connections. It was a tradition in her family to do good works overseas and, obviously, he had nothing planned after Yosemite/Yellowstone.

'It's my sperm,' he smiled. Malone had a disarming smile.

Her brow darkened. The trouble was that Kim looked even sweeter when she was mad at him. 'Oh, but it's not. It's me. They said you were normal.'

Now he laughed, but stopped. She often thought if he laughed he was laughing at her. She said by not taking things seriously he wasn't being true to himself. He had scraped into Princeton and studied psychology, specializing in animal behaviour, but his father and his uncle, another gentle giant, had taught him to fly. And because they had bought the Piper Pawnee crop duster together to conquer their morbid fear of heights, Malone was taught careful flying. Indeed, he always thought of flying that way. His mother had an uncle who had been lost in his Hurricane fighter over the English Channel, which was not careful flying. When he was young Malone used to lie in bed at night and dream that the Hurricane pilot might not be lost and come back one day and land in Rock Creek. His mother was not one for careful flying. He had woken on several nights to find her at the end of his bed, the perfume of the climbing jasmine coming in through the window, the hint of a smile on her face in the darkness. She had come and kissed him on the lips, smelling of musk and paradise.

To avoid the arguments and visiting lovers who pretended to be work colleagues, Malone had gone out into the local sycamore-clad frontier of Rock Creek, with its Perrier jogging track, and watched the birds. He used to go to a lost cemetery the other side of the Capital Beltway and sit and watch cardinals and chickadees.

It was a beautiful little plateau tucked right away on one bank, like a tree house with tiny, unreadable gravestones covered in moss and ivy, and he often put his nose into the mossy earth and breathed in; it had the scent of an older America that excited him, one where you could imagine red-painted Hurons or Mohicans round the next tree. Malone loved the birds there and anything to do with flight and had written a dissertation on 'Comfort Movements in the Winter Behaviour of the Male Loon'. The title had been set by his tutor. It was going to be mallards, or even crested pochards, tree duck, pintails or mangrove golden whistlers, but the tutor had insisted on loons. Loons went through all thirty-two types of coping behaviour, wing stretch, oil-gland stimulation and the like, when faced with failure in competition for a mate or after a catastrophic accidental landing on ice. But in the main birds tried to be careful flyers and not draw attention to themselves, except when mating.

Whatever else, Afghanistan was not careful flying.

Malone looked into Kim's china-blue eyes.

'They said my sperm was normal for Washington. Which puts me somewhere between Jefferson and Dr Strangelove, I suppose.'

His joke didn't improve Kim's mood.

'I think we should go home. That's what all this is telling us.'

'Don't get yourself excited,' he soothed.

'He's warning us . . .'

'Please don't cry, Kim.'

She shook her head. He was still inside her and for a second time was beginning to come.

The muezzin began his call to prayer again.

She lost her temper. 'Why don't they just shut the fuck up! We should ask them to turn it down!'

'They won't like that. They wouldn't go for that at all.'

The prayer call's volume increased. Malone came ecstatically with a shout. But he was looking at the face of another and it was not Jesus.

He hugged Kim to him.

'I want to go home, Malone . . . I know we planned to go to the frontier and all. That this was to be our frontier. But we could go to Alaska.'

In Alaska the temperature would always be correct to make blue-eyed Jesus babies, Malone mused, but did not say. And it was good for ducks.

'Why Alaska? Why not . . . Kansas?'

Malone had never had any connection whatsoever with Kansas.

'Alaska because some of my family are in Alaska. Because Alaska is a godly place to conceive a child! I don't even want to hear that noise with your sperm inside me any more. Kansas? You want to go to Kansas? Why?'

That night Kim tossed and turned and muttered in her dreams and Malone recognized the famous phrase from the 23rd Psalm. 'Yea, though I walk through the valley of the shadow of death, I will fear no evil . . .' It was half past three in the morning and he heard the muezzin start up again. The sound did not bother him and often he found himself projecting his own interpretation onto the endless, nasal ribbon of noise. Once it changed into 'Baba O'Riley' by The Who, a track he used to play over his headphones while flying the Piper. On another occasion he thought he was listening to a baseball commentary, where the New York Mets were winning.

The muezzin's voice did not stop as Malone heard the sound of three rockets exploding somewhere to the south, one after the other. There was a beauty in the way the sound of the detonations rolled and echoed across the mountains on which the city was built. Then heavy machine-gun fire was added and a siren. A minute later there was another, bigger rocket.

Malone smoothed Kim's hair. He touched her lips and felt her rhythmic breath on his hand.

It took, at most, ten minutes for the retaliation airstrike to come: one huge explosion which just went on and on like some perpetual amplified car wreck, and whoever they were, the bad guys, the Taliban, he hoped they were not under that exterminating angel.

It made Malone angry that the sacred gift of flight was used for such purposes. But he kept his anger to himself.

Kim shifted in her sleep, moaned lightly, and curled herself around his arm.

After the airstrike explosion there was a don't-even-dare-breathe silence. Then, as if nothing had happened, the call to prayer started again and Malone smiled.

Kim heard Malone wake and stretch. He did the same thing every morning. Malone left her in bed and eased himself from under the mosquito net. She watched him dress. She took in the lean lines of his back, his small bottom and wide shoulders. He had kept himself in tight shape, which was hard here. There was only one old rowing machine and they did not allow you to go running. These NGO compounds were a kind of prison. Some people did not go out at all. There was one older lady from Maine who worked for the UN photographic department and had not left her compound for six months after a suicide bomb had killed everyone else in her car but left her without a scratch.

Kim suspected Malone of walking to most places – they had argued about that – and even going jogging up among the houses and goats on the nearby ochre-coloured hills that looked down on the Intercontinental Hotel. It was no good. Whatever the two-faced heathens here claimed, they wanted to kill all white people, especially Americans. Kim sighed. Malone was too young for this, they both were . . . How had they got here? Kim heard Malone lift the latch and go out of the door. It was a sunny morning. Kim immediately turned over and stared at the mosquito netting. Why did she give him such a hard time? He was trying; he was trying all he could and, my, he had turned his life around from those dark times when she first met him, even though he had never fully let her in. He was so kind and gentle with her and so under-standing. So why had she not told him that Noah wanted her to go down to Kandahar?

She dug her nails into the heavy cotton sheets.

Everyone knew that Kandahar was dangerous and he wouldn't want her to go, but she also knew that he would not object.

Down in the garden, surrounded on four sides by the two-storey, mud-and-dung-walled fort, she heard a peacock scream as it was chased by one of the dogs. Kim often felt like screaming too. Perhaps she was just scared like everyone else. But really she did not know exactly why and that was the trouble here. No one ever knew anything for sure.

In the courtyard garden Malone was sitting on a raised dais covered in carpets, shaded by a golden cloth tied to four posts, watching the peacocks and listening to someone on the rowing machine, next to the hammam, where the woodpile to heat the water had a pleasant, fusty smell but which the gardener said meant nests of mice and snakes and scorpions. He did not explain to Malone how they all got on together. The swoosh-swoosh of the small chair running up and down the rail produced an endless sigh. The sound made the speckled doves that lived in a house on the roof wheel and turn and turn again. They then caught sight of a lone kite in the sky, probably thought it was a hawk and raced for the cover of home. There would be more paper kites as the wind got up. The children fought them, pretty paper square against pretty paper square. They smeared ground glass and glue on the kite strings to cut someone else's line. They fought dogs and cats and partridges and camels and bears when they could get them and even brightly painted eggs. They fought everything here, yet most Afghans struck Malone as being supremely un-warlike, certainly un-warriorlike. They did not brag. They did not talk endlessly about weapons or killing, at least not the ones he had met. He took a deep breath of the still cool air.

A man and a woman crossed the lawn arguing. 'I just can't do that . . . Tell me how you fucking expect me to do that . . .'

There was an undercurrent of fear and paranoia about the Fort, common to all NGO compounds, but not the unworldly strangeness he had felt at that club yesterday. Malone liked the Fort's garden with its peacocks rooting in the lush grass among the pomegranate and mulberry trees. He had been here a month now after a small, fetid stream had overflowed into a part of the house they were renting near the hospital. He had tried to divert the stream but the neighbour's wife had responded by putting a curse on Kim, who she said shouldn't be a doctor, and large, inexplicable sores broke out almost immediately on Kim's belly. The wife then denounced Kim to the street as an adulterer. After that it was fatal to stay. When Malone had first seen the inside of the Fort and come to sit on the dais under the golden cloth, he thought he was on a film set. Half of the courtyard garden's west wall was hung with Prussian-blue morning glory and the beds beneath planted with fragrant roses and the yellowest sunflowers on earth.

The Fort had been in ruins after the Taliban were defeated in 2001, and an Englishman called Sir Peter Rhind-Tutt had completely and lovingly rebuilt the hilltop structure, carefully researching the mixture for the human-dung-and-lime walls and carving the lintels over the doors and restoring the old windows and Mughal dovecote. A naturalist, Rhind-Tutt was continually getting himself into trouble trying to save animals, which was why there was a small menagerie, which included several Russian-speaking parrots and a blind lion called Charlie, who, it was said, had eaten a Russian tank commander. Rhind-Tutt was the son of a lord and an old Etonian who had taken a first at Cambridge, and everything was going well for him until he decided to walk across the north of the country from Faizabad to Herat near the Iranian border, completely alone, except for a small retinue of ten servants, and dressed as an endangered snow partridge (*Lerwa lerwa*). He had originally wanted to do the journey naked, as had early Afghan holy men, but his favourite cook persuaded him out of this suicidal plan. A fluent Dari speaker, Rhind-Tutt was feted in every town until a hunter, out of his mind on opium, shot the Etonian dead in one of the ancient, delicate Timurid squares of Herat. Afterwards the hunter was let go by the police who understood his dilemma on seeing a giant Dari-speaking snow partridge. It was not the tribesman's fault he had not been let into the *Englestani's* impossible story. The Etonian had blundered into his. This was often the mistake of the foreigner in Afghanistan, said the gardener who had told Malone about Rhind-Tutt. To get his story mixed up with those of the hills and their people.

Rhind-Tutt had left the Fort and everything in it to his charity and now a mix of folk were there: naturalists, occasional naturists, craftspeople and a group of engineers bringing the first sewage plant to Kabul. Their leader, Doktor Becker, had told him the clouds of dust that engulfed the city mostly at night were thirty per cent faecal matter. 'That is a shit storm, Malone. If you stay here long enough you will share everything with the population and they with you. With every waking breath!' The Doktor was not up and about yet this morning. Malone got up from where he sat and wandered over to a large table shaded by a trellis and a grapevine. They had been growing vines in Afghanistan since well before Alexander the Great was here.

An argument was in progress.

'I bought that bloody teapot at Fortnum's and it's very bloody expensive. Now I see that it is being used by everyone. And for poppy-head tea, which is illegal, I may add. I had some Ben & Jerry's ice cream in the freezer and that's gone too. It's not just a question of petty pilfering. It's a question of respect.' The speaker, on the edge of tears, was an elderly English lady, Miss Damaris Wace, who had a medieval fringe and whose speciality was teaching jewellery making to Afghans whose families had been producing fabulous creations for several thousand years.

The woman and the man she was arguing with left crossly and a familiar figure with a computer case approached.

'You don't mind me coming here to work, do you?' said Basil. 'I just cannot toil in one of those airless shipping containers they have given us . . . It's too hot and ugly.' The slightly plump man in cream trousers and a blue shirt was referring to what passed as the British Embassy, where he was a diplomat. He had a pasty, cheerful face and an awkward way of walking but was intellectually brilliant and the best company Malone knew in Kabul. 'We were going to move back into Lord Curzon's ruin and do it up again but the freehold has been swindled away from us by a Pakistani computer dealer who knows Hamid fucking Karzai . . . We cannot even hang onto our assets. A group of nice-looking young Afghans came in the other day and took lots of old pictures and silver away for cleaning. The security people let them! Do you want toast, Malone? You look pensive. Are you flying today? I wish I could do something useful like that. I wish I had a skill. I was useless at sports at school but I liked the place. I think it's why I enjoy pretending to work up here. It reminds me of my public school.'

The cook brought Malone two pancakes and he put butter and maple syrup on them.

'No, I'm not flying today. Don't be so hard on yourself, Basil.'

Basil sighed. 'I am hard on my utterly perfect self, I suppose. I just don't like the way things are going . . . I know I shouldn't talk about it. But General McChrystal-Meth . . . It's getting silly.'

'You said he wasn't as bad as the last one,' said Malone, trying to cheer his friend up. He was very fond of Basil, even though the Englishman did not understand Malone's total lack of politics.

'Oh no, he's worse . . . The other day one of his staff told the Indian election monitors that there was at least some chance for Afghanistan because they were descended from Alexander the Great and therefore Aryan, as opposed to the majority on the subcontinent. I've never heard a silence quite like that. One of the old boys from the Congress Party stuffed that one so far up his moustache he died of a coronary on the way to see his mistress. Poor old thing.'

Basil paused. The sun dappled through the grapevine.

'The trouble is my own people lie to me and repeat lies they have already put out and know to be lies as gospel. And even if you see a village murdered by the Afghan army, the minister denies it. "It is not happening like that, Mr Basil, you don't know these things because you are a foreigner." We don't actually know much of anything any more. This morning I had to deal with an airstrike that accidently killed another wedding party even though my staff say we never bomb wedding parties. We are losing so many soldiers to roadside bombs we've been ordered to send out only one patrol a day to cut casualties. The trouble is this gives Terence Taliban all the time in the world to plant more. I have to think of an entertaining diversion for the British public. I heard about that goose you rescued. Could I give it the Dickin Medal for animal courage for warning of a Taliban attack?'

Malone shook his head.

'The goose is an Afghan national who spends quality time in India. I don't think you can make assumptions about whose side he's on. He's a definite security risk.'

Basil sighed.

'It'll have to be another fucking bomb-disposal Labrador then. They never get blown up. The men do. The dogs are far smarter. One bitch has killed so many of her handlers, by wagging her tail and leading them over bombs, I think she's gone Taliban.'

'You shouldn't say things like that. It brings bad luck,' said Malone.

Malone wished he had not said the work 'luck'. They all tried to avoid it.

'Everything here is bad luck,' said Basil, as if tempting fate further, and they both sat in silence listening to the peacock.

'Sorry about that,' said Basil after a moment.

'Don't worry,' said Malone.

'So where's the goosie now?'

Malone told him about the girl.

'She's called Fatima Hamza and is doing research for her father who sounds a bit mad. She says he cut her toenails until she went away to school. Do you know about the Dead Officers' Club?'

Basil looked at Malone astonished.

'Yes, I do, and if you're planning to go to that club you bloody well shouldn't. You know who her father is?'

'Oh, he's retired and writing some sort of history of Afghanistan.'
Basil was shaking his head.

'I doubt very much indeed if Hamza Khan has retired from anything . . . He still has links with the intelligence services.'

'So do you.'

Basil fidgeted on the cushions. 'Believe me, it's not the same.'

'Her father insisted she stayed at the club. What is it, some kind of spook hotel?'

Basil paused.

'Be that as it may . . . There are said to be three secret American strike forces here and that's where the Kabul one goes to wind down.'

Malone shrugged. 'So the name's just military black humour?'

Basil sighed. 'I'm not getting through to you, am I, Malone? I put it down to this girl . . . Some say the Dead Officers' Club is so named because Special Forces hit squads in Iraq were making so much money certain individuals had to be taken off the books. They had to "die". Wives and children in the US think they are dead.'

Basil fiddled with his shirt cuff. He never rolled up his sleeves because his arms were very hairy.

'A lot of field officers in Iraq, elite Special Forces types, were given backhanders by the security or the transport companies to be there, or not be there, if you catch my drift. Huge amounts of money in suitcases. Anything your heart desired bought and sold in a land too dangerous for anyone to mind. Before long everyone was on the pay roll, in a roundabout way, of the big companies which were connected to the Bush administration. Halliburton and those lovely Blackwater guys. They're Christians but with the

Knights of Malta, or some such . . . And they could not stop making money. Instead of banking the dollars they set up an import–export scam with France and England where they exported and then re-imported non-existent goods, perpetually claiming the VAT, all through Dubai. They made so much money. They bought all sorts of crazy stuff. Remember those container loads of down-hill competition skis that were found in the desert south of Baghdad? They were theirs from a truck convoy that ran out of gas. They traded in gold, sold munitions back to the factories that made them and even guaranteed the entire Pakistani cotton crop for a boat load of antiquities they sold on to this wonderful old Japanese gentleman who had a collection of Scotch whisky you wouldn't believe.'

There was a proud desperation in the voice. 'In economic terms they were becoming on a par with Belgium. It was then that Cheney's people advised they may be better off dead. For tax reasons, if not for political necessity.'

Malone blinked. 'Cheney wanted to kill them?'

Basil stared at one of the peacocks. 'They came here, officially dead.'

'But their wives and families?'

Basil smiled. 'You'd be surprised how delightfully loose family ties are when huge sums of money are involved. And soldiers do die, after all. Families understand. There have been small, tasteful parades from Nebraska to Nantucket. And this is the new gold rush; the next staging post on the good old American for ever frontier. From the men who brought you Vietnam it's Tombstone Kabul!'

Malone didn't know what to say. Or believe.

'Imagine what self-interested men like that will do to protect their considerable assets when Uncle Sam asks nicely.'

Malone shook his head. He had trouble getting his mind around a group of zombie Special Forces.

'Fatima would never have anything to do with people like that.'

Basil took a bite of toast. 'Well, I'm not an expert on women, old boy ... Did you mention you're married? The locals get upset about that sort of thing, you know.'

Two jets flashed across the sky sending sonic booms off the nearby hill, covered nearly to the top in ochre mud dwellings.

'No ... It's not like that. She's taking care of the goose.'

Basil did not even look up. 'I'd give the place and Miss Hamza a wide berth.'

'She doesn't seem to know her way around ...'

Basil laughed and cast his eyes to heaven and smoothed back his short black hair.

'I'm going grey a little more quickly after what you've just told me.'

Malone grinned at Basil.

'I thought it was your tangled love life that did it.'

He saw Basil hesitate. The Englishman was very careful what he said among American NGOs because many were Christians. Malone had noticed that. But Malone had flown Basil to places that he was not meant to – not careful flying – more than once getting a bullet hole in the Cessna, and they had come to trust each other.

'Well, my boy, speaking of ...'

And then from a bag under the table Basil drew a shining blue teapot. It was the love token traditionally given in a homosexual relationship.

'Undersecretary to the Ministry of Justice! He shouted *"Allah Akbar"*, God is great, when he climaxed. In Kandahar. Where Kim's going, poor thing.'

Malone blinked.

'Kandahar?'

'Didn't she tell you? I could have sworn she was talking in the office the other day about going down there with her medical group. With that awful shit, Noah. I would hate to be on a fucking ark with that particular Noah. But then again I wouldn't exactly be in the two by twos, would I? I'm the last one for marriage guidance, old boy. But do not go back to that club. You have a wife, my dear. Now, I should shut up and go and get some of those lovely pancakes!'

Several days later Basil left to go upcountry. Malone waited until he knew that Kim had left that day for the hospital. He had not asked her about Kandahar. He did not want to have an argument about Noah; the sort his father and mother used to have. He didn't like Noah at all. Noah was a man from whom no light seemed ever to shine, and he talked a lot about evil.

Malone checked his phone closely. Fatima had not called him but she did not say how long she was going to be in the south. He went to the courtyard behind the main gate of the Fort to get a car and a driver. They always had to have a driver from the Fort because of the kidnappings. Taxis were not safe. Malone had a vague idea of stopping by the Dead Officers' Club just to see if she was still there and he devised a trip to the market as a sort of cover. When they got to the Kabul River there was a traffic jam of military vehicles. Finally, the driver had to stop completely and

Malone got out and lit a cigarette. He strolled over to the stream, which was perhaps the most naturally polluted in the whole world. A small crowd were standing next to an abandoned car and a dead tree. One of the many open sewers flowed into the black channel at this point, and a body was visible where it had fetched up against a little island made from a rotting vehicle someone had driven into the filth. A vulture flapped near by, unsure, not wanting to step into the ooze.

Even in death the body of the broad-shouldered man who had carried the cognac bottle around the club was impressive. The river was not wide, and Malone could see the eyes open and the mouth spread in the rictus of a whimsical smile. He saw that the man's throat had been cut in a similar crescent shape. Others from the club were there too, including the barman, who was clearly upset. One man, ignoring the stench, waded in and gently picked the dead man up in his arms.

There was an uneasy silence as the man holding his dead friend looked around at the crowd, not in anger but with a distance that brought a chill to Malone. For a second the intense blue-eyed gaze rested on him, the head inclined with an almost imperceptible nod, as if he were one of them. The man then turned and slowly made his way towards the river's bank and the shouting and screaming and the honking of cars began again.

Malone's driver moved close to him. 'They tell me it is a matter over a woman and she has been killed too, but not here. She was drowned by her family inside their house in a pee bucket. There's no more we can say as men. *Bismillah* . . . We'll go back now, Mr Malone? We have the dates to buy, and a chicken . . . Or do you wish to go to that club you are talking about?'

'No . . . Not now,' Malone said. Then, as he was getting into the truck, he saw the tall, thin Afghan again with the scar on his forehead whom he had seen outside the club. The man bowed slightly and touched his heart but there was a hint of a smile. Malone was glad when they drove away.

FOUR

'Malone! Malone! It's Fatima! I'm at the King's Palace out on the southern road ... My battery's running low. I'm in all sorts of trouble. Please come, right now!'

He had been in the hangar at the airport working with the engineer on the Cessna when she called a whole two weeks later. The Palace was on a rise and the roads beyond were in Taliban hands and he told his driver, when he came, to hurry. Anxious, Malone tried to call back but there was no answer. The driver sped across town until they turned past the university and were caught in a jam behind a rare American convoy out on the road to the south of the city.

Malone was breathless as he got out of the car at a ruined gatehouse checkpoint and told the driver to go. 'If I need you I'll call.' The driver shook his head and drove off.

Fatima was up ahead, standing by another checkpoint of rusting barbed wire dressed in black shalwar kameez and a headscarf.

'Malone!' she called out. Toto was beside her on a lead.

Malone ran up to her and then noticed two Afghan soldiers standing under a tree in the crisp shade of the massive Palace. He was so pleased to see Fatima, he nearly hugged her. She was surrounded by a crowd of fifteen or so children, shoeless in the dust. They wore clothes little better than rags and dirty shawls.

'I thought you were in trouble?' he said.

'I am. We need a talented actor and now you are here!'

'What?'

She laughed.

'I used to play in this ruin as a child, Malone. Come, we must make the film. *The Wizard of Oz* film . . . For my pops. You'll help, won't you?' She said the last words to the children in Dari, and they all yelled excitedly back as they scrambled through another section of barbed wire that said *Forbidden – Danger Mines*. The broken Palace ascended above them on three sides, a bit of decoration here, a neo-classical pillar there but mostly a tangle of stone and concrete splattered with shrapnel or melted by high explosive.

'Have you been here before?'

'Never.'

'It was built by a German architect who had all the money and materials he wanted, Malone, for the last Afghan king. Just imagine if he saw it now.'

Malone shook his head.

He had been really worried for her.

He shaded his eyes and gazed at the smashed rooms. Fatima held up her arms with a dreamy look as if pointing to a miracle.

'Even the Russians didn't break it down,' she said. 'They pumped in tank round after tank round and it still stands. I always think it is like a theatre where all the drama of this country plays out, where the ghosts enact our story endlessly while we are not looking. Or the crazed backdrop for a very violent opera . . . But I don't come here only to film.' She reached in her bag and half took out a handful of brown envelopes. 'I come here for the children. Inside are sweets and a little money and an address where they can find more if they promise to have an education. I do this to make up for not fasting in Ramadan. You see, I'm serious too, Malone.'

She touched him on the arm.

The day was very hot now and Malone wrapped his black-and-white tribal scarf around his head. From the Palace you could see most of Kabul and he had always meant to have a look. It was on a demarcation line. The mortars and rockets he heard at night were often lobbed over this ruined shell, heading for a tented American base near by.

The wind blew hot dust and Malone blinked and gazed up at what once had been three sides of a six- or eight-storey courtyard, each level with its own neoclassical pillars, some still whole, others blasted to smithereens by high explosive. Twisted metal protruded from the concrete like snakes and there were more mine-danger signs.

Malone could make out the remains of a statue and tried to remember the line of a poem by Shelley he had learned in high school. But the building was beyond poetry. It was a hymn in broken stone and broken promises to what mankind can do to itself.

'You really want to make the video here?'

'It'll seem so much more dramatic, don't you think?'

'Yeah, it certainly will.'

'It will.'

'You are kidding me . . .?'

'No, I am not, Malone.'

There was a shout from the children. One of them had jumped into a marble water tank, which may have once been an indoor fountain, that the soldiers had filled from a green hosepipe that came all the way from the American base. He looked at the impish faces. Convoys from the base had been attacked recently and ten soldiers killed in one suicide truck ambush.

Malone was almost able to make out Fatima's words in Dari.

'Oh, my little brothers and sisters, why do you shame me by taking my gifts and not buying shoes for your feet and not going to school?'

But the children answered in Pashto, a rapid machine-gun exuberance of Pashto, and he was lost. And a boy called out in English.

'Dollars, dollars, we want all your dollars.'

'Then you must work.'

Malone saw an aloof, middle-aged man standing in the shadows with Fatima's video camera by a pile of costumes on a marble bench. He was one of the waiters from the Dead Officers' Club. He smirked as Fatima handed Malone the lion costume and the children watched, wide-eyed. The waiter was still wearing his white shirt and black bow tie. It made him look like a phantom from the building's past.

Fatima then rummaged in her bag and produced madly smiling paper masks with rubber bands. The effect was slightly sinister. She gave them out to the children. 'Now you can all be Munchkins.'

'It's OK,' she said to the man with the camera. 'Malone's going to help out if he can get the lion costume on. I'll mime to the track.'

She looked at Malone pleadingly and he gave in.

Malone decided to take off his jeans to be able to get into the suit. He was wearing a pair of black boxers. He wriggled into the costume, which smelt unmistakably of goat, and she zipped him up.

He then reached down and put the lion's head on his own and the children all cried out in joy. A shard of broken mirror had been found and propped against a piece of concrete. The sight made him jump. He looked too . . . real. But the head was suffocatingly hot inside and he took it off again, momentarily, to a groan from the children and the sight of Fatima removing her layers of clothes and scarf to reveal her Dorothy dress underneath.

Several of the Afghan army soldiers appeared out of the shadows to watch.

'I will open my mouth wide so I can probably dub a Pashto version,' she said, and turned to Malone.

'Come over here, stand by me and put your lion paws around my waist. Let me pick Toto up. Quiet, Toto . . . Don't be shy, Malone. Just follow me with the dancing.'

The Cowardly Lion who was Malone nodded.

'Right . . . Action . . . Start filming,' she shouted at the waiter and she was singing.

' "Some . . . where . . . over . . . the . . . rainbow . . ." '

The beat from a ghetto blaster linked to her phone kicked in and Fatima was dancing around him. She grabbed hold of his Cowardly Lion's head. She stroked his whiskers. She let him go. She sambaed suggestively up to him and knocked her hips against him, wriggling her bottom, and planted a kiss on his whiskers. They then did everything again and again and again.

Finally, she grabbed his tail and then slipping around to his front threw herself into his arms and gave him another kiss.

Malone stepped back and fell headlong into the water tank as the children with their masks on danced around laughing and the waiter continued filming. 'That's great, that's great,' Fatima said, as Malone floundered to the side, the dun suit filling with water, and struggled out.

Fatima gave Toto the goose a big kiss and one for Malone. She went to her pile of clothes and took out a small vial from her bag and borrowed a bowl from one of the soldiers. She filled the bowl with water and added a few drops from the vial and put it on the ground in front of the goose.

'Drink, my pretty one. Drink . . . You'll find it quite tasty.'

'What is it?'

'A sort of rescue remedy.'

'What's in it?'

'Oh, mainly laudanum. Opium in a tincture of best rum. It will not hurt him. I was brought up on it and so were most of the Bhutto family. The Pathans used to give it to those they abducted . . . It will help as we film.'

Malone had wondered how she was able to keep the goose so calm.

The cameraman-waiter, irritated, said, 'We have to hurry up, please.'

Fatima nodded and turned to Malone.

'Now, can we repeat it once more with you as the Scarecrow and the Tin Man, Malone? Are you OK, Malone? We must be quicker. A patrol will come up here from the base and they're not always in a Hollywood mood.'

Malone took off the sodden head with difficulty, but he was laughing. He couldn't stop. He had not laughed like that for a long time.

Fatima was laughing hard too as he squelched about on what had been the reception hall of the Palace.

She had taken him by surprise when she had shimmied up to him like that. He had not expected such freedom because she was Afghan, he supposed. She sidled by and gave him another mischievous kiss at the side of the cheek. 'Let's wrap you in aluminium foil for the Tin Man bit . . . and then we'll do the Scarecrow.'

He and Fatima sashayed around the marble floor between piles of rubble, linking arms and singing with the children dancing after them. Toto the goose was being held by one of the Afghan soldiers and occasionally honked.

The video was finished before any American patrol could inter-rupt them and, covered in Scarecrow rags, Malone pulled Fatima into the water tank with him. The children watched amazed. Fatima put a hand gently at the side of his head. She had the most unbelievable eyes, eyes that you could look into for ever and remember the instant you closed your own. She was going to speak and then she touched his cheek again and heaved herself

49

out, the wet dress, ruined in the pool, sticking to her bottom and the water running down her bare legs.

'I must go and change in the army tent. Put your clothes on. I've somewhere I want to take you for a great treat. We'll go with my driver! Toto can have a little sleep in the car. We're going for a picnic!'

'Where?'

'Oh, the Barbur Gardens. But first we will give out the money and sweets.'

When she came back the children were beside themselves with excitement as they snatched the brown envelopes stuffed with Afghani notes and candy from Fatima, kissing her hands. Only one boy stood apart. He had a harelip and a black eye.

'Don't give them any dollars, man. They won't spend it on clothes. They won't spend it on food. Their elders will take it off them and spend it on opium and dope. Don't do it, man,' the boy said in English. Malone nearly dropped the remaining envelopes he was holding. It was not just English. It was English mangled into a rich Brooklyn accent.

'Who taught you American?'

'A brother down in the camp. He says he can fix my lip.'

Malone stared hard at the child. He was Uzbek or Hazara.

'And he's a good man?'

The boy nodded.

Malone felt a lump in his throat and had to look away. He was continually amazed at the generosity of the individual, ordinary soldier and it always reminded him of his own father.

'I don't take no charity,' said the boy defiantly, his chin stuck out as Malone held out an envelope.

'This is not charity . . . It's payment for acting. You're an actor,' he said.

'Payment?'

'Wages.'

The boy hesitated and then accepted the envelope.

Fatima took Malone's arm and they walked quickly away but the children started to run in the direction of her car. They clustered around shouting and banging on the glass and he saw one of the girls was in tears. Stones were thrown by those who had received nothing.

Malone watched the boy with the harelip as their driver carefully turned and the children let go before the car started to accelerate down the hill. The last glimpse Malone had of the boy was of him standing apart, silhouetted in the glare of the sun.

Inside the hot car Fatima seemed very pleased and was talking fast with her arm around the exhausted Toto. 'You're not like any of the Americans I've met here, Malone.'

He took that as a compliment.

'I used to adore the Americans I saw in the old films. I called them the Big People to Pops. He asked me what I meant and I said the immensely good characters played by James Stewart and Cary Grant in the old movies in his personal cinema, or ones he borrowed from the Sindh Club, like *To Kill a Mockingbird*. He thought I'd seen the giant US presidents carved on Mount Rushmore in one Hitchcock picture and was surprised when I tried to explain, aged fourteen, that the characters in those Hollywood films were more noble and thoughtful than characters in our traditional stories, who always end up doing murder before very long. Pops laughed and laughed and laughed. It was the same year we watched *The Wizard of Oz* for the first time and my father said the story had been shamelessly stolen from *The Conference of the Birds* by the twelfth-century Persian poet, Farid-ud-Din-Attar, about a group of birds who, looking for someone to solve their problems, find everything within themselves. He even wrote a letter to Hollywood saying that they should pay Farid's descendants. Pops can be quite eccentric like that . . . It was only weeks before my mother was shot.'

Malone heard the change in Fatima's voice as she said the words. He felt very close to her in the small car.

'She was shot?'

'It was in Clifton. Near where one of the Bhuttos was gunned down. They were trying to shoot my father.'

She was gazing at the seat in front.

'Who were?'

'His enemies.'

She turned to Malone, smiling again. But he guessed the smile was forced.

'Those children make me feel guilty at being so fortunate. We lived here for a short time before the Taliban. My family are Afghan. My father knows all the languages and the heads of all the clans. Thank you for going there with me. It is . . . too much. The worst thing, the very worst thing is that many people here will not accept help, even from their own. I don't know why . . . Perhaps they think it makes them slaves.'

Fatima took a deep breath.

She beamed at him.

'Now for our treat! We will go and find a cool spot. I have a picnic in the boot. Don't look so worried. Do not think so much, Malone, I have another favour to beg. That's what people say of me, that I expect and ask too much. In that I'm totally Afghan. I want everything, Malone. All your dollars! Your soul! I want to seize everything under heaven!'

She laughed.

'And this is only a tiny, tiny favour.'

'What?'

'First we'll picnic.'

'And you were going to tell me your secret. Was it about your mother?'

'No . . . But yes, I am going to tell you.'

In the icy sanctuary of the air-conditioned Toyota Fatima did not say anything more but he sensed that underneath she was very upset and she started to cry silently and shake and held onto Malone's hand. Hers was soft and bare of rings. The driver looked into the mirror and then avoided Malone's eyes. She did not stop trembling for a mile and he felt her emotion overwhelm his own.

They drove across town, most of the way in a traffic jam, trying to take a short cut through the markets beside the river.

'Did they tell you about the guy from the club . . .?'

She leaned over him and looked at the river too.

'Oh, yes. Poor man. He was very unlucky. What a truly terrible place to die.'

Along the river, stalls were mainly hung with bright cloths and carpets. A larger stall had five wooden prosthetic legs dangling from a crystal chandelier. A man without a nose held a pig up to the window and the dust rose in clouds. The driver then did a detour to leave a package for a friend at the Kabul Paris Wedding Palace. Outside the steel-and-glass office-like building were piles of yellow plastic dahlias.

Finally, they arrived at the long, high wall of the gardens, where young men, a fashionable few in their best Western suits in Day-glo silky purple or blue, and long, curly-toed shoes, paraded their masculinity. Malone had been before and dutifully walked around with a few of the people from the Fort.

Fatima took a cool-box out of the boot and handed it to Malone with an old tartan car rug. She then picked up Toto and they left the driver in the car and she walked past the queue and paid at the gate. The soldier at the booth hesitated at giving her the tickets ahead of a woman who had waited in the sun but Fatima appeared to charm them all.

'Go in, my daughter. It's all right. That is a splendid goose!'

'Everyone is so sweet to me here,' was all she said.

She led him up hundreds of steps past a channel of falling waters set into the marble to a mulberry tree, the fanlike leaves looking as if they had been made to shade them by gentle gods. Mainly men were making a slow ascent or descent of the stairs by the cool water, playing with strings of beads, talking and laughing and pointing at Toto.

The tree was not far from the perfect fretwork of the white marble tomb itself.

'This is where I used to have picnics as a child with my mother and aunts. Zahiruddin Babur conquered India in the fourteenth century and founded the Mughal Empire. When he started out he walked across Afghanistan and wrote it down in a journal. This was his favourite place. In India when his son Humayun was sick Babur offered his own life to God when he could have given the Koh-i-noor diamond. He walked around his son's bed three times. His son recovered but Babur was taken by God and is buried here . . . What a story! It's beautiful, isn't it, to give yourself so completely? The inscription calls it the light garden of the godforgiven Angel King. He's our Alexander.'

'It's beautiful,' said Malone politely. The tomb somehow seemed impossibly modest.

'He was a man who in life was not able to stay still. Perhaps the real reason he died was he had nowhere else to go. I fear my father may feel like that one day.'

She did a little pirouette on the short grass around the tomb and Malone felt the wind in his face from the snow peaks of Hazarajat. She took his hand, but only for a moment, and then gave a sheaf of Afghani notes to an elderly guide who blessed both of them and Toto for eternity.

She led him and Toto back to the mulberry tree and began to spread a feast out in front of them on the old tartan car rug. Under another tree near by a few boys were guiltily drinking Tajik vodka, which they poured into a teapot and then small glasses, as they played cards.

Malone stared down over the whole impossible city as she produced blinis and Iranian caviar and sour cream and smoked salmon from the cool-box. There was a flask marked *Coca-Cola* which she opened and a ready-made gin and tonic frothed out. He smiled at her amazed and took a glass which foamed over as she poured.

'We have to celebrate our debut in the movies,' she laughed, and they watched the home-made kites fighting in the clear blue sky.

'What's the favour you want to ask me?'

She leaned affectionately against him.

'I'm sorry. I didn't realize we would know each other so quickly. I am sorry. It must seem I'm bribing you with this hotel lounge rubbish. I don't mean to. I wondered . . .'

'Wondered what?'

'Before I ask you the favour I must tell you about my father. And my travels. I went down to Kandahar and to a place where our national heroine, Mailalai, yelled a famous poem to inspire our people to defeat the British . . . But don't worry, a family diplomatic friend was fussing over me. My father wanted me to touch the robe of the Prophet, peace be upon him, in Kandahar and I managed to charm one of the mullahs . . . They say Mullah Omar, the head of the largest Taliban group, is the only person Allah will allow to wear it. It's very dusty and smells of pear drops. And then I went into the mountains to Gandamak Ridge. You know the story, Malone: the biggest defeat ever for the British Empire. Sixteen thousand men, women and children slaughtered on a march through the mountains and only the American doctor surviving . . . Now you're going to think me and my family bonkers.'

Malone took a sip of the chilled gin and tonic. He was thinking that Kim was going to Kandahar and how they still had not properly talked.

'No, I won't think you're mad. Nothing seems mad in this insane country.'

She stared at him and took a piece of ice out of her glass and ate it.

'Well, every time my father starts to write his version of the Gandamak story, which he has been working on for years, he ends up writing down the future, the complete truth, often exquisite visions of great catastrophe. These prophecies have happened now many times in his life and he's worried it's all starting again.'

Malone did not know what to say. His own father had deluded himself more and more about the love of his mother but that was different.

'Is . . . Is he well?'

'He has never been better, except for this . . .'

Malone saw she was completely sincere.

'I really shouldn't tell you this . . . I do not know how you can possibly believe me.'

She took a delicate sip of her drink and continued.

'In *The Dostan of Amir Hamza*, which my father has always loved, the vizier Buzurjmehr comes into possession of a magic book and is able to foretell the future. My father truly believes that whenever he tries to put down the story of the retreat from Gandamak, he, too, writes down prophetic works. Word for word he detailed the shooting on Clifton that took the life of my mother with a bullet that was meant for him. My mother was a beautiful, beautiful woman who didn't give a thought for politics. She had a short career as a film actress and was only limited by a penchant for using foul language engendered by an English governess. But men wept at her beauty. In Karachi station a man was hit by a train and killed while staring at her, open-mouthed. My father used to go to the flower salesmen and buy her armfuls of roses on the slightest pretext. Basketfuls! Car loads! More than you can get on an ordinary donkey! More roses than in an English summer! He often needed three servants to carry them to the vehicle. But one day my dear father was sitting at his desk in his favourite smoking jacket and writing about the retreat at Gandamak and a young soldier called Captain Souter, who tried to save the women and children of the retreating British column, when he began to write of death in the street outside a house like ours. His own death, he thought. *Inshallah*, darling. As it turned out, my dear father was meant to have died in a hail of bullets on the very next scalding Karachi night outside Seventy Clifton, the home of . . . The same place one of the better Bhuttos was shot some time later . . .. There was blood sticky on the pavement, a tar-pit smell on that hot night and a passer-by shouting, 'It has clearly broken my billiard arm. The bullet has broken my arm.' That is what my father said. And then they shot the broken-armed man in the back of his head and laughed he did not need to go to the hospital now. My father tried to get to my mother, but it was too late. The bullets meant for my father had hit my beautiful, ethereal mother, with whom he was deeply in love and for whom he had only that day bought an outrageous basket of flowers in the shape of a swan. I wept for a month.'

Malone saw the pain in her eyes.

'That's horrible . . . My God. Please don't be upset. It's OK. I believe you.'

'But there is more, so much more . . . When my father was found on that frontier road as a little boy, his arms and legs had been broken to hasten death. My grandfather ordered the filthy foundling carried into the car and then he bit everyone. My grandfather was so impressed he adopted him on the spot. Each limb had been most carefully broken in two places and he was in considerable pain. He had been left certainly to die.'

'Why?'

Fatima sat there in the sunlight, sipping her drink.

'It is the punishment they reserve for a child who they think is a witch or is possessed by a spirit or a *dev*. Many children were abandoned as possessed after the obscenity of Partition. My pops is called Hamza because the *Dostan* was my grandfather's favourite book too and in it Amir Hamza is a foundling . . . His adopted father decided he must have been born on the 15th of August 1947, the earthquake day of Pakistan and our mad frontier's separation from India. Imposed insanity and schizophrenia. It is said that children born on that day have second sight. Perhaps now you see why he is worried when he starts to write down the future and it happens. People have said it is a trick and that he has been spying on them. But it's real and he has written down the greatest things before they have happened. Dangerous things. And how the world will change for ever . . . I shall tell you but not here. There are too many wicked ears, who may be listening among these innocent mulberry trees.'

She was silent again and Malone did not know what to say. He was beginning to feel drawn closer and closer to her and knew he should not. She then looked up and smiled a dazzling smile.

'Oh, and the favour . . . I was wondering. Can you fly me to Bamiyan?'

'Why do you want to go there?'

'I want to see where the Buddhas were. And I want to visit my young nephew who is there after a most unfortunate time. My father also gave me contacts in Bamiyan and in Faizabad . . . People I have to see for him. I may stay.'

Malone shook his head.

'I don't know. Both of our twin-engine planes are out this week. There is only the old Cessna and that needs good weather. There may be a medical-supplies run tomorrow. I hope you don't get airsick.'

She gave him a short and violent hug as they were already being stared at.

'I shouldn't ask you these things. I shouldn't take you away from your poor wife. From all the good you are doing.'

She poured herself another drink and topped his up and lifted her gin and tonic.

'May Zahiruddin Muhammad Babur the Conqueror of Death bless us in our travels!'

Malone walked around the hot streets of Kabul that night watching the greasy yellow car headlights emerge from the brown dust clouds that hung over the road in nightmare shapes. In the darkness those lights followed you like the evil eye. At night you got another picture of the city, of an ancient wickedness and complete degradation; of the most unpredictable place under the heavens.

But even a human scream in the night did not make an impression on him.

Malone was dreaming of Fatima Hamza in a perfumed garden when he knew he should have been thinking of Kim, who was still at the hospital and due to go to Kandahar tomorrow with Noah.

The crazy Pashtun girl Fatima Hamza possessed him. At her name his heart beat faster and he was flying in a wide blue sky and not the careful sort. He wanted to hear her tell more of her father's incredible story just as he had listened to his father's as a boy. It was a pull he could not resist, like that of the waning reddish moon, indistinct through the cloud and dust.

FIVE

'I've to go up to Faizabad more or less immediately after getting to Bamiyan. So you'll have to make up your mind quickly if you want to stay,' he said, too sharply. Malone had been up since four o' clock when he met Fatima at the entrance to the airport at seven. His goodbyes with Kim had been sleepy, monosyllabic and painful.

'Don't worry, Malone, I will decide. This is so exciting, isn't it, Toto?'

She smiled at him showing the gap between her front teeth. She was dressed in a black long-sleeved top and matching skin-tight jeans with Gucci sunglasses on top of her head and a pair of chunky, lace-up boots and a white leather backpack. There was a black-and-white-chequered scarf but that had fallen onto her shoulders. She flung her arms around him and kissed him inappropriately on the cheek.

Malone had not expected the goose. Toto now had a leather lead and a black diamanté collar. The goose nipped at his trouser leg.

'He's coming with us?'

'I couldn't leave him, Malone. Is everything all right?'

'Yes . . .'

They both stared down at the bleary-eyed goose, shaking slightly, probably from a need for more opium. His wings were carefully bound.

The guards knew Malone and nodded them past the armoured cars and machine-gun posts. They passed a battered old Soviet MiG to a U-turn in the road flanked by guard houses and Malone was waved and nodded through body searches of medieval thoroughness and indignity, with everyone staring at Fatima and laughing at the goose. A boy then took Fatima's rucksack and they walked to a rusting hangar outside which a Cessna and a twin-engine Grumman were parked. These were the total fleet of Astro-Nec, the air service he worked for, and both were constantly on the borderline of airworthiness.

The Cessna had crashed on two occasions trying to get to an airstrip in the Pamirs, the old engine unable to cope with the altitude. He had only just fixed it in time for today.

Malone spent much longer than usual doing the pre-flight checks. Fatima was the only passenger and sat just behind Malone's seat, holding Toto, who looked puzzled and a little scared as the engines were started. He then lay, ecstatic, with his head on her lap. Malone strapped himself in and grabbed the first slot. He was used to waiting for hours while dithering, multi-nationality military operations failed to make up their minds. He should have said more to Kim about Kandahar and Noah. But he had felt guilty and furtive about this trip. The engine caught first time and he let it run for a few minutes before upping the revs and taxiing out onto the apron. He then turned into the wind and pulled back the throttle.

'Wheee!' Fatima cried out behind him. 'Look, Toto, we're flying! We're off to see the Wizard!'

Malone pulled the plane up over buffeting pockets of warm air above Kabul's ochre hills and then the Panjshir range was below him and the Hindu Kush galloping out to the right, higher and higher to the snowfields of the Himalayas.

Fatima gently removed one of his earphones.

'Do you know Hindu Kush means Indian Killer?'

'No. I didn't.'

'It is so named when captives taken in India, too soft for the journey north over the frontier, perished in the high passes on their way to the slave markets of Samarkand and Cathay,' she said, and settled back down.

As they gained height the plane appeared almost to stop and they inched from razor-backed brown ridge to brown ridge over valleys full to the brim with low cloud. Here and there were patches of snow.

The ground moved under him very slowly and this was the careful flying he remembered from those lessons with his father and uncle, easing up along the Potomac, with the world slipping beneath him, in straight lines on a windless day, like the sea bed did when he was snorkelling. Malone had loved flying carefully over America until he had never wanted to land.

The engine reduced everything to noisy silence.

When he was very little he used to imagine he was flying in his bed, like Superman, long before his mother would come to visit him on hot summer nights, with her perfume and her disturbing,

speech-numbing curves. But up here was as secure as his hide-
away at the Rock Creek children's cemetery and Malone could
become cold, shiny metal like the plane itself. That chill was the
only thing which kept his family at a bearable distance.

The goose gave a gentle honk.

Malone banked the plane slightly.

The view never ceased to amaze him, the black rims of the
nearer mountains rising like waves. He glanced back and saw that
Fatima was gazing out of the window too, gently stroking Toto's
head.

The Bamiyan Valley was one of sand-coloured rock, honey-
combed with millions of holes. It was deep and protective and the
greens of farmers' fields and of stands of poplar trees stood out
below. He flew up and down the valley a few times and saw the
flag was in place on the runway. If there was fighting it was taken
down and he would have to divert to Faizabad. He tried the radio
and got a cheerful voice back.

'OK, Malone. You early. Fuck you . . .' The greeting then tailed
off into giggles and static. The place was not big on procedure.

But there was a commotion on the runway and he realized
that a flock of goats was crossing and he had to go around again.
As he did so he saw children flying kites in his path and a man
grin and point his Kalashnikov at the plane. If Fatima noticed
anything she did not say. As he came in the second time to his left
was the dark accusing finger, the empty exclamation mark, of the
stone recess where the great Buddha had been before being
dynamited by Mullah Omar. There was a gust of breeze as he
levelled the plane out and shouting mothers now dragged away
the kite-flying children and the goats had passed in a

brown-white, tail-wagging mass, hung with a small cloud of ochre dust.

Malone landed the plane with great care and gentleness, so as not to disturb Toto.

A team of Japanese archaeologists, who Malone had flown up with his fat, cigar-smoking Cincinnati boss, had found a reclining Buddha underground, which was even bigger than the standing ones. He braked the plane down to a full stop and turned it in a careful circle. He saw cars at the side of the runway and wondered if one was waiting for Fatima.

'This is your captain speaking. Welcome to Bamiyan . . .' Malone began but had to correct almost immediately for a skid and ended up feeling embarrassed.

He opened the cabin door and, with a wide smile, Fatima walked down the stairs onto the runway, leading Toto, who looked about him disapprovingly and lifted his yellow feet higher than ever on hot shale. He had preferred the perfumed lap of Fatima, who was waving at a boy standing by one of the cars.

It was easy to see that the boy she was meeting was not from around there and had once been much overweight. His face was drawn.

'Hello, Fatima. What on earth is that creature?'

He was looking down at the goose.

'Hello, little Aziz. This is Toto. And this is Malone . . . Where's the friend you were staying with? I have to give him a letter.'

Aziz nodded.

'He has already spoken to your father and says you must consult a man in Faizabad market if it is about your researching. When can I go back to Karachi?'

She shook her head and then winced. He was dressed tradition-ally in a shalwar kameez and a utility waistcoat, with a Pashtun hat on his head.

'Malone, meet my fat little nephew. He went off to become a jihadist but things didn't work out. A diet of rice and potatoes and running in the mountains is not what he was used to. More the television and computer screen. But you have lost so much weight, my nephew. All the girls will be after you! They'll swoon at your new shape.'

Malone wondered if Fatima was joking. The boy smiled. But it was not a happy expression.

'Please do not tease me, Fatima. I've had too much of the teasing. How long does it take to become a flyer?' he said to Malone.

'You want to become a pilot?' Malone was surprised. But then, the boy didn't look like any jihadist he had seen. This one bit his nails. He had thick dark hair and his eyebrows joined into one unbroken line. Even with the loss of weight he was almost as broad as he was tall.

'I want to fly away from here,' Aziz said with great finality.

'And you don't hate Americans?' asked Malone. The boy looked puzzled.

'Never . . . Not now. I want to go home.' There was a pleading quality to his voice and Malone noticed a scar on Aziz's neck like a burn. He guessed he had been through a lot.

They walked to a Toyota Land Cruiser and the boy said some-thing to the driver and they got in.

'You must have been very religious? I mean, devout. To go to one of those camps,' said Malone.

The boy was sitting between him and Fatima who had Toto on her lap. The goose let the boy stroke his head.

'It's not like that,' the boy said.

'What's it like then?' asked Malone. 'Were you suddenly converted?'

The boy sighed.

'I wanted to do something,' said Aziz. 'But I never thought . . . What it was going to be like. Most of the boys who came hated it all. And they told us nothing about religion. All they did was make us run, day and night, and do the forward roll which I could not do. And run and run and run. They said I was a Tali-tubbie. And they made me eat rat droppings to learn obedience. And smashed my iPod. I was a failure. They used to tell me that I would not go to paradise and have virgins and an everlasting orgasm . . . Truly, my aunt . . . And I did not care. All I wanted was to be back in my bedroom and eating a Snickers bar. I wanted my computer games . . . All I wanted was that. How shallow am I? They said they were going to shoot me. They are different, the people up there. I have seen a man run and catch an ibex. Catch an ibex and twist its neck with its horns! They do not need me, I told them. And then I was bitten by a camel spider . . . I have never felt such pain in my life. I wished to die. I did . . . And if that is to be a coward I want to remain one. But you cannot be a coward in Afghanistan and so I must go home in shame. And quickly.'

He turned and grinned at Malone.

'You do not have such camps in America?'

Malone was grinning too.

'Well, there are summer camps. But you get to meet girls there.'

'You do?'

They all got out of the Toyota on a path near to the cliffs pitted with holes and soon the alcove where the Buddha had been

69

loomed in front of them. The space was much bigger than anyone ever expected. The rock threw a cold shadow and there was the dripping of water from far above and a strange oily smell that might still be that of explosive. He stepped deeper into the shade and shivered from a sense of awe as much as the chill.

Voices echoed in the great chamber that had held the one hundred and eighty-foot statue of the Buddha and Malone had no doubt that he was at the scene of a crime. It was like one of those outlines of bodies chalked on the ground after a homicide but worse than that. It was an icon of emptiness.

Fatima's phone then began to ring and ring. She answered it briefly, promising to call back, and he continued gazing up into the void.

Malone felt a drop of water splash on his face and took a deep breath.

The power that had annoyed the mullahs about these shrines before they rocketed and dynamited the Buddha was only rein-forced. The absurdity of destroying an art work so ancient, beautiful and immense made him truly frightened. But the irony was that the black hole of its passing was now more powerful than the carving had ever been.

Outside again they all climbed up on a path marked with white-painted rocks, with Fatima carrying Toto, and entered the passages, once full of chanting monks and frescos, the latter all destroyed by the Taliban even after Genghis Khan had left them untouched. In the seventh century there were ten convents, a thousand priests and fifty temples. Malone had flown Buddhists up here often and they had shown him old drawings and maps.

He was never quite prepared for coming out above the head of where the Buddha had been and taking in the precipitous view of the sandy mountains flecked with green. It always gave the illusion that you could see for ever.

It was then he heard Fatima scream. At first he thought it was the goose trying to get away.

In the passage behind him she shouted in Pashto to her nephew. There were some words in Dari and he made out it was something to do with her phone. She held it up to the boy who laughed at first but suddenly stopped.

Fatima left Toto with Aziz and came running up to Malone.

She was crying. Tears stained her cheeks.

'What's wrong . . .? Is it your family?'

She shook her head.

'No.'

'So what is it?'

She was shaking her head.

'The *Wizard of Oz* video we made for my father, for Pops, is all over YouTube. It says my name and who I am . . . That waiter must have uploaded it as a joke or something . . . I know he was upset when I wouldn't have a drink with him but doesn't he realize what he's done? Singers have been attacked and killed for far less.'

'Shit,' said Malone.

She pressed the button on the phone and she was dancing in the blue-gingham minidress and Malone loomed into view wearing the lion's head.

Fatima was breathless.

Her phone beeped again.

'I have a text from my father. He rang to tell me this when we were down below . . .'

Malone saw her quickly reading. 'He says not to go back to Kabul. A mullah has already seen the video and has said dreadful things . . . Whatever you do, Pops says, don't go back to Kabul. That if possible to get back to Pakistan . . . That there are many who know who I am and will try and get at him through me! How could I be so stupid?'

Malone pondered what his friend Basil had said about Fatima's father's profession.

'There's not enough fuel to reach Pakistan . . . We had all better go to Faizabad. I've got a box in the back to deliver at the airport and another pilot who's up there can fly the plane back . . . Don't worry, I'll help. If there was only some way to explain . . .'

'Explain? Are you joking . . .? Explain? Look what happened to the Buddha.'

She shook her head. But it was the boy's expression that told Malone far more. The boy was terrified. He was almost in tears.

'Please don't leave me here,' he was saying and his small hands were clutching each other.

Fatima was staring at her phone in disbelief. 'It was for Pops . . . To amuse him. It wasn't for anyone else.' But then her nephew was urging her to return to the car and the plane.

'We should go back to the plane. I mean, I can try and sneak back into Kabul,' said Malone.

Fatima was walking quickly, back into the caves, holding the goose. He and Aziz kept up with her.

'No . . . I came here for a purpose,' she said breathlessly. 'If I go back empty-handed after our arguments I can never face my father. He said to me I was not sufficiently grown-up to come and make my way in a city like Kabul. And my God, I have proved him right! And he'll not be able to protect me when this gets around. Can you imagine what that means here? For someone like me? They'll stone me to death, Malone!'

There was no reasoning with her and Malone went back and sat in the plane. After walking off some of her anger she came and sat beside him and gave him the phone and he was able to watch the YouTube video again, slowly, as she stroked Toto, who nibbled at her sleeves with his beak. Her beautiful face was plainly visible on the small screen and Fatima was wiggling her hips like a belly dancer at one point. But it all seemed so completely innocent.

'That waiter had no right to do this,' said Malone.

There were tears on Fatima's cheeks.

'Nothing's private any more . . . The people who will condemn me will not care about such niceties. The Taliban are not in Faizabad so we must think what to do there.' She reached out her hand to him and he held it. He let go and started the engines and, checking behind, noticed that Aziz was sitting in one of the rear passenger seats, his hands clasped in prayer, his brown eyes beseeching.

A man in an extravagant white turban began to bang on the door with his stick and goats were drifting across the dusty runway again. A crowd was gathering. Malone pressed the starter switch and the engine fired first time. Malone turned the plane into the wind and took off, pulling the nose up fast as he caught sight of a car driving down the runway, a hand waving from one of the windows. Malone flew down the valley and the radio crackled.

'Charlie 2 6. You were not authorized at this time to take off. Be warned there is fast-jet military activity in the area . . .'

'Roger, control. I have a possible medical emergency . . . Copy activity . . .'

Malone had never wanted that dread-fuelled, godlike arc of the fast jet as you turn the afterburners on and for a moment the sky goes teasingly dark and the pilot must be at one with the friendly stars. That was not careful flying.

He did not want that. Or, at least, that was what he told himself.

Malone turned his head and stared at the great black gouge in the rock where the Buddha had been.

The darkness of the alcove seemed to be both accusing and warning him – he was not sure of exactly what.

Six

The ride in the minivan to Kandahar was not what Kim expected.

She had thought the entire team was coming in a convoy of Red Cross/Red Crescent-marked cars, but instead she was with Noah and an Afghan driver who she had never seen before. He smelt of sheep grease and only spoke Dari. She wished she had not left without putting things right with Malone. He pretended to be a tough guy but it was so easy to hurt him. She remembered how they had met on that wet vacation in Yellowstone and he was just wanting to be rescued in that little tent of his, waiting for her to come along and put everything in order. She had fallen in love with him immediately when spooked by a flash of lightning in a rainstorm she had stumbled over a tent rope and found herself in his arms. It was like discovering a wolf in the wilderness with a wounded paw and she was going to make the sadness better, she was. They had stayed in that campsite for three weeks and then she told her parents what she intended to do and they were delighted. She had gone and proposed to Malone in his small blue tent and the whole family had descended from the plateau to a river the next day, to a small and beautiful creek, where first he had been baptised and she had been taken under that wonderfully cold, laughing water again by her preacher father, before they were married next day in a car park, so an old aunt could be present. She was not sure Malone was going to stay serious through all the religious stuff but he did not seem to mind. One of the rangers had let them camp down in the creek. And she and Malone had looked up at the huge stars and the scientist in her wondered what she had done.

While she had been thinking about Malone, Noah had been speaking to her and she had not realized. The driver was grinning although he did not understand a word that was being said. They hit a pothole in the road and all the quotes he had from the Koran hanging from the mirror and the sunshades bounced around.

'I was talking to you, Kim. You are off daydreaming again. Just like that Malone. He's a dreamer, isn't he?'

She shook herself back to the present. Noah, although only thirty or so, had a thin face and a scrawny neck. He had black hair, thick eyebrows and a sallow skin. He was not tall but had an air of the Pharisee about him. He was from rural Tennessee. She thought that he meant well but had an unfortunate way of saying things.

'It's not wrong to dream.'

She saw the driver glancing back at her legs. She had put on jeans that were, perhaps, too tight.

'I know that . . . I know that. It's not wrong to have righteous dreams. But all Malone thinks of is those planes. All he thinks of is himself. I don't think even an angel like you has completely rescued him from falling into bad ways. You know I'm right. I see it in your pretty eyes!'

Kim laughed. If Malone had a fault it was that he hid from the world and that was because of his family.

Noah's voice was rising. The driver began taking even more peeks.

'Where are the rest of the team, Noah?' she asked.

He grinned nervously. 'They're coming tomorrow. This car had been hired by an important person who didn't need it any more. I wanted to talk with you.'

Kim felt a chill and goosebumps.

She had always thought that she was not as adept as she might be in sexual matters, although Malone told her she was. He didn't like all the business of the baby book. Malone liked things tender . . . But she had never been that clued up exactly about how men came onto her. She had read all those magazine articles but it still was a mystery. She found Noah a good colleague and he was far more committed to God's work than Malone but she never stopped noticing that scrawny turkey neck! She giggled to herself but kept her eyes serious. She was dreading what the minister was going to say next.

'You must know, Kim, that I've always had feelings for you. And now the Elders in our church have decided that if you were to leave Malone and . . .'

Kim listened in mounting horror, fiddling with her hair, as her mother told her not to. She had decided just to ignore Noah completely, when they came to a halt at the side of the road. She looked out of the window and they were in the middle of nowhere, except for a broken-down minivan. Noah slid open the door, got out and started shouting in Dari at their driver and waving his arms. Kim got down too and stretched and gazed up at the blue sky. She heard Noah continue yelling at their driver. All she understood was that he was telling him they should not have stopped in such a dangerous place. They were never meant to stop for broken-down cars as it could mean an ambush, Taliban or robbers.

Yet she was grateful for the interruption.

She reached inside the van and took out a bottle of water and drank. The day was pepper hot and although there were rocky outcrops around the road the country was like desert now. There was the occasional acacia tree, but everything was broken and fractured and waterless. To the north was an immense triangular-shaped mountain.

Kim had to do something about Noah.

There was a doctor she knew at the clinic who would drive her back to Kabul. She guessed the nerves and the loneliness had got to Noah. He had been here for a year and a half. She put the bottle to her lips and drank and the sun reflected through it. Then it was snatched away and the water ran down her blue shirt.

'Why'd you do that, dammit!'

She blinked, angry, but was looking into the face of a man with an assault rifle. The weapon was pointed at her right eye.

Two other men with neat black turbans had already secured the hands of Noah and the driver behind their backs. One was young and handsome, hardly more than a boy.

'I'm part of a medical organization that has set up a clinic . . .' she heard Noah say, in English and then in Dari, his voice angry. 'We're not with the military. The ISAF . . . My colleague here is a doctor . . . She's a doctor. Check her papers.'

Noah's face was then pushed flat against the red-hot bonnet of the car and he screamed and began saying his prayers and kicking, she was sure he was mumbling the 'Our Father', when a man in a black waistcoat produced a squat knife like a meat cleaver and chopped it down on Noah's neck with the casual skill of a farmer butchering an animal. There was an exhalation of breath and a frantic kicking of feet and then more sawing with the knife. Blood pulsed and bubbled across the steaming metal.

'No!'

The minister's head was then held up into the sun by dark strands of hair, teeth chattering, the blue veins in the temple standing out ... Kim wanted to scream. But she was determined she was not going to show fear as her right leg started to shake. She had been told that was the worst thing to do. Tears burned on her cheeks and she started to pray. To say the 23rd Psalm silently to herself. ' "The Lord is my shepherd, I shall not want ..."'

Then the man in the black waistcoat tossed Noah's head into the dust at Kim's feet and despite her best efforts she fainted.

Seven

The ancient northern town of Faizabad was hot and quiet and Malone was propped under the shade of a tree by a line of wooden shacks that were mainly grocery shops. He had delivered his box – surgical stuff for an aid team – but he could not leave Fatima and had handed the plane over to the relief pilot, begged a lift into town and sent a message to his boss that he would be back on the next UN flight. Fatima was in a makeshift store buying nan bread and another card for her phone, which was not working well. Aziz, who looked like he had won the lottery, had bought a paper wrap of sugar-coated peanuts. In front of the line of the shops and fruit sellers with glistening yellow melons was about four hundred yards of an aid-funded two-lane highway, leading nowhere, on which honking cars and donkeys were coming both ways in both lanes at the same time.

Malone shook his head.

A boy sitting at a stall selling only Tajik cigarettes waved him over and, finding the tree uncomfortable, he obeyed the summons.

Why was Fatima taking so long? Malone didn't like the look of the chaotic modern hotel that was down a slope away from the road on the other side of the highway, set back about four hundred yards. That was where they were headed. He went and stretched out on the carpets in the boxlike construction behind the stall.

'You American? You English?' said the boy who had invited him.

'Something like that, Irish ... Irish American. I live in Washington.'

'Washington. Do you have many donkeys in your city?' The boy who asked him wore a black turban and dangled his wide feet over an open sewer as he sat on the edge of the stall. Malone followed the boy's eyes to a biblical procession of men with henna-dyed beards on small donkeys tapping the animals' necks with a stick, while their wives in sky-blue burqas hurried along behind with baskets and boxes.

'Are there dancing places where you can meet pretty virgins in their night-shirts?'

The boy had not got his words out before there was the flash of an explosion, followed by the pressure wave and eventually the sickening bang.

And then silence.

The air was filled with dust and so were Malone's eyes and nostrils. All the cigarettes and the other contents of the stall were now with them in the box.

Malone blinked and looked around for Fatima. She had been blown off her feet beside another stall. He staggered over to help her but Fatima insisted on calming Toto.

The goose nipped Malone hard at the side of the face, as if the bomb was his fault.

Glass clattered down on the nearby highway like hailstones and the sound echoed around the hills. A woman began screaming and then another. A column of lazy smoke rose from a building near the modern hotel across the highway. The boy was already running towards the scene and Malone, Fatima and Aziz, holding the goose, sat on the stall with their ears ringing finding it difficult to breathe as if the explosion had stolen all the good in the air.

Dazed, they watched the ochre haze settle.

'This was not about us,' said Malone, trying to reassure Fatima, but she turned and smiled and sang, 'You're so vain, you probably think this bomb is about you . . .'

Even Aziz laughed and then they just sat there, staring out at the day; the urgent silence ringing in their ears.

In about five minutes the boy from the stall returned, excited.

'Very good news! It's not the hotel you will go to. It's the head-quarters of the Freedom Party! The Freedom Party! There are eight people being dead from a woman suiciding bomb pretending to be pregnant! The Taliban do not like Freedom Party very much.'

'There are Taliban here?'

'Oh, yes. Much. Not before, but now they are strong here. They like it here because the Germans can only fight them in the light of the sun.'

'What?'

'It is written in the book of German rules. And they must let go men who say they are not Talib. Oh, yes.'

The boy smiled as he said this. He went and pulled a rotten piece of wood off a crate, as if he was arming himself. He then threw the piece of wood away and spat into the open drain.

In the street two dark-green jeeps of the Afghan army raced past, machine gunners in the back, followed by a rusting ambulance with an American siren. Toto was not happy, putting his long neck close to the ground and pointing his beak upwards.

'Will you help me get to America?' said the boy. 'I should very much like to go to Hollywood and be in the movies! If not I'll go to Washington and be President.'

'And I thought this town was peaceful,' said Fatima, mainly to herself.

'How do I get to America?' repeated the boy.

'It's a question I've asked myself too many times,' said Malone, picking a splinter of glass out of his hand. He certainly could not leave her now.

Fatima walked with Aziz and Malone, carrying Toto across the two-lane road and over the waste ground littered with glass and metal towards the hotel. They skirted a stagnant pool where children were trying to sail a paper boat, and squeezed through the guarded metal gate of the Aria Hotel. A boy showed them into a large reception room which smelled of damp, and where a sign proclaimed *PANIC BOMB SHELTER* in English, in large, red, handwritten letters. A woman was sweeping up glass and in one corner was a gift shop where lapis lazuli and uncut rubies still embedded in quartz were jumbled in among African carvings. A man in white shalwar kameez with a black waistcoat beamed at them. He was young with shiny black hair combed straight back.

'*Salaam alaikum*. It gives joy to me that you come for a few days' rest in our town of great tourist potential! How long will you be staying? Do you want one room, or two? The management apologizes for the unfortunate detonation which was beyond our control. Do not worry about the bomb as we are perfectly safe here. We have the three-star UN disaster rating and the shelter. You are safe here. And there is never more than one suicide bomb a day.'

The manager spoke to Fatima in English. Malone was about to ask a question but she spoke first.

'We want one room. I don't know how long for. We want one double room. Can we see it now? And one small room for my nephew.' Aziz had gone to sit in an armchair. The bomb had worried him and he was eating his peanuts even more quickly.

'May I compliment you on an excellent goose. Do you want us to cook him?'

Toto opened his beak.

'Certainly not,' said Fatima.

The man shrugged and led Fatima, Malone and Toto up the wide stairs to a room with a television and a large fan. There were purple curtains up at yellow-glass windows one could not quite see out of. On the other side of the windows he made out the shadow of a blast wall. It was possible to smell the toilet from the door. There was a smaller room near by but Aziz had stayed downstairs.

'There's water, even hot when the electricity is kind and Allah smiles on us.'

'Is there electricity?'

The man sighed.

'Allah, peace be upon him, is not smiling at this particular moment.' Doves cooed on the roof.

'That's fine,' Fatima said, and the manager left and she shut the door.

There was a single open window in the toilet bathroom and the air in the rooms was very close. Malone heard the sounds of children playing and someone was practising drumming for the feasts after Ramadan. Fatima put Toto on the floor and the goose had a cautious look around before taking up residence under a cracked glass table, turning its flat head this way and that.

Fatima turned to Malone.

'I'm sorry,' she said. 'I didn't want to be on my own.'

'No . . . I understand.'

'Do you? You don't know very much about me or my family.'

He grinned.

'I thought you were worried about . . . the bomb.'

Malone felt so big and obvious in the small and strangely lit room. Fatima stretched out on one of the single beds and began to call her father again but he was not picking up.

There was a knock at the door and it opened. A boy came in and brought them tea, nan and a dish of yoghurt and then disappeared again. Two jets screamed overhead and the windows rattled. Malone got up from where he was sitting on the other bed and looked out of the small window in the toilet but the planes had already gone.

'You really like flying, don't you, Malone?'

'Yeah, I suppose I do.'

She broke a piece of nan off and dipped it in the yoghurt and handed it to him. He thought about it for a moment and then ate. Fatima threw a piece to the goose under the table.

Malone lay down on the other bed. 'I shouldn't be in this room with you. Should I? What will Aziz think? What are the hotel people going to think?'

Fatima shrugged. 'Probably that I'm a rich kid working for an NGO. They don't think of me as a woman. They say there are three sexes here, male, female and female aid workers. Yet if I was wearing traditional clothes the mullahs might come and take me out and stone me for committing adultery with you.'

Malone must have looked worried because she gave him a melting smile.

She laughed. 'And we don't need to have sex. It's enough to be alone together . . . Especially near a toilet.'

'My God.'

She laughed.

'No, mine.'

At that moment a nearby mosque started the call to prayer and she had a fit of the giggles that petered out into silence. Then she was off the bed and rummaging through the brown-paper bags.

'There is no point in being down about all this . . . *Inshallah,* darling. How about a gin and tonic? They had a fridge at that shop and I have got lime and olives and pistachios. I do not need to use the water filter and the soda stream because they even had tonic and bottled water ice!' To his astonishment she produced two metal beakers and set about making her favourite drink. She laid out pistachios and stuffed olives on little paper plates.

She handed him a drink. 'My pops will be very grateful for your help, Malone.'

He clinked glasses with her. 'Your father, eh? So, tell me what else he has predicted?'

She sighed.

'Well, I shouldn't really tell you this . . . He's a remarkable man . . . An educated man from the North-West Frontier. A

Pakistani diplomat, soldier, loving husband and unpublished writer who has always been suspicious of prophecies and phrases like "So, it is written". So . . . That's what they always said in stories around the hunt fires. And after my mother died so cruelly he was sent to New York by our Foreign Service where he became a shadow of himself and began to drink and consort with girls. However, the stories did not leave him alone, this he told me. He had been up early one morning writing away at his Gandamak history and then he ran into his bedroom and started shouting about the Twin Towers to a girl in his bed. Yes, the Twin Towers. It was the 11th of August, a whole month before, and the last words he had written on the British retreat from Kabul to Gandamak had been about a Captain Souter.

'He ran out onto his little balcony and stared at the World Trade Center and it was still there and the Polish girl who was sleeping in his bed thought he had gone mad. "It's going to fall," he said. "Like Babylon!" But she just turned over, yawned and went to sleep again. She was used to my father saying very strange things as he claimed at times he had sat next to his dead wife Leila in Central Park but my mother had ignored him because she was still upset at her murder out in a common street. "With nowhere clean to fall down, Hamza! What sort of death is that for a fucking actress!"'

Malone was staring into his drink. Her words had taken his breath away in the hot room.

'Your father predicted 9/11?'

Fatima nodded.

'Absolutely. On the morning of the 11th of September he was in his apartment, late for work as usual, having not told another soul because they probably would have thought him insane and thrown him out of the country at least, when it started. He was looking at the TV at the bottom of the bed, and saw the first plane exploding into the north tower of the World Trade Center . . . and then ran onto the small, chilly terrace and stared amazed at the plume of smoke which stretched across the sky, itself a kind of script. The roaring he could hear, like the Djinn laughing, were metal girders failing. He picked up a pair of binoculars from the terrace table and watched unblinking until his eyes were sore and marvelled at things he had been able to foresee. Can you imagine?'

Malone stared at her.

'I had sent him a recording from my school musical in England only the week before. 'Somewhere Over the Rainbow', from *The Wizard of Oz*. He said the tune began to play in his head, over and over again. I think I told you we used to dance around to the songs. He scoured the buildings for the first sign of weakness, his own eyes watering. He knew what was going to happen next and that was the problem. He had written that too. He was the prophet of this surprising doom.'

'What did he do?' asked Malone.

Fatima shrugged. 'What could he do? What would you have done? It was like having a ringside preview seat at the plagues of Egypt or Pearl Harbor, depending on your side, and he had none. The Polish girl with straight, reddish-blonde hair, whom he had been making love to, whose name he couldn't quite remember for me, came out onto the small balcony and stood next to him, also naked. The warmth of her body reassured him, he said. It made the event more human. My father observes certain things in minute detail. Often embarrassing detail for a daughter! Pops told me one of the girl's nipples was pierced with a thin gold ring. Her toenails were carefully painted lilac. She was slightly stoned and, trembling, asked if it was a movie.

'My father shook his head. "No, my dear. This is real and the end of the world as we know it! The whole direction of everything has changed! And I told it first . . .!"'

Malone lay back on his bed and she on hers and he began to wonder what he had got himself into. What was he going to do, how was he going to get her back to Kabul? It went out of his head that Kim had not called him.

'Darling. Do you want another gin and tonic?'

His mouth was open. He did not know what to say. He had a headache and the day was becoming too much, even for Afghanistan.

Fatima got up and switched the Chinese-made fan on and off several times and nothing happened. Children played in a yard outside but the room was stifling.

'Come on,' said Fatima. 'Let's walk into the bazaar. It's a good market and it's too hot in this room. I can't make that fan work. There's a man in the market who may help me. I will give Toto some sleeping drops. The old town will be too much for him after the bomb.'

Malone got off his bed. The goose was going through every one of his thirty-two comfort movements.

'There won't be any electricity until five or six and then it goes off at eight. I was here three weeks ago and got stuck in this place for a few days.' He stood up and grabbed his jacket.

'Shall we get a taxi?'

'No,' she said. 'I want to walk.'

Downstairs Aziz was in an armchair with several plates of food in front of him, fast asleep. The guard with a Kalashnikov at the gate nodded to them and they walked across the wasteland to the two-lane highway.

Malone walked fast, an easy loping stride, and she kept up with him step for step as they went down onto a dirt track and then a bridge which crossed the Kokcha River. They both held onto the rail as a string of camels passed and then gazed down into the ice-blue waters. On one of the banks a boy was fishing and by him a friend was shouting as he pulled in another fat trout. The boys saw they were being looked at and held up more than half a dozen foot-long fish threaded through with line.

'I used to go to the trout rivers with my father too in the hills north of Islamabad and we caught so many he gave those we could not eat to the poor,' said Fatima. The boys by the river were laughing and shouting. Malone fingered his phone. He had not heard from Kim.

Fatima took her own tiny video camera from her bag and began to film.

They walked up a hill where buses were parked, through the stench of sewage, to the roundabout and the start of the market. There was a mass of people thronging around the vegetable and meat stalls that were full of goods. There were two Afghan soldiers, sleepy at a guard post at the start of the market, but nothing more. Men sat around a little square, most in upper-floor cafés, but with no food in front of them, no cups of tea or pieces of nan, as this was Ramadan. They sat talking with their fly whisks and worry beads.

The heat of late afternoon was still intense. Malone's shirt was wet with sweat and he had put on a droopy blue hat, not a baseball cap. The hat looked like something an American might wear on a beach. It was faded and denim. It went with his working boots.

'Do you feel the heat, Malone?'

He was thinking about what she had said. About 9/11.

'Yeah . . . I feel the heat. I can get too much sun.'

She laughed and they plunged into the bazaar. Three men were being photographed with a pinhole camera that gave sepia images straight from the nineteenth century. Old men sat cross-legged in front of stalls selling spices, or donkey saddles, or any type of clothing, in particular the Taliban organizer waistcoats, in which you could carry a suitcase full of all your worldly possessions, and a bomb. Fatima had put on more scarves and wore dark glasses but the way the men looked at her, even stepped out of her way, meant that they thought she was a foreigner. A few of the wives followed their husbands. Only one was arguing.

'You are a stupid man and it's a stupid car. Just like you, it has never gone far in its life. I have had better donkeys and camels than that car. What other wife has a car which has to be pulled by a nomad's camel! I'm a laughing stock. I should have married your brother whose brains are in his head and not his backside.' Her husband's head was wound around with a white turban, his thin lips were pressed together and there was merriment on the faces of those around him.

A young girl in a white burqa was sitting by the side of the road, staring at the mud. The girl's eyes were momentarily raised and Malone felt their incandescent teenage anger and then instant curiosity at seeing Fatima and him. A donkey plodded by them with panniers loaded with melons and greens and a dishevelled man from the Afghan army was shopping and asking for razor blades. 'So you can cut your throat before the Taliban cut your balls off?' teased one shopkeeper.

'You've been here before, Malone? I do love markets.'

'Not this far down.'

'I'm told there's a wonderful hotel built out into the river.'

'Yeah, but no one stays there now.'

They stopped at a shop, a simple wooden box open at the front, raised up from the road with places to sit. The shop made saddles and Fatima left a letter from her father for the owner, who was not back until the next morning. The black-veiled woman who snatched the envelope was not friendly and they walked on. Nearby she haggled for a pair of red-sequined slippers.

'Just like Dorothy,' she said. 'Now I have two pairs.'

Up ahead a crowd was blocking the muddy path.

What's that?' said Malone.

Two German soldiers from the nearby base edged around the boys and men, who were craning for a view into a shop and did not give them a second glance, even though both of the soldiers were in combat uniform and an interpreter trotted at their side with a giant packet of peanuts. One of the men was tall and obviously an officer, the other was short and fat and kept his hand on his .45 pistol in a holster on his hip. His face was twisted into what was meant to be menace but was simply fear.

'Hi there,' said Malone, as they passed the Germans.

The officer stopped.

'We cannot give you any assistance,' he said, and strode stiffly on.

They walked on to a shop where meat was hanging, covered in flies, and Fatima asked a boy who was working there a question. Malone was surprised that she used Pashto instead of Dari and two men came out and stared hard at him and then waved them through more hanging carcasses. The smell of rank blood and dung was nauseating and they came face to face with a man who was wiping a long and bloody knife on his apron. He was middle-aged and his head was bald and his face and mouth were cruel but then they cracked into a huge smile and he embraced Fatima.

'Daughter, welcome,' he said and there was much exchanging of pleasantries as he put down the knife and took off his apron and led them through into a carpeted room. They were brought tea and after waves of talk and laughter between Fatima and the butcher, he spoke in English and did not object to her little camera. The butcher turned to Malone.

'Her father taught me English when we fought the Russians. It was a good time and we killed many. But what she says is true about him looking into the future.' He motioned to a boy sitting at the side of the room and was handed a small box out of which he took a piece of paper that had all but disintegrated. 'One night Hamza came to me and said, Abdullah, you have no teeths . . . They are gone with living in the mountains. But tomorrow we will take a Ruskie column. We will get thirty-two bottles of vodka. We will kill nine soldiers. We will kill the commander and you will have his teeths. The commander is a cruel man and has destroyed many villages. You will possess his skull also and will paint it green to honour Allah's battle flag. It is how he said here. And so it is written . . .' The man's eyes glowed and he took out his teeth, which were a little too big for him. The boy then came up next to

94

Malone and was breathing heavily, holding another, larger, red-lacquered box. Malone looked at Fatima who was filming the delighted butcher with her little camera. She nodded at him and he opened the box. Inside staring back at him was a skull, covered in pitch and painted a luminous green.

'Please be careful, my daughter, in this place. There are many who will not be so glad to see you,' said the butcher and as they were leaving Malone saw she handed him a small envelope. 'From my father,' she said simply. They then went out through the swinging carcasses and the flies back to the press of the market.

'He's a true believer in my father's powers.'

'Every time he eats a steak,' said Malone.

Fatima and Malone laughed and joined the mêlée outside the shop to see what they were looking at and then he noticed the satellite dish on the roof of a small hotel. The crowd was watching television. He leaned over a group of shaven-headed little boys and saw a small screen in the back of the shop showing an epic of ancient Egypt. A man was suspended on a rope above a town square and the pharaoh's guard had just slit the back of his ankles so he would bleed to death very slowly in the afternoon sun in front of his family. The little boys were in rapt attention and Fatima gave one a sugared peanut from her pocket.

The boy nodded his thanks to her as the news bulletin exploded over the television, interrupting the execution.

A car bomb outside the Justice Ministry in Kabul had killed three. But then there was soon a cacophony of music and a girl was dancing on the screen. The quality was poor but with a horrible empty feeling Malone recognized the song and then Fatima recognized herself.

'This song was uploaded to YouTube. That is what we are hearing. It is to be confirmed as is the fact that the girl is the daughter of Hamza Khan, a hero of the fight against the Russians and the former head of Pakistan's ISI intelligence service, who has in the past been accused of helping the Taliban . . . A girl who was mistaken for the singer was attacked for bringing shame on her family and has died in hospital. It is only now they have found out their mistake and her cousins have pledged vengeance on Fatima Hamza. Her video shows scenes from the Hollywood musical *The Wizard of Oz*, where a man dressed as a lion is dancing with the girl. This has been denounced by several mullahs, who refuse to watch it, as depraved pornography, an affront to the decency of Afghan women, encouraging bestial acts and, of course, witchcraft. They call for Fatima Hamza to be put to death as soon as possible. The video, the so-called Dorothy Tape, is also being condemned in other countries because it is a symbol of American idolatry and beloved of homosexuals worldwide. One cleric in Iran has said it may, indeed, if viewed with impure thoughts, cause earthquakes. Fatima Hamza was educated in England and it is said she has worked as a bathing-suit model. She is part of the old Western elite in Pakistan that is out of step with the radical winds blowing through the region . . .'

The crowd of men and boys around them had gone silent.

'I think we had better get the hell out of here,' whispered Malone.

A tear was running down Fatima's face. He felt an ache in his sternum. Malone just knew that someone in the crowd must have recognized her. She pulled the scarves closer around her face. The boy she had given the peanut to began to follow her. She gave him another, half turning, and her scarves fell away.

'It is her . . .! It is the harlot from the news!' said an old man in a low voice.

'Do not be foolish,' Fatima snapped. 'I'm a doctor from Tajikistan, a paediatrician, helping in your hospital. I have never been to the capital. I have never been to Kabul, I prefer it here. What's all this Talib talk? This used to be the town of the Northern Alliance.'

Malone was trying to follow the words. She began to walk faster and dropped the bag of sugared peanuts.

'It is her! It is her!' yelled the boy.

'Who?' a shopkeeper shouted.

'It's the whore! It is the woman from the YouTube! The one the mullahs say must die. She must die! She's responsible for the death of an innocent girl!'

Malone was so scared he could hardly move. It was a long way out of the market and everyone was edging towards them, but he caught a hint of hesitation, and told himself all they had to do was keep walking as if nothing was wrong. To keep walking to the square with the restaurants and the guard post and he saw the German soldiers up ahead and began to make for them as the first stone flew overhead, missing Fatima by inches.

Malone was right by her now, looking around. He was thinking of what the news reporter had said.

'Your father was the head of . . .?'

She sighed.

'He was,' she said, a little embarrassed. 'He's never one to boast . . .'

They were within ten yards of the Germans and the boys were screaming at them now and men had joined the crowd.

'Take her! Take her! She must be brought to the river and stoned!'

Malone grabbed Fatima's shoulders and propelled her past the Germans who turned just in time to see the mob breaking on them like a wave. The small sergeant took out his pistol. Then she was running for her life towards the square and Malone pushed her into the first taxi and said in a calm voice, 'Aria Hotel,' and they were away. A rock hit the taxi and, angry, the driver braked.

Behind them, Malone saw a tall man with a terrible scar on his forehead walk in front of the crowd and hold up his hands. He was dressed in rags and capered like a lunatic and said, as a mullah, he wanted to sit in judgment. The mob faltered.

'Drive! Please, driver. The German troops have assaulted a woman!' Fatima cried out as another rock hit the roof of the car, and Malone realized she was trembling.

When Kim woke she was in the back of a 4 x 4, her hands and feet tied, looking into the eyes of a trussed chicken on the floor. They were driving fast on a very bad road and being thrown about was what woke her. For a while she did not speak, couldn't speak as she remembered what had happened. Kim almost became hysterical and then resorted to the deep breathing one of her sisters had taught her after the birth of her fourth child. She prayed. She tried to keep track of time as they bounced along, but her watch was gone and so was the cross around her neck.

It was then the radio burst into life. She heard music she recognized as Kyrgyz. As far as Kim could tell there was only the driver in the car.

From where she lay on the back seat she could see eyes looking at her in a driving mirror decorated with fake flowers. It was the young boy from the ambush. She was glad it was not the older man.

'Do you like the music?'

'No.'

'It is good music.'

She didn't think music was permitted in Ramadan but there was a smile on the young man's face. He only had a small, trimmed beard and was in his early twenties. His rifle bounced about the passenger seat. There was a bullet hole and a large crack along the windscreen and an amulet hung from the driving mirror.

'Where are you taking me? You speak English?'

The boy nodded.

'We are going to the north. Many miles . . . Many miles . . .'

'To where?'

'To maybe Kunduz. Maybe mountains.'

'Kunduz?'

The town was infamous in the north as a Taliban centre. Aid workers had been shot down without explanation. She had read that for hundreds of years the town had been a centre for brigands and robbers.

Malone was probably not so far from there though. If he had gone to Faizabad.

'My . . . My hospital will pay no money . . . But if you release me, I will make sure you are well paid. I will. I've some money in the bank which you'll not get if you kill me,' she said in Dari.

The boy shook his head and smiled into the mirror. His manner was surreally jolly and, Kim thought, totally inappropriate considering what had happened to Noah.

'You're from America?'

'Yes.'

'I was to go to America and study before there was the last invasion. My cousin went to see some of my family in Los Angeles. Very beautiful city. Very nice people to me, Americans.'

Kim took a deep breath.

'Then please let me go. You can say I slipped away. No one will know.'

'I will know,' he said. 'And so will Allah, peace be upon him. So please, do not ask me the question again, please. It is not permitted.'

She fell silent after that and it may have been the overarching rhythms of the music or the rocking of the car but she slipped into an exhausted doze. When she awoke the boy was next to her on the back seat and a date was being pushed into her mouth. 'Eat! It is the time to eat. Rice is being brought. I will be untying your hands and you will drink water. It is good water from American filter . . . But please do not run. If we did not shoot you, you would certainly die out here in these mountains. This place fatal for Americans. You are alive for one reason.'

'What's that?

'Because you surgeon doctor.'

Kim looked up and saw the moon and smelt the woodsmoke. It was a luminous dusk and she made out several shacks by a stand of trees and a crowd of people came to peer at her in the car. They were in the mountains and there was a chill in the air and the overwhelming scent of herbs.

A smiling woman with a broad face clambered onto the back seat and untied her hands and feet. She then took off Kim's trainers.

'Please don't take my shoes.'

But the woman placed them on the front passenger seat. Another man was now sitting in the driver's seat as the young man squatted by a fire outside. There was no road, not even a track.

'You cannot run here without shoes,' laughed the woman in Dari. 'You cannot run with shoes.'

EIGHT

'I have to go out and get food,' said Fatima. They had not left the stifling hotel room for three days because of what had happened in the bazaar.

'Don't go,' he said.

She smiled. 'We have to eat. We came past a modern provisions shop which the boy downstairs says has tinned peaches . . . And I have to see how things are . . .'

He nodded. Whatever attraction they felt for each other had been lost in the code of mutual politeness imposed by the small space where they were trapped, unable to see outside. The hotel manager kept promising them a car that never turned up and all the time the television repeated the hysterical bulletin about Fatima's Dorothy video.

She put on her burqa and she and Aziz both went out to buy bottles of water and food at the modern provisions shop by the stagnant pool of water, while Malone waited in the lobby of the hotel.

Ten minutes later she came running back past the guard at the gate.

Fatima put down two bags and took a moment to get her breath. 'There was talk at the counter of a story in the newspaper where a misdialled number answered by a man's wife led to accusations of adultery and an hour-long gun battle between the families, leaving four dead. Then I realized that they all knew who I was and what I was accused of. Even the children stood in silence and I was so nervous that I put a can of tomatoes back wrongly, because of the gauze on the burqa, and brought down the whole pile. When I bent to pick them up everyone was staring at me. They know. They all know. We have to get out.'

In the tiled-floor cool of the lobby Aziz was sweating, terrified. He said, 'The man whose house I was staying at in Bamiyan has a family who will shelter me in the part of the town above the market. It will help if you take a smaller car. Please leave word where you are going and look after yourself. It's just that I would prefer to try and get on a flight than go through the Taliban areas. Be careful, Fatima. I'm sorry I am useless and weak.' They all embraced and he quickly shook Malone's hand. Aziz then went up to his room and took his small pack and was gone.

Malone and Fatima went upstairs to find Toto had taken up a defensive position on one of the beds and he heard a cat on the hot corrugated-iron roof outside the broken bathroom window. There were goose footprints on the walls, though these had not joined the mysterious boot marks on the ceiling. The goose held its long straight neck parallel with the bedclothes. Fatima went immediately over and stroked the soft feathers of his head.

'Look how frightened he is.'

'Yes.'

She had been telling Malone more and more of her father. How former heads of the ISI never retired because they were so in fear of their lives. Malone quit worrying about how his unexplained absence from work and his disregarding of regulations might harm his flying. Anyway his phone signal was not strong enough to get a call through to Kabul and the hotel's computer did not work, let alone connect to the internet.

'I'll give Toto more of the serenity drops,' said Fatima.

'Save some for me,' said Malone.

Fatima poured a little of the laudanum into a dropper and coaxed the goose to drink as the young man who was the owner of the hotel drifted silently into the room. His brilliant-white shalwar kameez was so starched it crackled.

He stared at the goose now with disgust rather than interest and said, 'The two German soldiers from the bazaar are in hospital and one is not expected to live, *inshallah*. It is not safe for you here and I cannot let you keep this creature in the room he is dirtying. I have a car for you. A 4 x 4. Where do you want to go?' There was a smile on his face that Malone did not like.

'Ishkashim,' said Fatima. 'We can go to Ishkashim. I want to go to the Pamirs. You do not have to come, Malone, darling Malone. You have done enough.'

He sighed. If he went he had no idea what Kim might do, let alone losing his job.

'I might as well try to complete my journey,' she said bravely. 'My father has given me a contact in Ishkashim and in one of the villages before you get there.'

The manager began to shake his head.

'This is a dangerous journey in normal circumstances and expensive. It is many, many miles and the rivers are flooded. And then there is the Taliban quite suddenly in possession of much of the land in between now. This is also Ramadan and it is so hard to get a reliable man who will drive all day in a hot car without the food and water.'

'How much?' asked Malone. The manager raised his head and smiled broadly.

'It is meant to be two hundred dollars each but I let you all go for four hundred American dollars cash and I'm losing money. Or you may decide you are perfectly safe here. The government radio says the small incident at the Freedom Party headquarters was due to a cooking-gas explosion and that there are no Taliban here.' As he finished, in the hollow distance, there was another explosion.

'Another mishap in the kitchen?' said Fatima.

The manager nodded.

'We'll go right now,' said Malone. He did not want the young man with the slicked-back hair to change his mind or raise the price.

'Yes, now. It is possible better now.' The manager touched his starched and ironed shalwar kameez over his heart as Malone counted out the money from a slim wallet in a zip pocket of his jeans.

An hour later they left the hotel compound, crouched on the back seat of a battered white Toyota Land Cruiser as they splashed through the stagnant pool, sinking home-made boats and sending children running. Malone glimpsed several men lounging by the supermarket, like those who had been part of the crowd that had chased them, who did not have the look of men around here. They all wore the flat, dun-coloured Pashtun hats and had beards.

One began to point at the car.

Had the manager of the hotel betrayed them already?

The driver turned onto the potholed highway and the men were out of sight. The two-lane road quickly ran out and the car bumped along the mud track which led back to the town bridge. They next turned onto a dirt road going along the river and when he looked at his phone there was no signal at all. They had passed a point of no return.

Fatima reached down and touched Toto the goose, who nibbled her hand. She now stretched back across the seat and appeared to be enjoying the journey with all the enthusiasm of a child, even though there were men out there who meant to stone her to death.

Momentarily her warm hand touched his.

'I am so glad you are coming with me, Malone. You are so brave to help me and come with me. You must have such other plans.'

'Yes.' But it was impossible for him to leave her now, all alone. He wanted to put his arms around her, right there.

The future excited and terrified him. Perhaps at last he was having the adventure that he had always avoided and had avoided him. Now there were no plans, only hers and the open road.

The goose honked in the hot car.

Malone watched as they passed by another bridge and the famous hotel, surrounded on three sides by the river. He wanted to take Fatima there, to spend a week, or maybe two, enfolded in the crisp sheets and hidden behind the roar of the waters of the duck egg-blue Kokcha River. He did not want to have that thought for Kim's sake. Yet the joyful ease of Fatima's smile sent a shiver through him. One moment he was glad he was sitting in that back seat with her, stroking the head of the goose, and then he wasn't at all.

'Malone, I am so grateful to you for coming all this way with me. But you are in danger, Malone. I think perhaps you should go.'

He laughed.

'I think we're all in danger from here on in.' He saw the driver half turn and wondered how much English he understood.

'Yes,' she said.

'I don't mean to worry you but a bus was blown up north of Ishkashim. They killed twenty-seven . . . And there have been other ambushes. We have to go that way, through the villages of the Warduj.'

She smiled. Then her lips began to tremble.

'So what are you saying? Should I put on my burqa? Should we have brought the lion costume?' She began to rummage in her backpack and he put his hand on hers.

'No . . . But we could double back to the airport and hop on a UN plane.'

Fatima shook her head. 'No, that's a bad idea.'

She was right. They might wait at the airport for days for the intermittent UN flight to Kabul. And be seen.

'Well, there's this new little airstrip in the Wakhan. But it's only taken a few aid flights.' Malone realized they had a less than zero chance of getting on a plane there but he felt he had to reassure her, and himself.

Fatima did not say anything after that, filming the countryside as they crossed the river. At the other side of the bridge at a checkpoint a bored soldier from the Afghan army demanded to see their work permits and Malone produced his. Fatima did not hand over her passport, wisely, as the soldiers were apt to steal them just for a photograph of a woman, but produced a letter of invitation. The soldier scowled because he could not read. But then he saw the goose, smiled and began to talk so fast in Dari, Malone could not keep up. A quill had fallen on the floor and she gave it to the man who looked eternally grateful and went into a green-painted shack and came back with a handful of fresh white apricots.

'His mother raises geese,' said Fatima. 'He knows these geese. His mother tried to breed them once but they did not stay. He says they are the best of geese.'

'Toto has friends everywhere,' said Malone.

A young American soldier, who appeared from nowhere, then looked into the car.

'You American and she's with you?' asked the soldier.

Malone glanced at Fatima and she inclined her head slightly.

'Yes, we are aid workers,' he said.

Malone was about to try and ask for help. But this was not even the American zone. The soldier was probably from a Special Forces unit and Malone and Fatima might be handed over to the Afghan army, who, after listening to the TV news, would sell them to the family of the dead girl.

'That's good, sir. Have a nice day,' said the soldier and waved them on. Malone noticed another up by a Humvee with Delta Force markings.

'Thanks, Malone,' said Fatima. 'My father says telling your troubles to the army always makes things worse. That's what armies are for. To make things worse.'

They drove on up an incline and past field after field of Kyrgyz nomads who had brought their camels to race, fight and sell.

Malone saw smoke rising from the black yurts and a girl in front of one in a purple robe dancing to a small cross-legged band. The driver stopped, as fascinated as they were.

One of the nomads' great, dark woolly-brown camels hauled itself up on its legs and bellowed and chased after another.

A girl in saffron yellow was capering with a broad pink ribbon past two enormous, greased wrestlers, who glistened in the bright sun. The snow peaks shone on the far mountains and old men with wispy beards sat around fires telling stories and smoking pipes full of the hash that grew by the side of the road where a man was juggling with black-and-white baby goats while holding another in his mouth.

Malone felt suddenly alone and vulnerable in the back seat of that car with her; he did not need to tell her that he was attracted to her. She already knew.

The driver started again, reluctantly. He shouted words into the back of the car that Malone did not at first comprehend.

Fatima laughed.

'What did he say?'

'Oh, that he will get sick of his wife one day and go and run away with the nomads and live the way a man should. Free. Free of everything.'

'I've always thought that a great idea.'

'But have you? Have you ever let go of everything, Malone?'

After many drowsy hours at the top of a rise they halted to buy melons from a man sitting in front of an orchard. In between the melon beds at the other side of the road were fields of twelve-foot cannabis plants, which at the moment fetched a better price than the opium that only sold for two dollars a kilo. The driver gestured at them he was going with the melon seller and they were left in the Toyota in the hazy golden sunshine, out on that road alone, as a small man trotted past them on an ivory-coloured donkey and his two wives walked behind, laughing, each one in an identical blue burqa made of a shiny cloth; the women nodded to Fatima as they passed and stared at Malone.

The man on the donkey stopped. He was in his sixties and his wives were in their teens. The man tapped his donkey into the side of the road with his stick, tied it to a tree and went into the orchard where he peered into several of the fruit trees, as if he was going to steal the apricots. He then took off his jacket and used it as a prayer mat, turning west to face Mecca.

In Afghanistan, Malone realized for the first time, Mecca was in the same general direction as the Rocky Mountains.

The girls giggled as their husband went through his *raka'at*, standing and crouching and bowing, submitting himself to his God.

A stream gurgled down from the melon patch to the orchard through a culvert under the road. Malone opened the door and got out of the car and stretched his legs and smelled the rich cannabis pollen on the wind as the dark fields ran on and on to the foothills of the mountains. On the other side was corn stretching down to the river, and in its season poppy, although that was usually further south. Fatima got out of the car too and Toto immediately spread himself out on the back seat where Malone had been.

111

'He's taken your place, Malone. You can ride in the front if you're not scared.'

In Faizabad the hotel manager had told Malone to do the whole journey lying down out of sight on the back seat. Aid workers suspected of informing on the drug crops had been shot or, after they were spotted, their cars blown up by improvised explosive devices as they left a village, the explosive encased in ancient pressure cookers.

'I will wear my headscarf,' he laughed.

'You'd still look American in my burqa.'

'*Inshallah*, then.'

She giggled. '*Inshallah*, darling.'

A warm wind blew down the road. There had been no other traffic but the donkey and the man and his two wives. Fatima turned around and around in the wind. The girls giggled some more. Their husband went on with his prayers. The driver then emerged from the field above with an armful of yellow melons that he could not eat until the sun went down. Malone had a feeling of peace in this place and from some way behind them, from the fields of the nomads, he heard the playing of music and the banging of a drum.

She stepped up to him and he smelled her perfume.

'Tell me, Malone, will your wife be worried?'

For a second, he hesitated. He knew what his old roommate at Princeton would say. He would have said no.

'Yes, she'll be worried. She's not answering her phone.'

Fatima smiled.

'But will she mind?'

'No, she will understand,' he lied.

Fatima was standing very close to him, her face turned upwards towards his.

'And she'll not mind you going off on an adventure with a strange and deranged woman? The daughter of a former head of the Pakistan intelligence agency who is losing his mind because of his predictions about the future? A silly girl who has got herself into big trouble with the mullahs due to her liking for *The Wizard of Oz* Hollywood movie?'

Malone did not reply. He wished Fatima took things more seriously. The driver threw melons in the boot and started the car. Malone got into the front of the car and occasionally glanced at her as the day turned more golden.

'Please do not look like that, Malone, or I will believe we are doomed. My father says trust in Allah but tie up your camel. There is only so much we can do. *Inshallah*, darling.'

Fatima then stretched her long legs and fell peacefully asleep as Malone almost went cross-eyed scanning the road ahead for possible ambush or hidden bombs. Several furnace-like hours later they stopped at a garage in the chaotic market town of Baharak and the driver waited twenty minutes for another man who was meant to do the rest of the journey. It was blisteringly hot even in the shade and the metal on the outside of the car was painful to touch.

'Let's get out and take a look around. I want to go to the shops,' she announced, quite fresh, dabbing her face with a wipe and offering Malone one.

'Our driver may just take himself back to Faizabad.'

She shook her head. 'He'll stay,' she said. The goose was asleep in his bag. She woke Toto up and put him on his little lead. She got

113

out of the car and went up to the driver. The goose trotted after her.

'Shall I bring you a Coke from the market to have later?' she said to the driver. 'You'll drive us the rest of the way if your friend does not come? I'll reward you.' The driver nodded and touched his heart with his right hand.

Fatima then opened her phone and there was not even a weak signal and she pulled the scarf across her face as a veil. There were television antennae and dishes on the roofs and for all Malone knew the men in the garage, in the street, had seen the offending film. Yet everyone welcomed Toto and because of Fatima's Western clothes assumed she was American or European. No goose would have survived Ramadan in an Afghan family.

The town, like many all over the North-West Frontier, was built around a crossroads. In the middle of this crossroads was a small glass house of a police post, outside which dark-green-uniformed Afghan army soldiers squatted on the pavement, playing backgammon, their rifles in a heap. Cars came through, and motorbikes with up to five passengers, but mainly donkeys and people on foot, who stopped to buy the piles of fruit and vegetables that tumbled from stalls overflowing into the road. The colours were brighter here and the scarves of the women a vibrant blue or red. There were nuts and figs and mulberries and even lemons and oranges. One shop was hung with the crimson Chinese lanterns that were used for wedding decorations and baskets and baskets of artificial flowers. Bags of rice and red beans were marked *US Aid: A Gift from the American People*. A cat stretched out on one of them and yawned and then, eyeing Toto, decided the goose was a dream and went to sleep again.

They walked up one street and back and tried another where farming tools, fabrics and brilliant red carpets were being sold. There was a tea shop on a balcony where men sat over empty glasses with their worry beads and walking sticks, all with the distant, hungry stare of Ramadan. The men watched them pass but not with any hostility. Fatima bought bread at one shop and a packet of processed cheese, which she bargained down, and some cans of Coke. As she found the side street with the car breakers and garages again Malone was glad to get back into the oven of a car, which had the same driver, who politely turned down the can of Coke. He was strictly observing Ramadan.

He started the car and drove off and three girls sitting on a rock shouted to them as they left the town. The girls here were not even wearing a headscarf. Fatima filmed them with her little camera and they waved. In the drowsy heat he expected her to be on edge and worrying about the video but she closed her eyes and drifted off to sleep and they drove steadily for about a hundred yards or so and then bumped, bumped over a culvert. The driver slowed and eased his way over another culvert, muttering either a curse or a prayer. They did this for mile after mile and hour after hour and his mind began to wander to the little cemetery on Rock Creek past the Beltway where he used to go and hide when his father and mother were having a row, or she was entertaining 'guests' from New York.

It was another two hours at least before they stopped again. Malone blinked. He was looking into Fatima's smiling face. She stretched, relaxed and they got out of the car, followed by the goose. Fatima let Toto drink water from her hand.

115

'You like geese a very great deal, don't you, Malone?' Fatima asked him.

'Yes.'

'Is it because they are free? Do you want to suddenly take off? To spread your wings?' she teased.

The driver was looking at one of the tyres and shaking his head. He then vanished completely under the car. Fatima was standing very close to Malone and he did not know what to do. He went over to a wall but she followed him. They were not as high up as they had been after Faizabad and the fields were greener and down by the river the stands of poplar trees shimmered silver in the light. At the other side the hills rose up quickly.

She smiled; a radiant smile that seemed to take the world by surprise. He lit a cigarette and inhaled the smoke deeply. He had been trying hard to quit but now did not seem the moment. He wanted her to be right next to him but then it was too much.

The driver reappeared from under the vehicle and nodded to them.

Malone got into the back with her and the goose and they rattled along in silence. Everything in the car smelt of the golden-yellow melons in the trunk. The road veered away from the river and to the right there was a fertile plane with grassy fields, some full of a fragrant clover, which smelt like jasmine with gardenia and frangipani thrown in. Every now and again he had a breath of it over the warm smell of the melons. There were huge walnut trees lining the road and more stands of poplar and fruit trees in the meadows where the harvest was taking place and boys and girls, unveiled except for the hijab, were hurrying home from school to help. They pointed at the car and laughed. The driver began to shout at himself and the car and they came to a halt again. Malone thought he was able to feel too much of the road.

He must not allow himself to fall in love with her.

'What's the problem? Is it a flat?'

'Yes . . . I am most sorry. And the exhaust. And our other tyre is not so healthy. It is good for a few miles but no more.'

The man was half under the car again and then wriggled back out.

'Where are we?'

'We're in a place we should not be. We are in the Warduj. That is the name locally. The army moves from here at two. Everyone is meant to be off the road by two. It is now three. We are in the wrong place at too late a time.'

When they had stopped there had been no one around their car. Now men and boys had appeared from the fields as if they had stepped out of the stones and were sitting along the wall watching them. An old man crouched down and squinted at the wheel with the puncture and shook his turbaned head and made an up-and-down motion with his arm as if operating a car jack.

Malone nodded. He noticed one of the men on the wall had a Kalashnikov lazily cradled in his lap.

A young boy by Malone had a length of rope that had a wooden hook on the end. The boy saw that Malone was looking at the rope and made as if to toss it into a tree and giggled. He understood Malone's discomfort instantly. The contraption was for gathering walnuts, not hanging infidels. The boy threw the hook into the branches and clawed some of the fresh green nuts down. He brought them over to Malone. He then handed Malone a few dried nuts from his waistcoat pocket.

'*Tashakor*,' said Malone, and everyone on the wall began to smile.

Another boy came up with a donkey and motioned to Malone to get on. He hesitated. He did not want to make a fool of himself but Fatima who was standing near by jumped on, rode it up the road and turned it around with her knees like an expert. She dismounted laughing and Malone got onto the animal, which seemed very small, and the boy whistled and the creature took off like a rocket. Malone only just hung on, digging one of his knees into the animal's shoulder. He had learned to ride as a child but never well.

When he managed to bring the animal back he saw Fatima had her arms folded in a determined way.

'We've to go into the next town. Our spare has a flat too and there are all sorts of other things wrong with the car. We cannot drive on a flat tyre on these roads and have to get some special rubber to mend it. Or else we have to wait for the bus to come past.' She took her phone out of her pocket and Malone saw the disapproval of more or less all around.

'There's no signal here. I've been trying to text my pops.'

She was holding Toto on his lead and several of the little boys were admiring him. One stroked his head and giggled.

'The grown-ups don't like phones,' Malone said.

'Why?'

'You can get a fix on them. You can home a missile on a phone.'

Fatima gave a nervous smile and put the phone away.

Two of the boys who had been leaning on the wall rode on top of their Toyota as they limped into town. The village was only a mile down the road over a series of culverts around the last of which there was a collection of turbaned men, a few of them armed. The men peered into the car and the driver waved a greeting to them. One of the men, Malone was sure, would be ready to complete the circuit on the bomb in the old pressure cooker, the improvised explosive device they were probably driving over, if ordered. There would be another cluster of mines leaving the village. The village picked off intruders at will in this way, but the men let them through. Perhaps that was why the boys got on top, to grant them a safe passage. The village was a strip of wooden houses and shops but with stairs from out in the street leading to the first storey.

They stopped and he got out for a moment.

'Why are those stairs like that?' he asked one of the boys in Dari.

'Oolf,' said the boy. 'Oolf.' And he grabbed at his own throat as if a wolf's jaws had closed around it and grinned.

In the cool of evening they then drove into a little compound where a mechanic said he could not mend the tyre and they would have to go back to Baharak. They stretched their legs and Toto began to nose around in the grass.

Malone saw the driver's face was white with fear. He turned and the armed men from up the road were coming quickly towards them. They were smiling.

'You have goose?' one said in Dari.

'His name is Toto,' said Fatima.

'You will come with us, please,' said a precise-looking man with a brown tweed jacket and a black turban. In the buttonhole of his jacket was one of the fragrant white pea flowers.

'We have to stay here,' said Malone.

A rifle was pointed by another gently smiling man.

'No. You will come with us. You will come now,' said the man with the brown jacket.

NINE

It was over.

Malone was so afraid he found it impossible to speak and so apparently did Fatima as they were taken to a battered red Corolla and she lifted Toto into the back by a sack of grain. He saw her fighting it, trying to look as serene as ever. He had the ridiculous but paralysing thought that they might search her pack and find her gin-and-tonic kit and shoot them on the spot.

The red car pulled away and then turned off the road and onto a two-wheel track which led across the fields of bean, alternated with those of wheat, which was being harvested. Backs were bent and the scythes darted while at another part of the field men directed four donkeys to crush the ears of corn and an old man threw the wheat in the air to let the wind blow out the chaff.

Her hand was now gripping his very tightly.

Malone tried to concentrate only on what he saw.

The way of the harvest had not changed since the invasion of Alexander, nor had the love of the people for their precarious earth. The men with the scythes smiled as the car drove past and Malone imagined the family had owned the land possibly not just for centuries but for millennia, despite the invasions of the Greeks or the Persians, the Mongols of Genghis Khan or the bony, pink-kneed British. When the invaders had either gone home, or settled and become part of this land, the backs were bent and the scythes began to dart again.

The sun had almost gone down between the gap in the mountains, turning them a rosy colour and magnifying the green. Malone tried to breathe deeply.

The car stopped again by two boys who were doing cartwheels in one of the fields of fragrant pea flowers.

The two men in the front of the car began a loud conversation and Fatima turned and spoke in a low voice.

'I love this scent. This flower grows on the other side of the border. A princess in one of my father's stories when I was a child was told by a *dev* that a love philtre could be made from the flower, only by the light of the full moon, and only by the pure of heart, that made the coldest person fall headlong in love with the first being he or she saw. That was how the moon fell in love with the sun. Forever chasing each other across all time . . . Lovers gave the flowers to each other. The old kept them pressed in ancient Korans.'

Malone noticed Fatima's left hand begin to tremble.

'The pea flower has a practical use too, Malone. The pea is a nitrogen-fixing crop for the opium poppy, which will soon be planted again in these fields. The villagers get so little for their poppy crop nowadays that they bury the opium under their barns, waiting for better times.'

122

Malone wondered if the men were going to shoot them by the river.

Growing up in the city he had always wanted to live in a valley like this one, like the valleys where he had been taken as a child, real or imagined, the hard mountains giving way to soft greens. Here was land worth fighting and dying for, unlike the Pashtun sandboxes in the south in Helmand.

He looked at the handsome young boys in their clean white shalwar kameez and the fields rolling down to more walnut trees and the river. Men were fishing there, trousers turned up, sitting on their haunches, and it was hard to imagine they were engaged in a war at all. One of the boys gave Fatima a posy of the pea flowers through the open car window and ran away laughing. To Malone it was like a Muslim vision of paradise. It must seem like that to Fatima, he thought, although somewhere along her education she had stopped being a practising Muslim, part of a mosque. Another boy got into the car and sat on the knee of the man in the front.

Surely they would not be executed with the boy watching?

No words had been spoken and they started off again and the car bumped gently along the track until they reached a bridge over the river, which had split into several channels. The bridge was about fifteen metres across, fenceless and made of green tree trunks lashed together with jute rope.

Malone realized that it could be drawn up by ropes attached to a huge walnut tree.

The car stopped and the engine was switched off. He tried to disappear into the sound of running water.

Was this where it was going to end? Malone knew Fatima was thinking the same. He felt it in her hand.

The men and the boy got out of the car and gestured for them to do so. Fatima carried Toto as they all crossed over the bridge. When they reached the other side her phone was sticking out of her jeans pocket and she forced it back down. The man in the brown jacket saw her and held out his hand. It was not an aggressive gesture and she passed the phone to him. He nodded at Malone, who sighed, and gave the man his. The man put his hand on his heart and pointed to the sky. He put the phones on a rock and smashed them both with the butt of his rifle and threw them into the foaming, surging water.

'I am sorry,' he said in Dari. '*Tashakor.*'

Malone smiled as if it were nothing.

'May I keep my camera?' Fatima asked. 'I have to have a camera. I am making a record of my journey for my father.' She took the camera from her bag and showed it to him.

Surprisingly, the man said yes and she took a short film clip of the bridge and the leader.

'I told you they don't like phones,' Malone said to Fatima.

'What are they going to do now?'

'I don't know.' He was breathing the cool air of the river in fast, looking at the poplars and the willows, searching for a place to run. But he would have to leave her . . .

Then the leader motioned with his hand towards the car, which had been driven slowly over the bridge after them.

Relieved, they both swallowed and smiled and got back into the car and were driven for about ten minutes to a large fortified farm behind a high wall and gates that were guarded by armed men. The house backed onto a rock wall that was riddled with caves. A village with a meeting house and what looked like a school straddled along the mountain base and there was a path leading to another smaller village higher up the mountain. It overlooked a lesser valley, which ran at a right angle to the main one, heading west.

'We will find you the mendings for your tyre in a day or two. Now we all go and eat and sleep,' said the man in the brown tweed jacket and Malone thought his legs were going to buckle under him. He had expected to die by the river.

They were led into the compound where they were greeted with both hands by at least twenty men before being shown to a stone hut with a smoking chimney.

Inside the guest quarters there was the traditional raised floor with carpets and shining emerald and gold bedrolls. Fatima clapped her hands with joy and a girl came in and tended to the fire. The perfumed air blowing in from outside was much cooler now.

Immediately overhead came the scream of jets, the sound of a sonic boom and then nothing.

Malone ran outside but the planes, flying low, were already gone. Fatima noticed that the girl who had brought the firewood was shaking.

Fatima then took her shoes off and sat on one of the carpets and Malone did the same and the girl returned with an old silver pot of green tea and some nan bread which was freshly baked and a bowl of curd. A man brought a box and two sheep hurdles in and put them in the corner of the room for Toto and Fatima placed him inside with a piece of nan.

The girl smiled this time as she left. The stove was warm but smoky and as they sat there they could hear the sound of a stream outside. After a while the girl brought them a huge dish of lamb pilau and two spoons and lit a small oil lamp before leaving them again to the sounds of the evening, the croaking of frogs and the last song of birds roosting. Here there was no call to prayer.

'Eat,' Fatima said, picking up a spoon.

'Do you trust them?'

Fatima smiled.

'We can trust them, Malone. They have not killed us. They have taken us into their house. They have to look after us. And I think they want to. I would trust them with my life but we are doing that already. Perhaps a man who asks a question like that does not trust himself. *Inshallah*, darling.'

In the corner of the room the goose made a contented honking noise.

After they had eaten, the girl scurried in with more tea and another intricately decorated silver teapot full of water. She then went and arranged the mats, duvets and pillows for the night in the corner of the room and bowed to them with a smile. A posy of pea flowers had been placed on the bed.

Fatima giggled and stared at Malone.

'I think Dorothy just got married.'

'What do you mean?'

'The flowers . . . To put them on a bed like that. They are usually for a young couple who are together for the first time.'

He felt himself begin to blush.

They sat opposite each other, watching, as the light fell and the sounds faded and the noise of the stream, which ran through the fortified compound, took over, and became music. They heard voices passing and the barking of a dog and the slow, long howl of

126

what was, unmistakably, a wolf. The girl had put a fragrant root on the fire which mixed with the perfume of the fields to produce an incense-like scent, but more stimulating. In that time Malone never took his eyes off Fatima. He watched that enigmatic smile on her face as it faded from view as if it was going to be the last time he ever saw her. His gaze lingered on her pale skin and he realized that he was more than a bit in love with her, and what such love meant to him.

He watched her lips, those full lips, curl a little more into a smile. She did not move and her eyes did not blink and he knew, he knew to the bottom of his soul that if he did not make a move they would stay apart for ever, the two elaborate teapots and the tea tray between them. The light was all but gone now and there was the silvery hint of the moon in the small open window of the hut. Her smile had vanished in the darkness. He could just see her pale skin and, with a rush of cool breeze outside, it was gone too.

And then there was the door opening and Fatima silhouetted against what was left of the light.

'Goodnight, Malone . . . I have to sleep with the women. This is a dangerous place . . .'

'Fatima, you can't go . . .'

But she had and he was in darkness and alone, except for the occasional movement of Toto in his box.

In the night he awoke and there was a presence by him. Her wet mouth found his and he did not hesitate for an instant and was kissing her back and they were rolling onto the invisible embroidery of the mats and blankets in the darkness. In the narcotic scent of the stove and the fields they took off each other's clothes

127

in a rush and he was kissing her breasts, and then she grasped hold of him and her mouth was around his penis. He pulled her up to face him again, kissing her again, as if he meant to kiss their lips away, for nothing to stand between them. With a motion of her hips she mounted him and the perfume of the fields enfolded them both and they shouted together as one. He collapsed in her arms and paused there locked in eternity until the figure changed and he was looking into the laughing face of his mother. 'What did you expect, Malone ...?' and he woke from his dream, covered in sweat, the light of dawn appearing around the door.

Fatima opened the door an hour later and looked down at him. He was so grateful to see her. He could not help a tear, many tears, suddenly coming into his eyes. It was so absurd. To find another person like this, in these circumstances ... He loved the innocent mischief on her face. He heard Toto move in the box he had been put in. He blinked away the tears.

'Good morning, Malone. What's the matter?'

'Smoke in my eyes. From the stove.'

What had he even been thinking of? A married man, he had wanted to sleep with Fatima in the heart of the most militant Islamic area of Afghanistan, and yet last night, for a moment, it seemed not only morally right but beautiful.

'I'm going to wash,' she said.

She picked up the water teapot and a small towel and a wash bag from her backpack and stepped out of the door. He got up and went to the window and saw her crouched at the stream, splashing water on her face, and then she walked to the gate of the compound where the guards were wide awake.

'*Salaam alaikum.*'

'*Wa alaikum as-salaam*, Pashtun sister. Go to the left by the bigger stream for washing. There are no wolves there. At least not on four legs.'

She laughed.

'I am not scared of your wolves. They are probably too little for me to see.'

They gave a whoop of laughter and she went off. Malone watched until she came back. The boys let her in.

'We will go and fetch you breads and honey and curd from my mother's house in the village,' said one.

The girl brought it five minutes later and she and Fatima came back into the hut and Malone smiled as Fatima immediately gave some of the nan to Toto. The bands on his head stood out in the gentle morning light. His brothers and sisters up in the Pamirs would be thinking about flying south now, over the Himalayas to winter on the hot and dusty plains of India, and make love. The goose nibbled Fatima's hand.

Fatima poured a cup of green tea and took it over to Malone, who was now lying on his back on the bedroll.

She kissed him gently on the forehead.

'I've been up half the night talking to the girls. The daughters of the headman. They would not go to sleep. It was like a slumber party.'

'You could have stayed.'

She shook her head.

'Not here, darling Malone.'

She winked at him and offered him a piece of the fresh-baked bread.

'Eat, Malone. The sun is rising. We have to eat before it does. There will be no other food from these people during the day in Ramadan and even if you are not a Muslim it's insulting to eat when they do not. It always seems cruel to me when this month coincides with the harvest. But I suppose when you are faint with hunger everything becomes more real, more intense and more beautiful. Please, Malone, don't look at me like that. What's on your mind cannot be, here.'

She dipped the piece of nan in the yoghurt and then in the almost narcotic honey, which was as rich as cognac and tasted as if it had been fermented. She took a small bite and then placed it in his mouth.

'The villagers here make honey from the flowers of the poppy and from those of hemp. Did you know that?'

He shook his head.

'I knew from the first you were a pilot, Malone. But I didn't realize you were a poet also.'

He gave a self-conscious smile.

'How do you know that?'

'Your notebook fell out of your pocket.' She saw his face fall and then he realized he was being teased. 'Your writing is very strong and beautiful. I used to try and write . . . My father has always prized writing almost above life itself and I think I am probably trying to please him. I want to put poetry into my documentary. I love the Pashtun landays.'

'Say one.'

She laughed.

'May you turn into a wayside flower,

So that I may come on the excuse of taking water and smell you.'

Malone raised his eyebrows and laughed.

'They go straight for it, don't they,' he said.

He got up on one hand and took a deep drink of tea. He started to put on his shirt.

'You read my poems?'

'Yes, Malone, I am a wicked woman. I have no shame.'

'And these . . . What do you call them?'

'Landays.'

'Who writes them?'

'The women do mostly, Malone.'

'I had no idea.'

Fatima sighed.

'Some have even been killed for it.'

She looked sorrowful so he said, 'My stuff's very juvenile . . .'

She stood up and gave him a kiss on the cheek.

'No, I don't think so at all, Malone.' He was starting to reach for her but she went and sat down again and her mood seemed to drift.

'My father threw a salad bowl at me when I announced I was coming here. Did I tell you that, Malone? It was because he had been writing about the retreat at Gandamak, thinking he was going to predict the future of the frontier . . . But instead he predicted mine. I was called to him, we were staying up at Islamabad and he was pacing around the garden. At first he said he had seen his wife, Leila, my mother. He said she had told me not to come to Afghanistan. I knew this was not true. She always told him things were going to be all right and I think ghosts take a longer view. A mynah bird then landed on the table from one of the many feeders. It hopped over to where his fountain pen lay and with a flick of its beak pushed the pen off the table and flew away. I picked up the pen and rested it back on the paper and saw what he had written. I remember the words: *The girl is dead and nothing can be done for her. She lies by the drainage ditch in the open. She was not aware of her own passing. The fires in the village are still burning.*

'It was after that we went in to lunch and he threw the bowl which contained an avocado salad . . .'

A shiver ran through Malone. His mother had to stop his father telling him ghost stories when he was little. 'Aren't you worried?'

'Not with you to protect me, Malone.'

He fell into a silence and Fatima began to eat more of the breakfast as he stared at the crumbling lime of the wall. The light was growing outside. Soon the girl would come back for the tray.

Malone lay back on the cushion thinking of being up in the air, taking life in slow motion, in his Cessna; of the difference between that and of looping and dancing and writing the name of Fatima Hamza across the sky.

Fatima sprang up and said, 'Let's take Toto outside,' and they watched as the goose nosed around by the little stream, followed by the smaller children. She then carried the goose inside and put him in his box. When Fatima came back he was gazing at the high range of barren mountains to the east and she touched him lightly on the shoulder and they crossed the stream and went through the gate of the compound and into the fields where the families were already working. It was so crazy to have been brought together in a place like this. The sun was warming the greens of the valleys and the water in the torrents was an impossible blue colour. He gulped in the cold air.

At the very top of the brown-shale peaks there was snow but the mountains were dark and it was a darkness that seemed to come from within. He turned to her. She was so beautiful as she stood in the clear pink light of morning but there was a fierceness, a sharpness in those blue-green eyes that told him this was for real and not another way of escape.

She took his hand and led him back into the compound and to the guest hut where the mats and bedrolls had been stacked along the walls. The sunshine came through coloured glass in a vaulted roof and played in pools of blue and green on the red carpets. He hoped they were going to make love.

'Now, there's something I want you to do, Malone,' she said, and he swallowed hard.

He was about to bend down to kiss her but she then began rummaging in her bag. Next she took off her black boots and her pretty pink socks. She shyly handed him a pair of nail scissors.

He saw her face was pleading, and a tear at the corner of her left eye.

'I want you to cut my toenails, Malone.'

Her toes were long and soft and brown and he took hold of her left foot.

Malone opened up the scissors.

Tears were teeming down her cheeks.

'So, Malone, it is as I told you. No one has ever cut my toenails but my father until I was eight . . . I have never told that to anyone else, Malone, and I told you the day I met you. You know my secret. I trust you. I am a modern woman who has been educated in Europe but I think my father would like still to cut my toenails when he calculates they are too long, as if I am eight again! What does that tell you about me? About my country? Please do not laugh. It is not a cause for laughter. Those who know him do not laugh. But now I want you to cut my toenails, Malone. Cut! Not because you control me, but because I want you to understand.'

TEN

Kim slept fitfully and on her own in a corner of a hut in the mountains. The boy who had brought her had gone and the only man who remained spent his time in a mulberry tree that had fruited a second time, knocking down the blood-red 'black' mulberries into panniers below. The girls gave her walnuts and white mulberries that had been dried last winter and at first she had refused them, it was all she could do to stop her mouth shaking like it did when she was very young and frightened. The women watched her closely, but not unsympathetically, and said, *'Mish mish,* eat, good.' She was given wide bowls of milky tea. They spoke to her in a mixture of Dari and Pashto but never English. She considered escape until she had been allowed a few steps outside in her bare feet and had seen how the village hung in space on a cliff above a valley full of trees and surrounded by dark-brown mountains. There were paths going down to the east and others to the north and south which gave the place, she guessed, its strategic significance.

Kim marvelled how the boy had ever managed to get the vehicle he stole up here. Outside the open door she saw that it had snowed very hard this morning. She wished she had got a message to Malone and then began thinking of Noah and all that foolishness and pride about going off on her own. The picture of those last moments of the ambush lingered in her mind. Kim had tried to rid herself of them through prayer but they did not go. She prayed and prayed for Noah and remembered the argument between the boy who had brought her here and the horrible creature, the fat man, who smelled of rose water and sweat. She shuddered and then shivered.

Kim was not dressed for the mountains and the women had given her a leather coat and had brought her warmed water to wash her long hair which interested them and they combed it for her after bringing her food. Mostly she remained inside in the door of her hut, looking at the mountains before being locked in at night. Today, it was two weeks since she had been taken and they gave her back her shoes, satisfied she was not stupid enough to tackle the mountains alone. She went outside and looked at the houses, stone with wooden doors built against the savage wind and blending into the landscape under the mulberry trees as if they had been camouflaged. Children peeped out at her and she was given a scarf for her hair. The old man high up in the tallest mulberry tree shouted down and she noticed he had a wooden leg which poked out from under his shalwar kameez.

It was not a prosthetic leg from a hospital but a simple one, part of a tree, like a pirate might wear, just like his eye-patch.

He grinned down at her but in a friendly way and dripped red mulberry juice. She was then led down a path, the side of which fell away in a precipice, and was at first scared and suspicious until she found she was to help by carrying water back up to the little village. A spring gushed strongly out of the rock and two cows looked at her, their noses steaming in the cold air.

Kim had prayed but no one had answered. She had expected the soldiers to follow them, American soldiers to track them as they did in the movies, but no one came. She sighed. The soldiers only went out on the same short patrols and never up into the mountains. But Malone would. The minutes had at first seemed like hours. She had hoped so much that he, at least, would be on her trail.

Or perhaps everyone thought she had died with Noah and she was in this godless country alone.

If she could only get the boy to give her back her phone then she could call for help, or failing that call Malone. He would know people who would know what to do.

The handsome woman who had been taking care of her looked at her closely in the face.

'My son. He comes tonight ... With other men ... With the mujahedin. Do not be frightened, little one. My son is your protector.'

But Kim was frightened now.

She carried the heavy goatskin of water slowly back up towards the houses, every muscle and sinew in her arms and back aching. She stopped and gulped in breath and saw a pair of eagles below her, the sunlight catching the tawny brown of their wings. Only at

137

the top, standing in the bright sunshine, did the probable meaning of what the woman had said dawn on her.

Had the boy taken her for himself? Not just to save her but off to this village hanging off the mountainside . . . for himself? Had she come all this way to be a heathen's wife in a place so far from everything no one could get to her? Where was Malone? He was going to be so worried about her. Where was her Malone?

Fatima and Malone were lying side by side in a field of the pink and white pea flowers, their index fingers just touching, after helping clear a drainage ditch and make a stack of wheat sheaves. He stretched back content if not totally happy in a way he never remembered being. The sky was the same blue but it shouted to him and he could keep looking at it for ever. All he wanted to do was stay in that field of flowers with her, even if he could not love her fully. The scent rolled over their bodies and he felt that they were both drifting off to sleep.

They then heard voices.

He saw strangers coming across the field. Malone and Fatima had been there nearly two weeks now and he did not want to return to anywhere just yet. He wanted to keep the drawbridge up over the river to the rest of the world and he knew many of the villagers by name and liked them. He understood why they wanted to defend their valley against outsiders and planted bombs on the road between Ishkashim and Faizabad.

He sat up quickly. He instantly knew one of the approaching figures. It was Fatima's nephew, Aziz. The boy was almost running.

Malone also recognized the beanpole of a man next to him, dressed in rags, who seemed to skip along. The two were accompanied by several men from the settlement on the main road. Malone nudged Fatima.

'It's Aziz. And I think I have seen the other man before.'

The boy embraced Fatima. The tall man stood by smiling. He had a terrible scar on his forehead.

'What are you doing here, Aziz?' asked Fatima.

'The family in Faizabad threw me out. They said I was eating too much. It was not true. And I met this poor man on the road.'

'*Salaam alaikum,*' said Malone to the tall man. He remembered now. This man was outside the Dead Officers' Club in Kabul. And by the river with the dead man . . . Perhaps he had even seen him in Faizabad. 'Who are you?' Malone said.

The man shrugged, as if he had expected the question.

'Who am I? That is a huge matter for a man like me.' He touched his scarred forehead. 'Maybe you are going south and need a guide? I told you, my name is Amin Beg.'

The man spoke in very formal Dari despite his rags.

'You never told me your name,' said Malone. The man's presence unnerved him.

But then Aziz interrupted.

'The cousins from the television are coming after you to kill you. Traditionally, it is always the cousins here who bring vengeance. I heard people talking on the old bus that brought us. You must go from here. If anyone here was to know your identity they would take you before a Sharia court and . . . We must go . . . We must go to the nomad areas. Up in the Wakhan and the Pamirs beyond. The high valleys. Only there will you be safe because the passes are so high and the way so difficult the cousins will not follow. Even their hatred is not equal to the path.'

Malone had never been there. He only knew it was the other side of the Hindu Kush.

Fatima looked excited. 'We can let Toto fly away and find his love up there. That is where I have to go anyway. For my father. That is where my Yellow Brick Road leads, Malone.'

Amin Beg gave a nod. There was a knowing smile on his lips which Malone did not find reassuring. Yet there was such intensity in those blue-green eyes. A black-and-white scarf was loosely tied around his head.

'The cousins will not follow us there,' repeated the boy Aziz.

'It's probably so,' Amin Beg said, tapping the ground with his stick. 'But you never can tell.'

'Your driver came with us on the bus,' said Aziz. 'He now has the parts for the 4 x 4 but it may take days.'

They all then went back into the compound and the visitors' hut. Fatima sat down next to Malone while her nephew took a drink of water. Amin Beg took nothing and the villagers played with Toto.

Amin Beg smiled at Malone. He had all his teeth and they were very white.

'It's Allah's sacred will, peace be upon him, that we meet again,' he said, anticipating Malone's question. 'I am travelling up to the Wakhan. Perhaps it is there I have a house and family and many horses, I forget. It is a very good place for horses. I was a guide, or a donkey man, when the climbers used to come.'

140

Malone noticed that Amin Beg wore a pair of old rubber beach shoes.

In the distance there was a roaring noise and then the jets Malone and Fatima had heard when they arrived thundered overhead, causing a sonic boom that shook the building.

Malone was outside in time to see the flare of one of the afterburners as the planes flew down the valley. They then powered straight up into the sky before swooping back and a child screamed as more booms echoed off the mountains.

'Get out! Come on! Get out!'

Malone took hold of Fatima's hand, as she scooped up Toto in his bag, and they ran through the gate and to a ditch in the open fields. The others followed. There was a complete silence as the planes disappeared upwards once more and were gone.

Fatima's nephew got up and Malone pulled him down as Fatima was struggling with the frightened goose.

They crouched in the mud and running water.

'They're beginning a bombing run,' Malone said. He had seen them practise up at Bamiyan.

As he spoke the words the village in the gap in the mountains high above their compound exploded in flame.

Malone ducked down, even at this distance feeling the heat against his face.

A second strike of multiple bomblets tumbled down the mountainside. The main house in the farm compound disintegrated before his eyes and the brick and plaster caravanserai, their guest hut, became dust in a puff of white phosphorus smoke.

The village above them was hit again with a bigger bomb, which sent rocks cascading into the river. The sound of the explosion was immense and echoed and re-echoed off the peaks all the way up and down the main valley as if the mountains themselves were complaining.

Everyone was running from the buildings and into the fields to escape the planes and Malone heard a roar again high above and the earth rose up from the fields, and he saw a group of children engulfed in what looked like shiny streamers and he knew were ribbons of razor-sharp metal from the bomblets.

Malone's head was down in the stream as the earth moved around them all, and the two planes then came in for a low-level attack with a high-pitched whistling that sounded like an incoming rocket. Miraculously, when he dared to look, he saw that machine guns and rifles were opening up on the aircraft from the lower village in a brave but futile attempt at defence. To his surprise, Fatima took a Kalashnikov from a fallen man and pointed it at the planes and started shooting. The two boys he had met on the first day jumped into the ditch by them and he grabbed one of them.

'We've got to get nearer the river,' he shouted.

They scurried head down and then he flattened as he recognized the growl of one of the planes' miniguns which could put a bullet in every square foot of a football pitch simultaneously. He tried to picture the impersonal view inside the cockpit, the screens, the switches, the displays. But flying was so very different for him.

He glanced back and saw the bullets bouncing off the buildings and the rocks of the lower village. He urged everyone on and they came to the little dam where the river joined the main drainage ditch. Fatima was holding the goose tight to her body with one hand and had the gun in her other. A group of armed men from the village were behind the walls of a ruined shepherd's hut.

They had wooden-stocked Lee Enfield .303 rifles from the last time the British were here. The villagers used them to shoot the wolves that preyed on the chickens and even the donkeys and, it was said, took children. Malone expected another run from the planes to machine gun again or drop a blast bomb but they had gone.

Fatima put her arm around Malone as they stared back at the burning village and at the bodies in the fragrant pea fields.

Malone felt the tears start to well up in his eyes. The trees, the hayricks, the shura building, where they held village meetings, everything, was burning or completely destroyed. A black ribbon of smoke from the upper village obscured the sun. Women and armed men were running out to the fallen and, as an American, he felt very much alone until one of the little boys came and held onto him too.

'This is not war,' began Fatima. 'It is murder.'

But Amin Beg stood up in the ditch and pulled her down again.

'Do not be talking!' he said sharply. 'Get down. It is not over. Listen!'

Even the goose was silent.

Malone listened hard and then he heard a helicopter, perhaps more, approaching from the south. They wheeled in over the river, landing in front of the compound. Troops in camouflage uniforms fanned out from them and the two craft lifted off again. The troops made straight for the lower village, firing at anyone who got in their way. A woman went down and almost immediately a boy got out of the ditch and ran towards the firing. One of the soldiers who had stayed back in the drop zone saw the boy and was going to level his rifle. Malone was sure the man was American and stupidly scrambled out of the ditch too.

'Don't fire! I'm an American. Do not fire!' he shouted. He felt certain that the soldier was from the Dead Officers' Club and had pulled the broad-shouldered man out of the Kabul River. The soldier hesitated, his blue eyes surprised, as at that moment Toto started to honk again.

The shepherds who had been behind the pile of stones with their ancient British .303 rifles fired and both men on the landing zone fell dead, while amongst the remaining village houses there was a series of small explosions and then the soldiers in camouflage ran back spraying bullets in every direction and carrying large sacks. They didn't pause for their fallen comrades. Malone saw that Fatima had taken up her rifle again.

The two helicopters hardly touched the ground to pick the soldiers up before wheeling away, expertly hugging the contours of the hills and flying along the valley that led into the interior.

And then there was a silence so total it hurt.

Malone took a deep breath.

He was still holding onto the boy who twisted out of his grip and ran over to the soldier who had nearly shot them and grabbed his M16. The boy kicked and kicked the bottom of his bare foot into the man's face and then spat on him.

'Oolf,' he shouted, shaking with emotion and anger. 'Oolf!'

ELEVEN

Malone scrambled out of the drainage ditch, his clothes soaking with water, his whole body shaking. He checked one of the small boys for wounds as he was crying but he had only cut his leg on the sharp stones of the stream. Malone hugged the boy to him and the child put his arms around Malone, tight.

He gently left the boy with a woman by the brook and walked out into the field to where Fatima was standing with her rifle and the bag containing Toto, who honked when he saw Malone and nibbled at the pea flowers. She and Malone stared and stared at what was left of the village. The explosions still rang in their ears and the silence was clenched like fists around them, any moment threatening to strike again.

Several little girls dried their tears and began to stroke the goose and feed it corn. They kept hold of him as he clambered out of the bag and his large yellow feet parted the grass. One of the girls started to smile.

Except for two concrete houses that had not been directly hit all those built wholly or partially of wood or straw and mud were on fire, as were the trees and the storehouses in the caves behind.

There were cries and screams and men running frantically from one building to the next.

Malone saw a cow bolt out of the compound gates, one of its rear legs shattered, bellow and then, with a burst from a Kalashnikov, be put out of its misery by the headman, Hakim.

His shots were joined by those from within the lower village and the fields, as if they had beaten the invaders off. Fatima did not fire her Kalashnikov. She smiled at him and then looked down at her hand.

'I've broken a stupid nail,' she said.

'We were lucky,' said Malone. 'Where did you learn to shoot?'

She shrugged. She rested the steaming barrel of the rifle against the grass.

'Oh, my pops taught me. Endless shoots in Sindh when I was little. I wanted to keep up with my brothers. We shot quail and snow partridge up in the mountains. I was always a better shot than they were. My father is mad on shooting. He once had a nasty dream when he fell asleep after eating too heavy a lunch at the Sindh Club in Karachi. He's not a greedy man but he has a passion for quail pilau. In his dream he had come back as a quail and all his human friends were trying to kill him. He woke and leapt out of his chair shouting, "I am not in season! I am not in season . . .!" The club has been there since the Raj and no one passes any comment on eccentric behaviour. And it did not stop Pops shooting . . . I suppose we get it all from the British.'

Malone thought he saw a tear in her left eye. But she began to move towards the houses.

'Does he often have these dreams?' asked Malone.

She looked at him a little annoyed.

'They are very different from what he writes down . . . What he writes down is serious like this is serious.' Fatima pointed around her with the rifle barrel. 'It is not silly dreams about quail. I still have not made you understand my father, have I, Malone?'

He did not reply.

The air had the sickly smell of high explosive mixed with the astringent one of phosphorus. Yet already the scent of the pea flowers was returning and the wind shimmered the leaves in the poplars as the smoke rose and joined that of the village halfway up the mountain above them.

They left the goose in the middle of the field with Aziz and the little girls and boys who had been in the ditch with them.

'You'll go to the ditch if the planes come back,' Fatima said to them, as if warning of cars on a busy road in Karachi or England. Two of them nodded but Aziz said, 'I will come too,' though Malone knew by the fear on his face he did not want to see inside the village.

'You stay with the girls,' said Malone. 'You watch out for them.' Amin Beg had already run into the burning houses.

They walked quickly over a bridge to a drainage ditch in front of the metal gates, which had been blown off their hinges. Already men and women were laying out the bodies, mostly children, who looked like they had gone to sleep. A woman was crying hysterically.

'He was in the school. My son was in the school with all of the other children. He was with the mullah . . .' She began to scream and a boy of about five, neat in a new coat, lay with his eyes open

149

as if he were listening to what she said. She sank down on her knees, silent now, and raised her arms towards heaven.

The headman, Hakim, was with them as they went through the gates. The two young men Fatima had joked with in the early light of dawn were both dead, together, in a puddle of blood which stretched around them. Their faces looked older and weary and one's arm had been completely severed by the ribbons of metal from the bombs.

Fatima and Malone crossed the stream and the guest hut was now so much powder, but strangely, the bed he had slept in was untouched as was a silver teapot and two cups of green tea. Their packs were half buried in the rubble.

A hush had descended and but for the crackle of the flames and the occasional cry of the women, the difficult, angry silence descended again. He stared at a young man on the ground whose face was gone but his hands were still around his Kalashnikov and he had fallen still firing, covered in brass cartridge cases that glistened with his blood in the hot sun.

Hakim paused.

'These Americans who come are bandits. They come to steal our opium and they not get it all. They not kill the great man they want who is in the top village and now has gone far into the mountains yesterday. The planes come to kill him but then men in the helicopters do business for themselves. They kill children to put money in their own mouths. We shall put money in their mouths and hang them. If they come back we will kill more of them.'

Yet Hakim's voice was calm, almost weary.

Malone nodded his head but he did not say anything. They came upon one of the attackers in camouflage fatigues who had been shot in the chest. He had the fresh-faced, preppy appearance of all the other boys at the Dead Officers' Club. Hakim's son kicked the body.

'We never leave our dead,' Hakim said in disgust. He stopped outside what had been the largest structure in the village which was now a burned-out ruin. Men were retrieving sacks of what Malone surmised must be opium from the cellar. He recognized the sweet burned-chocolate smell from the tea houses of Kabul.

'They did not get so much,' said Hakim's son.

'So they will be back,' said Hakim.

They walked on towards the school and from a line of poplars a flight of choughs took to the air and started wheeling and crying to them. It made Malone jump but then he looked up and there were more birds in the sky. The birds had come back to the poplar trees and were singing. A young boy ran up to the headman and he threw his arms around him. The boy had three orange-and-black-and-white hoopoe birds strung on a fishing line. He had a catapult in his belt.

'Praise be to Allah the merciful that you disobey your mother and go hunting!'

The boy was one of Hakim's other sons.

For an instant there was pure joy on the headman's leathery face.

The school was a concrete building and the roof had partially collapsed. Women sat outside, rocking back and forth, fully veiled. Malone went inside the building and wished he had not. He came straight out again and sat down on the ground by the women and Fatima. The men made stretchers and in the end there were six small bodies and nine adults laid out along the drainage ditch past the field of pea flowers.

When the corpses were in a neat line prayer mats were fetched and the men began their prayers, facing west. Was it Malone's imagination but were the bowing and the supplications more violent than usual?

He sat on the grass and the boy who had been crying and had cut his leg held Malone's hand. All his life his father had been trying to tell him about his brief adventure in Afghanistan, about a land where the moral and the amoral collide so closely and absolutely; where the good is truly magnificent and the bad is Satan himself. Malone had just seen both.

Yet he no longer wanted to shed tears. Fatima, beside him, was surprisingly calm, and talking in a low encouraging voice to the women. The day was hot and his tears had dried on his face. Malone stared at Fatima. The village added to what she had begun in him. He no longer felt the emptiness he had tried so long to keep. But what was replacing it hurt.

The women left and she turned to Malone and smiled.

'Are you all right?' he managed to say. He glanced back at the fields and Aziz was where he had left him.

Malone wanted to reach out to her but could tell she did not want to be touched, kneeling as she did on her haunches, squinting at the smoke.

Hakim came walking up to them. There was blood on his scarf.

'You have to go now . . . The two of you. We have much to do. I am going south with some of our people. Others go north to block the road if the Afghan army comes and then gather the other militias. Thank you for your help, both of you. But you must go from here now. Others are not as welcoming to outsiders.'

Hakim took Malone's two hands in his own. Malone did not say a word as the emotion rose up in him.

He was sure the headman saw this because he nodded.

Hakim did the same to Fatima. Malone noticed that the headman held her gaze even longer. As if a message was passing between them. Then he gave a brief nod.

They went and collected their packs from the rubble of the destroyed guest hut and walked over the undamaged drawbridge, back through the fields to the village on the main road. The driver of the car who had returned with the new spare tyre was trying to get back to his 4 x 4. But a group of armed men with green combat waistcoats stuffed with spare clips of ammunition stood in his way and he began to argue with them. He was weeping with frustration.

'I'll get in trouble with my boss . . .'

'Your boss can go and . . . Are you an Afghan! Are you a man! Are you a Muslim? Will you tell Allah, peace be upon him, at the gates of paradise that you are only a driver and your boss will be angry? I will show you anger.'

A rifle butt was smashed in the driver's face and he went and sat down at the other side of the road, his head in his hands. Malone was not about to go over but, in case he had any thoughts to intervene, he felt Hakim's restraining hand on his arm.

'We will travel in that big truck,' he said, pointing to an ancient lorry.

Once the new wheel was in place, the group of armed men got into the Toyota 4 x 4 that Malone and Fatima came in and roared away. The headman anticipated the question Malone wanted to ask.

'They will go to meet whatever soldiers come from the north. But two of them will take the car back to Faizabad and explode it on the German base there.'

Malone looked deep into the man's eyes.

'And you do not care that I am an American?' he said in Dari.

Aziz looked at Malone as if he were mad.

'No,' said Hakim, in English. 'We do not fight *against*. We fight for. And that is how we win, Malone. That is how we win. That is when the Americans won, when they fought *for* something. When they fought for their own land. Yes? Anyway, our daughter Fatima says you are Irish, who have been fighting everyone so long that you are natural brothers with all rebels. You are welcome, Malone.'

And then Hakim laughed and they all did, as he, Malone, Fatima, Amin Beg, Aziz and eight others plus Toto the goose, kicking his yellow feet, got into the disintegrating three-ton quarry truck that groaned and rocked its way along the increasingly boulder-strewn road, heading south.

Malone knelt in the back of the truck and looked at the village where they had stayed. He stared at the remains, watching the smoke rising and turning from black into white as if the prayers and the saving of souls in the ruins were already having a benign effect and were chasing away the evil of the planes, until the truck rounded a huge vertical cliff and they were out of sight.

He put both hands on the tailgate and noticed they were now very seriously sunburned. Malone looked at them as if they belonged to someone else. My God, they had been lucky. He and Fatima had been so fucking lucky. He tried to breathe deeply to calm himself and did not stop thinking of the village. He had never taken risks like that in his life before.

Malone shuffled over next to Fatima and put a scarf on his head and pulled down his sleeves.

They watched a boy playing with Toto with an ear of corn. At least the attack had not burned the harvest in the fields; just as it had not touched the eternal nature of the fields. Malone wondered if, up in the mountains, the man the planes had been after had got away. Then Malone let the old truck rock him into a state between melancholy and a trance. All the time her hand was around his.

'I want to go home,' Malone heard Aziz say, mainly to himself in English. 'I want to go home right now and I do not want to be a fucking hero. I have had enough of this frontier shit. I want to go home and overdose on television and pizza.' Those around him who understood laughed quietly and took out their prayer beads.

Malone wondered what Hamza might predict for them next.

Several hours later the truck stopped in a narrow gorge where the sides of the valley went up vertically for three hundred feet.

A large boulder had been placed in the middle of the road.

The road itself was a track composed of gravel and stones that ran along a small cliff, which dropped down to the waters of the Kokcha. On one of the flat, grey granite shelves in the river was the angular, modernist form of what remained of a Soviet armoured car, water gushing from holes where men had once thought they were safe.

Ahead, a fat but strong-looking man in a small turban, a black waistcoat with gold embroidery and striped trousers which ballooned in the hot wind was straining at the boulder with a length of steel.

At the side of the track there was a battered white car behind which a man stood, scowling at first and then raising his rifle. In front of the car wires ran to a point in the middle of the road and disappeared into the ground. The men had just buried a bomb and the rock was to stop anyone innocent disturbing them. The wires continued in the other direction from the car through bushes and up to a scrubby plateau that could have concealed an army. Everyone got down from the truck to help the man move the boulder.

Another bomb, a mess of wires sprouting from an old pressure cooker, was taken from the truck's cab and put in the white car. Malone had not realized they had been bumping along the road with a cargo of explosives.

'Come on, you lazy dogs, heave,' the fat man called in a deep and jolly voice. 'Only the woman is working. Only the women work in this country any more.' He raised his eyebrows at the presence of Malone but said nothing. He heaved and heaved with his burned hands until the boulder crashed past the dead tree on the rim of the precipice and down into the ravine and onto the armoured car.

'It is my hope the fat slug, my brother who has become the head of the border patrol in Ishkashim, will try and come past here and I can give him a bath in the lovely river. I can blow his arse over the moon and back! Oh yes, it is written. He will pass this way, will my brother ... He fucks boys and when he cannot get them he fucks sheep. Do you understand me, blue-eyed man, believer of the book? I do not understand myself most times but you are welcome. Not like these dogs who cannot do a day's work? Do you understand?'

'I do,' said Malone in Dari, and the man kissed him on both cheeks.

They went on their way and much later Malone was jolted awake as the moon came out from behind the mountains and lit up layers of mist in the cliffs above them that glistened like the web of a giant spider. It was cold. The metal of the lorry had lost its heat and he moved closer to Fatima who was looking at the dark ridge towering above. To their left the rocky plane of the river shone in the silvery light. Fatima's face had seemed frozen since the raid. He had seen bombs in Kabul, a blanket being put hurriedly over a body, but never anything like that, never anything so powerful or intimate. He still felt the shock of the explosions in his chest and saw the pink, unbelieving faces of the dead children in a field full of flowers.

'This is not the right road,' someone was saying.

'It's the right road. Show me another? I have driven this a million times, donkey man. You should be in the mad place.'

'The bridge is down.'

'It is a new bridge. We are only an hour from Ishkashim. The bridge cannot be down.'

'In the name of Allah the bridge is down. The road goes to the river and stops. There is no bridge. So the bridge is down. Where is the bridge? It is up your immense anus!'

The man being addressed got up from where he was sitting cross-legged and peered over the cab. Fatima leaned out of the side of the lorry as it groaned slowly along a causeway. Toto nibbled at her leg.

'The bridge is down,' agreed the man looking over the cab.

'Thank you for your expert opinion.'

The truck drove nearly to where the road stopped in darkness. Malone saw a knob of white concrete sticking up like a molar under poplar trees that were catching the moonlight several hundred yards away across the river.

'Has the bridge been exploded by the planes?'

'No, they need the bridge,' said another man.

'It has been swept away by the waters. It happens every year. Every year they pay money to the fat dogs who run the province who buy bad concrete. Every year after the rains in August the bridge comes down. It is known. It is written, it is written in the heavens.' He laughed and so did others, eager to relieve the tension of the air raid.

Everyone got out, suddenly experts, and peered over the edge into the dark water, which looked even deeper and faster flowing. The roar of the river churning the smaller boulders mingled with the higher notes of the wind in the poplar trees. But the moon shone down and the night was clear. Malone gazed up at the stars, stretching in a band across the sky. Fatima came and held his hand, as if he were a child. They stood on the lip of the abyss together.

'We must get back into the truck,' said Hakim. 'We will ford the river downstream.'

Everyone clambered in and the man who had not seen the bridge was down said, 'We will never get across.'

'We will,' said the headman, irritated. 'We have to get a message to our friends and brothers in Ishkashim about what has been done. We have to get more men and weapons.' His tone was weary but firm.

'Anyone who doubts it must swim across,' said another voice with a giggle. 'Who knows, you may suddenly find yourself in the Aral Sea in Kazakhstan or paradise. It's a good night for a swim.'

Malone watched Fatima hold onto a puzzled Toto as with painstaking slowness the truck reversed along the causeway and then, with the help of a man who had dismounted from the cab, turned off onto an impossible incline over the stones and boulders that surrounded the stream. The old truck groaned as if it did not want to go. Malone had seen trucks and even buses split apart in the fast-flowing rivers of the frontier but he had never seen anyone cross a river like this at night. There seemed to be no path. Everyone was wide awake now and peering at the stones.

Finally they got to the river's black edge at a point that all claimed was wider and shallower but already the tyres were failing to grip on the wet stones. There was a chill over the water that was blown back towards them with the wind. A bag of dates was being handed round and then nan, which Fatima gave to Toto, but everyone was more concerned with the river. Malone knew nothing about rivers but he was convinced that this one, the Kokcha, that became the Oxus, the sacred Amu, was rising. As he looked down at the white stones in the moonlight he saw black channels which had been separate a moment ago combine and had been told by his father (who had rarely been under canvas) never to camp near the beds of rivers as flood waters can come down the valley in a moment. That was clearly what had happened to the bridge, swept away as completely as the sea obliterates a sandcastle on the beach.

Fatima put a date in his mouth.

The driver revved the old truck's engine and the wheels sunk deeper into the stones of the bank and then released. All at once they were fording the river like an old elephant.

'I never doubted it. We are going!' said a voice.

No one else spoke as they inched out into the middle of the river, the engine labouring, and then they were deeper, the water pressing on the truck and coming through holes in the side.

The water was icy cold and sloshed around his feet and made them both shiver. Soon it was a foot deep and they seemed to sink lower and he felt the river's power as the flow pushed against the side of the truck and the big wheels were swept along the stony bottom.

Malone's heart was pounding but then the truck groaned onwards. A man cheered but immediately the moon went behind a pearlescent cloud and they started to sink down between the stones of the riverbed, and with the water coming over the sides the engine stopped completely.

All at once there was only the sound of the river and Fatima gripped Malone's hand harder as the torrent drove them sideways again and the truck began to tip. It was black around them and it was impossible to see either bank in the fast-flowing water, cascading here and there over rapids. He heard the driver desperately trying to start the truck. Fatima held Toto above the water level in his bag and he stayed quiet.

'Don't worry,' said Malone.

Aziz had his hands over his eyes. Amin Beg was grinning at the moon.

Next to them a man was clutching his beads and praying. Malone added a prayer and he saw Fatima's lips moving too.

160

The truck tipped at a crazy angle and a man fell on top of Fatima and Toto honked.

Had they escaped the raid on the village only to be drowned in a river within walking distance of a town, a place of safety from where they might be able to get home?

The moon came out from behind the cloud and illuminated the faces of the men from the village, who were doing their best not to show fear.

'What we need at a time like this is a swimming camel,' said one man. 'They are marvellous swimmers in the deep water. It is because people do not take them swimming more that they become disagreeable. I have heard they are descended closely from the whale. A mullah told me.'

'You are descended from camel dung.'

Another man started to rummage in his coat as if attacked by bees. He pulled out something and dropped his rucksack into the flooded back of the truck where they were all standing.

The moon was bright again and Malone saw it was an amulet.

The man kissed it wildly and then put it first against his forehead and then his chin and the two sides of his face and each eye in turn and began to kiss it all over again. Hakim saw what the man was doing and pulled a donkey whip out of his own bag. He repeatedly struck the man who did not break off his ritual.

'Stop that, apostate, or you will feel my wrath before Allah's!'

But as the headman was about to bring down the whip again the truck's engine started and the clutch was let out slowly and everyone seemed to sigh at once as they began their progress towards the other bank and shallower water.

'I never turned my face from Allah!' said the man putting away his amulet. 'But at times in Afghanistan he is very busy and I only try to help.'

A roar of laughter greeted the words. The headman laughed too and they were even more relieved when the truck gained the safety of the other bank and the water began to drain from the sides. Malone sat down on the wet metal. He saw a broad smile spread over Fatima's face that lit up the faces of the men across from her as Toto nibbled at them both with his beak and Malone experienced the wave of relief and, he strove to find the word, closeness, that swept through the back of the truck, now that the story of the truck crossing the river had come out right.

'You've crossed a river, Malone,' Fatima whispered in hushed English into his right ear. 'You've crossed a river that you've wanted to cross all your life.'

TWELVE

The first Kim knew that the boy was coming back to the village was that there was a single rifle shot and then one in answer, which echoed around the ridges and sent the two eagles far aloft, screaming.

Men in black turbans wearing blankets over their shoulders were coming up the zigzagging path from the east. Kim went down the path every day to fetch water. She wiped her hands on her dress. She had been given one of the women's mulberry-coloured dresses and a white headscarf, so as not to stand out if planes or drones photographed from above. She began to breathe fast and had to calm herself down.

Kim had not yet stopped praying for a miracle.

But then the boy's mother took her roughly by the arm and hurried her into the hut and the door was slammed and padlocked. She was left inside in the semi-darkness, the only light from a small, high window, a spluttering fire below a crude metal chimney and a roughly galleried hole in the roof. She went and banged on the door.

'Let me out . . . Let me out! You cannot keep me here!' she yelled pointlessly, and then went to sit down on the mattresses and pillows beyond the fire.

There had been laughter outside when she shouted and one of the girls said, 'She is waiting for her beloved.'

Why had her country done nothing to capture the men who had killed Noah?

She shivered as she remembered the broad knife and the cutting.

Kim went to the other side of the room and stood on a can of vegetable oil and peered out at the men and women talking noisily under the mulberry tree. She recognized the boy, who had a rifle slung over his shoulder and a small, round hat at a rakish angle on his head. He was standing by a tall, young but very dignified man, who did not have a rifle and did not look like a fighter. He was not saying much but the rest of the mujahedin seemed to be deferring to him. The young man appeared to be in pain and was clutching his side. He was nodding and then the boy tugged on the man's sleeve, held up his hand in apology, and pointed to the hut. The whole party appeared to be coming towards her and she fell off the oil can and retreated to the other side of the fire and the musty darkness.

She heard the padlock being removed.

The boy and the tall young man stepped inside with the other men clustered around the door. The boy came to the fire and gestured with his hand.

'See, she has blonde hair.' He did not say anything else. He did not say 'Hello' or '*Salaam alaikum*'. It was as if she was not there. 'She is a doctor. A surgeon.'

164

The tall man looked at her. He had a beaklike nose. His eyes seemed to peer into her soul.

'Good,' was all he said. He went out and the boy followed him. She heard the padlock being put on the door again. No one came into the hut that night and she was not fed. She stood on the oil can again and saw that the men were feasting. They had killed several goats and were spitting them over a fire and the women were serving bowls of rice. The young man did not eat and his face was very white. Kim lay on the bedrolls at the other side of the room and fell into a fitful sleep, expecting the men to come for her, constantly rousing herself. She occasionally heard laughter in the night and the howling of wolves in the mountains.

She woke and drank water from an old teapot but no one came. The next day she was kept isolated and alone and only fed by the boy's mother in the night, when she heard the men talking under the mulberry tree.

'Why am I being kept in here? Why?' she asked the woman.

'It is for your own good. And to look inside yourself.'

At those words Kim lay down on the bed and cried. Increasingly, she felt anxious and afraid and the tears rolled down her face. She tried to calm herself and to pray but she could not seem to; the Lord's Prayer came to a halt at 'deliver us from evil'.

It just would not go on after that and she remembered when she was growing up kids at school said only witches and the very bad were not able to say the Lord's Prayer.

Was all this a punishment for her anger, for her spite?

And she had treated Malone so poorly these past weeks. Had she really meant her trip with Noah to Kandahar as a lesson for him? Malone had been so distant at times. She knew he was different and did not fit in with the path her mother and father had chosen. But she loved him.

Why was this happening to her?

If her kidnap was meant to test her faith she felt that God had abandoned her.

For a while she sat on the bed, trying not to think at all, but wondering if the young man had ordered her execution. She tried to put away the idea but it held her on the edge of panic. When the key was turned in the lock and the door opened she jumped and had the childhood fear that she might wet herself.

'You will come,' said the boy. 'The man who came last night is a very important man and he is most sick. He will die if you do not help him. His side is going to burst like a ripe melon!'

Kim blinked and put on her shoes.

'Hurry.'

She followed the boy to another hut where the young man was on a bed in considerable pain. At first he said words in protest but was shouted at by the boy's mother. The longer Kim spent in Afghanistan the less she understood about the place of women. She approached the bed.

'May I examine you?' she said in practised Dari.

'You may,' said the man.

She pulled up the shalwar kameez he was wearing and his belly had the unmistakable signs of a swollen appendix.

'You have acute appendicitis,' she said in English. 'We must get to a hospital.'

He understood and shook his head.

'Operate here,' he said in English.

'You may die.' She looked round for the boy. 'Tell him he may die if I operate here. I have nothing to operate with.'

The boy spoke rapidly to the young man who repeated his words in English.

'Operate here.' He then added others in Dari, which she could not catch. The boy came over to her.

'He says you have your medical bag which was taken with you. We have more supplies and morphine. It is better that you operate . . .'

Kim was staring at the men that surrounded the bed. The scene might have been out of an illustrated Bible.

'What if he dies?'

'Then it is God's will.'

'*Inshallah*,' said the man on the bed with a hint of a smile.

'You have not the choice,' said the boy, and there was an urgency in his voice. His mother's eyes were pleading too. She sighed and nodded.

'*Inshallah*,' repeated the man on the bed mat.

Once the decision had been taken she felt relieved. She told the men to go and the boy's mother chased them out and brought a case that had been with them in their hire car, which had her medical bag and, luckily, plastic sheeting. First she washed the man and covered the area in surgical spirit and laid him down on one piece of sheeting. The boy had already rigged another piece to stop bits dropping from the roof and he had brought in a strong light that he told her was used for hunting. The young man who was her patient was looking at her with steady eyes. If he was frightened he was not showing it and did not flinch when she put the line into his arm. She connected it to a full morphine syringe.

A thought passed through her mind that this man was probably an important enemy, that she could kill him by giving him the full syringe of the drug.

But the thought went away.

'Count down from ten,' she said. The man on the bed looked puzzled. The boy laughed nervously. Kim repeated the phrase in Dari.

The man got to six and was unconscious.

She could hear the concentrated breathing of the mother and the boy as she operated fast. There was no oxygen, no anaesthetist, and he could not be out for long. His chest slowly went up and down but she knew this could stop any moment. She cut firmly with the scalpel and removed the swollen appendix into a kidney dish and was sewing up the wound to gasps, prayers and cries of 'Shahbaz' from the mother and boy who were smiling. She tied the last stitch and changed the syringe to a light dose of adrenalin.

'Stay with him. Stay with him and get me if he stops breathing, or when he comes round,' she said to the boy. They both nodded and the boy's mother hugged her hard.

'That is good,' she said pointing at the bed, her eyes wide. 'That is good.' Kim was pleased. Coming from the boy's mother that was a compliment indeed and she was pleased too. She crossed the compound back to her hut with her instruments and even with her scalpel and felt the spring-heeled delight of achievement she used to feel high jumping. The men with beards knew now and she heard words of adulation. She slept soundly that night and no one locked her door. The next day she was called when the man woke and he held onto her hand and nodded his head.

'Tashakor,' he said.

'I am a doctor,' she replied.

'I would have died?' he asked.

'Yes,' she said.

'It is the will of Allah when we die. But it is good to die not yet,' he said in English.

'That is true,' she said in Dari and smiled at the serious young man. She wanted to ask him many questions and for an instant felt she might and then the brown eyes retreated back behind his unflinching purpose.

'You'll be OK now,' she said, after examining the wound.

'*Tashakor*,' he repeated.

Kim nodded, turned, and went out of the door.

It was pitch dark when, two nights later, she heard the replaced padlock on her door being opened. There was a figure in the doorway and she was instantly awake. The moonlight behind the figure silhouetted him against the sky for a second and then he tiptoed into the hut and bumped into the stove and put something down before closing the door and drawing the bolt from inside. She scrabbled for a fork with which she ate her food and then there was the sound of a match striking and a small oil lamp was lit. It was the boy. It was the boy who brought her.

'*Salaam alaikum*,' he said. The words were so stupidly formal she laughed.

Kim just stared at him and held onto the fork.

'We go tomorrow. All the mujahedin go. We all go together. You are coming too.'

The boy moved onto the carpets where her bed was. In one hand he held the lantern, in the other a box. He placed the lantern on the carpet next to the bedroll. 'Everyone is pleased with you for what you have done. I have brought you presents. Look on them. I have brought you dates and sweets from the markets.'

One by one he took trinkets out of the box. There was a very old necklace and earrings.

She took one of the dates and ate it and then another.

Next, he brought out a bottle of perfume like a conjurer. Then a lipstick. Last he laid on the carpet a large plastic rose. He leaned over and touched her hair. She took another date.

'You are beautiful. You are the most beautiful girl I ever see. And you are skilled as a doctor. You have many gifts . . .'

'Where do we go tomorrow?'

His rifle was still on his shoulders and he took it off and put it by the bed.

'We go to Baghlan, maybe Kunduz. The man who is here that you healed is very important. He's one who only answers to Mullah . . .' He did not say the full name. 'He is very important. You are to travel with us and then it looks like we are working for the aid business. He's a clever man. And we nearly lost him because a melon pip goes in the wrong place . . .'

She stared at the handsome face in the silence that followed.

'And then?'

'Then you are free,' he said. The words were both enthusiastic and regretful.

She took his hand.

Kim could hardly speak for joy.

'Truly, you will let me go? You will not kill me?'

The boy smiled at her, his eyes soft.

'I cannot do hurt to you. I feel love for you. I cannot do hurt to you. They say they will let you go to reward you for the operation.

Even your friend wasn't meant to be killed. That man in Kandahar is a mental man. And if they not let you go, I'll let you go. I will fight them and kill them. I will take you to a dispensary at Kunduz where there are good ladies who do good work. I will take you there. Do you like me? I know your name is Kim. Do you like me, Kim?'

And then he began to caress her arm and she lay back on the bed and looked up through the hole in the roof, unable to believe the words he had said, unable to believe that she was going to be free.

He stretched out next to her, propped up on one arm.

'I am going to be free?'

'Free . . .' He did not sound sure of the word.

The boy had answered her prayers in the damp, cold hut that smelt of rats' droppings and when she felt his hand on her knee she did not move away. She felt she was in a dream and he was the only way she was going to wake up. He was saying things but all she could think of was being free and then the terror of how she was going to reorganize her life now, she could not go back to her old ways, what she had thought before . . . It was not just God . . .

His hand was on her thigh now.

She had never let herself feel the reality of things. There was always a barrier in the way like her parents, or high jumping or God or Malone, or doing good works in a foreign land. The masks she put on. Kim breathed in and his hand stopped and then continued up and rested on her left breast.

Kim looked at him, this frightened boy with a rifle who had not told her his name, and she raised her face to his. He was terrified. She turned slightly and blew out the lamp and began to kiss him.

171

It did not seem alien or wrong in the soft darkness. He froze like a cornered wild animal.

Slowly, he started to kiss her back, kiss her mouth with such enthusiasm. He showered her face with kisses. Kim was not sure if this was exactly the right decision but it was now unstoppable.

'I am loving you!' he said in Dari.

'No you are not,' she said in English. 'But we sure do need each other.'

He took off her headscarf and her thick coat and she let him. He lifted her dress above her head and seemed to start fumbling with the matches, wanting like a schoolboy to see her naked, but she pulled him back. His hands were shaking as he removed her panties and she had to help him with her bra. She undid his shirt, button by button, and he peeled off the rest of his clothes and they were kissing on the bed.

His penis was so hard against her thigh and she put her hands down and gripped it.

He kissed her neck and started to suck her nipples as she eased him on top of her and guided him inside. She was wet and he thrust his hips forward and she answered with every stroke, just for the pure pleasure of the moment, to be free, to be alive. They came and he cried out and a wolf howled in the night and they both laughed and, almost immediately, they began to make love again.

She knew she was the first lover for the boy and in between their lovemaking he wept and she rocked him tenderly in her arms.

Kim knew, she just knew, the boy had made her pregnant.

A mountain boy, a Taliban boy, fighting against all she had ever stood for. One of those who had ambushed her and beheaded

172

Noah . . . She still did not know the boy's name because he was playing at soldiers and he had made her pregnant. The boy was not the only child inside her now.

He nuzzled her neck. She stroked his hair and felt him becoming hard again.

'Ahhh,' he said as if it was a force of nature he could not control.

Kim giggled.

She was happy. In that dark hut, in Taliban captivity, she had found a measure of freedom she never had before. She watched the pale pink of the September morning through the hole in the roof with eyes wider than she had ever thought possible.

It was her new dawn.

Thirteen

'We are here,' said Malone.

He and Fatima arrived in Ishkashim with the rose mist of
daybreak swirling through the wood and stone houses, with the
impossibly high mountains dancing away to the west. Down a
dark alley in a muddy courtyard was a guest house. They were
shown to a room by an old man sitting outside in the cold, barefoot, half-asleep and mumbling to himself, while a large white
dog barked and wagged its tail at Toto and howled fitfully at the
moon. Amin Beg and Fatima's silent, shivering nephew, Aziz,
were put in a small annexe. There were no locks on any of the
doors and the door of their room did not even shut. Exhausted,
they fell into separate beds and what belongings they had were
with Toto underneath Fatima's.

When Malone woke, hours later, he just lay there, looking at
her. The room was clean and had two metal beds with mattresses
and a wrap-around duvet and a pillow. Toto was up and about,
examining his yellow feet against the red, carpeted floor. The

small guest house smelled of fresh baked bread and bleach. Malone attempted to call Kim on a phone he had borrowed from the night porter and got the signal but the number was unobtainable.

Kim was always switching off her phone and they had rowed about it. Even if he got through he was not sure what he was going to tell her but he tried to avoid lies. He thought hard about the airstrike back in the valley and what was starting to happen with Fatima. He had begun to feel like a human being and not just a shell. It was as if an explosion had begun within him and was filling his head with a new world.

Malone took his wash bag out of his sodden pack and a very small towel and went to the communal bathroom. At the door he slid a pair of plastic sandals onto his stockinged feet. The floor was slippery and wet because a party of merchants who were travelling up the Wakhan Valley had had a communal bath after their Ramadan breakfast. A wood boiler was roaring away but in order to get to the toilet he had to crouch down under the pipe to the hot-water tank and burned his arm. Inadvertently, he put his wash bag on a high windowsill and disturbed several hornets which had been nesting and they buzzed menacingly around the room. He kept an eye on them as he pulled down his pants, his nose only inches away from the boiler, and shouted as someone else tried to come into the room. When he was finished he stripped off and washed all over in the Afghan style and doused himself with the water. He grimaced in the mirror and shaved. Shaving always made him feel like a kid but his eyes had a startled look he was not used to. He used an old Gillette travelling razor that had belonged to his grandfather. Two pieces of stainless steel made a sandwich of the razor blade and you screwed on the handle to tighten it all, it was simple and beautiful. The harsh mountain sunlight came in through the window and a hornet buzzed past his head as he rinsed his face. He was shaking a little and cut himself.

He went back to the room, surprised to find Fatima absent and Toto patting around on his yellow feet. Malone lay on the bed hoping that now, in this guest house, he would have time alone with Fatima.

But through the half-opened door he heard Fatima talking in the entrance hall of the guest house. The hotel was run by a young, neat Pashtun man with a brown shalwar kameez, a black waistcoat and a serious expression. He was shaking his head at the news of the airstrike.

'I am hearing the sound of the bad explosions in the valley. They were far away. They were bombing the Warduj again. The last time they bombed was when a bus had been blown up on the road. It is a dangerous place even when it is peaceful.'

'It's very beautiful,' said Fatima, and Malone smiled. It was exactly what he expected her to say.

'I have been to the Warduj once,' said the manager. 'They were suspicious of me because I was from the south. They grow drugs very good as we do. They are suspicious of everyone as we are. You are lucky to be alive. First from the Taliban. Then from the planes and last from the river. That crossing has killed a lot of people only this summer. No one knows how many because the bodies were never recovered. They are eaten downstream by the wolves and leopards. I think the people in the villages weaken the bridge so it is washed away and they can steal from the trucks that are turned over.'

Malone was waiting for Fatima to argue with the manager but she did not. The very idea that the men and women they had been with would steal from anyone made him angry. Most of all he wanted her to come back to the room without locks. He wanted to make love to her.

'Do you know this address? Can I go there?' asked Fatima.

'Oh, yes, I know this person. But I think he is not a good man. You must not be going alone. I will bring you breakfasting first. Who gave you that address?'

'My father.'

Fatima eventually came back into the room after going to the communal washroom and sat down on the bed opposite Malone, her hair wet and gleaming.

She was wearing only a towel wrapped around her thin body. Malone took a step towards the bed. But a boy arrived with a silver tray and a thermos teapot through the unlockable door and Malone sat back down on his bed. There were several large nans, a plate of creamed milk and a pot of cherry jam next to a roll of soft purple toilet paper. The youth, who was missing his front teeth, beamed at them and left.

They began to eat.

'Do you think the men who want to stone me are still following us? The cousins of the girl who was killed?'

Malone shook his head.

'The only way is past the village where we stayed and I wouldn't like to try. My guess is they will blow up any car that comes down that road. At least until Hakim gets back. Maybe we have a day or two.'

He sat down next to her and put his arm around her shoulders.

'Could you not get through on the old man's phone?'

'No. The network is down.'

Malone kissed her tenderly on the cheek.

Fatima looked very agitated.

'Not here, Malone.'

She moved away and looked pleadingly at him.

'It's not just there are no locks on these doors ... It is the bombing. You do understand, don't you, Malone? Sweet Malone? I close my eyes and I can see those poor children ...'

He sighed.

'Yes, of course. Of course. It's affected me too. I woke up thinking about it ...'

Fatima took a deep breath and crossed her legs. She rubbed the side of her forefinger.

'What is it?'

'Oh, I burned my hand on that rifle.'

'You certainly know how to shoot.'

She smiled.

'I told you, my father taught me: "Look at the bird, little Fatima. Too many people forget that. They look at the gun. Look at the bird. The tigress does not look at her claws!"

'We always went on the northern road to Hyderabad out of Karachi and I'd be peering out of the tinted-glass windows as we approached the slums where seventeen million souls live. This was the danger area, the place for car-jacking, the crowds seething around the stalls at the side of the road. I remember seeing a boy speaking into a phone while leading a blind man towards an open sewer and a tiny girl with a blonde wig pulled two lepers by a long stick. Pops says, amongst it all in a clean, pink-painted room in this Pashtun suburb, is the Taliban leader, Mullah Omar, who had been moved by the ISI from the northern Pakistan city of Quetta to protect him from American drones. The brown kite birds wheeled in the blue sky . . . I can see it all so clearly. Pops is appalled by his adopted country but at the same time completely proud of the boundless energy of even the poorest.'

Fatima paused for a moment and examined her toenails and Malone wondered whether he should try and kiss her, despite what she said, but she began talking even faster.

'When, after hours, we reached Hyderabad, we would turn under a ragged brick arch covered in the posters of dead Bhuttos. Benazir stared down on us accusingly. I'm certain he was not responsible for 9/11 as he was not responsible for the tortures and murders he was accused of. He only ever talked in a pleasant way to prisoners and left all the other stuff, the threat of needles down the sides of their thumbnails and the like, to their imaginations. It was all a question of isolating them in a vessel of nothingness, he would say.'

She stopped again and looked out of the window at the large white dog who had barked in the night. 'Soon we would be out of the Bhuttos' town and driving down a rutted road towards the Indus. Our driver then turned off onto a sandy track between low hills, which gave way to cotton fields and where the hazy distances blend into subtle blues, where you can smell the water in the ditches and the tanks. Even in this flat farmland I saw the frontier was his soul. Very early in my life my father made me realize that without that endless sweep of mountains, the torrents, the game, the mulberry trees, the echoes of ancient battles and eternal loves and the stories that grew from them in a *rabot*, a shepherd's refuge, or by a line of singing poplars, or from the dung left on the road, we are without identity and honour. The frontier is all, Malone.'

He nodded and she continued.

'But there is no passion in the shoot in terms of blood for him. No blood lust. Nothing tribal. His passion, and it's a passion, is in doing things well. It's a forensic coldness that takes him away from everything, an ecstatic void. He feels it in his work. Above all, he feels it in his writing. When that chill descends on him, like the air coming up off a glacier, things start to happen. He is like this when he writes his predictions. The paradox is that only when you stop staring and stand aside can you really see, and take your advantage, or shot. Pops said it is like the difference between the wide-eyed Ghilzais, blood dripping from their beards (they drank the blood of the British infants to keep themselves warm), who had chased Elphinstone and the British garrison, and their smiling, detached leader Akbar Khan, who stood apart shouting "Spare them" in Dari and then "Kill them all," in Pashto.'

She sighed prettily.

'I believe in his written predictions, Malone. In the *Dostan* we read of Buzurjmehr, the Emperor's vizier, who can interpret dreams and see the future and secured justice for his murdered father. You must understand, visions for us are not the swirling fogs of Nordic and European culture. A proper vision in these mountains means you can count a houri's eyelashes and pinpoint the shop in the bazaar where her belly-button jewellery was made. And Pops knows an immense event is going to happen, an event far greater than what he most clearly predicted in New York . . .'

Malone gazed at her, astonished as much at her passion as at what she was saying, while at the same time wondering if she was being entirely serious.

The boy came back and handed her a bottle with bubbles in it. Fatima looked up and gave him a smile which lit up the room and, when the boy left, reached into her pack and brought out two glasses. 'I think we should have a gin and tonic, don't you, Malone? Don't worry, the ice is from filtered water.' Expertly, she mixed two drinks.

Malone took the glass she offered. 'Did your father want to be in the ISI?'

Fatima looked out of the window at the cloudless blue sky.

'After the Twin Towers – my father's story habit was uncovered after an embassy drugs search and his girlfriend questioned – the Pakistani government had no other course than to bring him home and promote him. In the ISI he rose without trace. The story of his prediction got around and there were very wicked people, including some Americans, who thought that he had masterminded the whole thing. I think he started to believe it for a time.

'When he came to retire he was not able to rid himself either of the curse of power or prediction. He stepped down from the service as its head several years ago but is as active as ever and most of his subordinates do what he asks of them. This is true for other former chiefs. In essence the state of Pakistan has five secret services at the moment but that is nothing to, say, the poor Palestinians who at the last count had twelve.'

Malone sipped his drink.

'And does he . . . do stuff?'

Fatima nodded. 'Oh, yes . . . He has planted several bombs to scare the bad people employed by those on the extreme right wing of the American army and CIA. I have only known him once act in a selfish manner and that was when he blew up the golf club in Islamabad.' She laughed. 'He simply cannot stand golf . . .! Gosh, is that the time!'

Fatima wore a headscarf and sunglasses as she and Malone, together with Aziz and Amin Beg, walked out onto the muddy main street of the town, past shops selling provisions and camel and donkey saddles and saddlebags.

The deep reds of the carpet material of the bags made the place seem festive and the men sat cross-legged and barefoot on the raised wooden sidewalk. Malone began to wonder if they had seen Fatima on TV. But the hotel did not have an antenna and there was no connection there with the internet, even though it was boasted of in a brochure. The brochure, from the days before Ishkashim had been cut off from the rest of the country, also promised hot water. The town was now more accessible from Tajikistan, just over the river, than Kabul. Perhaps they were safe. He wanted to walk hand in hand with Fatima but thought better of it. They stopped to buy dates.

'Where is the house of the Wali? The administrator of this area?' she asked the shopkeeper.

Wali meant friend of God.

The man scooped their dates into a cone of newspaper and scratched his head.

'You must let a servant go there for you. He is an unpredictable man. Some say he is a *dev*.'

'*Tashakor*. Thank you. But we have to see him ourselves.'

'If you want a permit for the mountains I can get one for you. If you want to travel to the Pamirs? The lands beyond the rainbow? When it is raining in the entrance to the Wakhan Valley there is always a rainbow,' the man offered.

Malone laughed. He was thinking of *The Wizard of Oz*.

'No, thank you, but no.'

All of the men who had been sitting cross-legged were standing now, interested. The shopkeeper grinned and put dried mulberries and peanuts in with the dates. Amin Beg greeted a friend who was leading a donkey and a horse, kissing him on both cheeks.

'Greetings, teacher,' Malone thought he heard the man with the animals say.

He saw that Aziz hung back, unsure what to do. The men were thin and rough but had piercing eyes like Amin Beg and the same disarming smile. Amin Beg was looking into the horse's mouth.

One man said, 'If you follow this road, the compound of the man you want is on the left by an acacia tree. Amin Beg knows the house. Amin Beg knows many things. You must take him with you.'

Amin Beg gave Fatima his empty, delirious smile.

They walked on, past a butcher's shop where a struggling cow was hooked onto a rail and slaughtered as another group of men watched, kicking stones into the stream of blood from the neck.

A woman was coming towards them, red-faced, in a rough purple dress with a huge bundle of firewood on her head. The men did not give her a second look. The tang of the fresh meat blew into the street and a boy was poking in one of the puddles, which had turned crimson with the blood. He was wearing a silver-beaded waistcoat and beyond him Malone saw the gap in the mountains that led to the Pamirs, the high valleys of the nomads, and ultimately to the Chinese border, the new frontier. Malone turned to Amin Beg. 'You know a lot really, don't you? Do you know this man we are going to see?'

Amin Beg shrugged.

'It's often bad to know things.'

'He's not a good man? Like the people say?'

Amin Beg then spoke with unaccustomed fluency.

'This Wali once tried to kill me at my sister's wedding. He tried to sneak up on me at night. But he was drunk and taken with opium and he made a noise. He stabbed my sleeping bag with a long knife but I was no longer there. I hit him on the head with an old British toilet pot. He's a boastful man and always insists he killed me that night of the piss pot even though we have met at the mosque several times. It is hard to deal with men so stupid and corrupt. I suppose it's why I do not sleep so well and can be found on my bad days talking to the wind.'

They went through a blue-and-red painted door in the thick stone wall of the Wali's house, into a garden of apple and pear and peach trees, with bushes of hibiscus along one wall and a small goat straining at a rope. Aziz looked uncertain.

'I will walk back to the hotel,' he said. Malone nodded, and Fatima gave a carefree smile. Aziz seemed more and more nervous.

An old man, who smelt as if he was rotting, led them through the orchard and past a snarling dog to a cool veranda. Here they took off their shoes and went into a Pamir room with a raised sitting area around an old stove, carpeted and smothered in damask cushions and gold-embroidered sleeping mats, and a vaulted window in the roof, glazed with blue glass covered in silver stars.

On a small brass table were many bottles labelled in English *Very Good Sweet Sherry – China*.

In the corner he noticed a hubble-bubble pipe and saw a large belly stir and then a tousled head and heard a low laugh.

Malone caught the burned-chocolate scent of opium he had last smelt in the village. On the floor he saw a rug showed the bombing of the Twin Towers and very fat men falling out of the windows as the two aircraft struck. In the bazaar in Kabul they decorated the usual 'war carpet' with helicopters and AK-47s. But even Afghans had to ask for the Twin Towers separately, and in a hushed whisper.

An expensive pink-silk turban had half unravelled and on the Wali's stretched-out feet there were red slippers with magnificently curled ends. The Wali's hair was cut in a Western style and a pair of thick-lensed glasses was perched on the end of his hooked nose.

'*Salaam alaikum*,' the man said in a lazy, educated voice. 'I've been expecting you for some hours. You've been having adventures and desire my help. First I think you have a note and questions for me from the esteemed Hamza Khan? And you are the beautiful Fatima . . . I am speaking English to you. See if I can't.'

Fatima passed a note to the man and he held onto her hand as he took it. He peered at it through the thick glasses. The expression on his puffy face was not a nice one.

'Ah, Hamza, your father, my old comrade in arms. We are all a little scared of Hamza! And you are the hangman's beautiful daughter! I honour him. I do. You are making a film and want to know the true Afghanistan? And you want to know if he predicted the future? They say he came out of his mother's womb predicting Pakistan and that was why his parents tried to kill him. He was a bore even then. Ha! But truly I have known him scribble things in his books and be able to predict exactly who the Russians might bring against us . . . And now he is so powerful he arranges the future himself. So what does he want with me . . . ?'

'He's interested in what you remember of his earliest predictions.'

'Why?'

'He wants them to stop.'

'Does he? And what awful things does he see? He has seen many awful things, your father. And done even more. It must be of the greatest importance.'

Fatima did not answer him and the man took a deep drink from a glass.

'Well, I can tell you one thing . . . It is not possible to get you back to Kabul. The road is blocked with an ambush before the

Panjshir at Dasht Parghish . . . I would not want to travel myself even though I have known the family in Dasht for many years. I hear you have come through the lands of the opium farmers and survived many things, but you would not survive in Dasht. The sheikh there has a man trained as a dog who bites the flesh from human throats. Afghan people are so hospitable, I hear that all the time. Maybe it is not so . . . Snap!' He lunged forward at Malone, snapping his teeth together and then collapsing into giggles.

A spectral white Russian-looking girl peeped out from behind a screen and hid herself again.

Dreamily the Wali took out a phone and pressed several of the buttons and a downloaded video began to play.

'Somewhere over the rainbow . . .' The song came loud and clear on the soundtrack. The Wali had a wicked smile.

'I captured this earlier before the network came down. I don't think you can stay in Ishkashim. They're a bunch of easy-going dung-jugglers, my Waki peasants, but they'll discover your secret sooner or later and here it doesn't matter who your fucking father is. They'll skin you, Fatima, as your father used to skin the Russians. Of course, Fatima alone may stay with me under my protection. I perhaps can communicate to you, in a personal way, what you seek. Stay here with me and I'll show you a true picture of my beloved country that will stop your father writing down his prophecies.'

The Wali's mood changed when he saw this was not at all possible from the expression of Amin Beg and Malone.

'You seem to be surviving well, despite your rags, Amin Beg. Despite the further hole the Ruskie cannon shell made in your brain.'

'I survive, despite you,' said Amin Beg in a quiet voice that was on the edge of being mocking. 'And who needs a brain in Afghanistan these days?'

The Wali sighed. He turned to Fatima. 'If you got this far, though at the time no one expected your video and death sentence, I was to advise you to go up to Sarhad-e Broghil, to ask the proprietor of the first guest house for the whereabouts of the Thanador. He is the one to ask about prophecy. And if the proprietor is not there you will have to go over the high passes and up to the far lake, Lake Chaqmaqtin. Even I have never been there. I hear you have a sacred goose? There are many such geese on the lake . . . But it's not possible for you to reach it so late in the year. It's not possible. You'll die and your father will mourn. This country's too unforgiving for fairy tales. Stay with me . . .'

The Wali stopped what he was saying and laughed with his mouth wide open and the Russian-looking girl brought him a tumbler full of sherry and began to light the pipe.

Malone did not want to spend another moment with the Wali. Just then there was a noise outside and Aziz ran back into the room.

'Has someone eaten your goose?' said the Wali.

'What is it?' asked Fatima.

Aziz was trying to get his breath.

He whispered, 'We must go. Those who are following us, the four cousins of the murdered girl, are broken down just the other side of the river that nearly was our end. They will be mended soon and may be here by nightfall. I heard this in the hotel from a man who swam his horse across.'

Fatima looked very concerned.

'She travels with an American and a goose,' continued Aziz. 'They did not mention me or Amin Beg. They'll be here, they'll be here by nightfall.'

The Wali finished the tumbler of sherry and began to chuckle.

'Something wrong? You can always stay with me, my pretty, pretty. You will be perfectly safe. Now put that camera away . . . You can stay, you know.'

In an hour the four of them were driving in an aged 4 x 4 up the road into the Wakhan Valley, into the narrow piece of land that stretches out like a finger towards the Pamirs and China. Toto the goose was in a basket in the back of the Toyota where Amin Beg sat cross-legged and unmoved, his eyes staring away into infinity.

Occasionally, the goose nibbled at a coil of rope by the basket. Fatima and Aziz also sat on the back seat while Malone was in the front, by the driver who was constantly changing the music from his phone, which was plugged into the car's stereo, but had for the moment settled on Kyrgyz dance tunes.

The road was a good one for a few miles but then petered out and they were driving up the bed of the Wakhan River, although the main channel was to the south. At first they passed through villages where children waved and ran along beside them. There was already a difference in the features and both boys and girls wore embroidered waistcoats. Only a few of the girls had headscarves.

Malone turned around to Fatima.

'Do you think they'll follow us?'

'We can look after ourselves if they do. There is a rifle. I have seen it in the back with the tents,' said Aziz, trying to sound brave.

They had borrowed a number of items left by mountaineers at the hotel, promising to return them to the scrupulously devout and trusting manager.

Malone ignored him. 'They'll follow us,' said Fatima. 'It's as certain as the mountains.'

Malone nodded. 'I'm glad we didn't have to stay with the Wali back there.'

'So am I,' said Fatima.

The car hit a bump and they were all thrown up in their seats.

'But he mentioned something I had not heard of before. What is the Thanador? Who exactly is the Thanador?'

It was Amin Beg who answered and Malone felt a chill as he did so. Increasingly, Amin Beg was not the idiot he pretended to be.

'The Thanador is an ancient title in the Hindu Kush. The Thanador is the Keeper of Nothingness. To even understand the Thanador you've to go through the thunder passes into the mountains and it can be dangerous. Perhaps your father is playing games, Fatima. The weather's changing and it may be safer to turn back now, even if we have to fight.'

They all were silent for a long time as the car threw them this way and that.

'We must go on,' said Fatima, refreshing her lipstick. 'We shall go and find this Thanador who lives on the old Silk Road, on the roof of creation. My father mentioned him often. The Keeper of Nothingness, who dwells in the Pamirs and blows stories of his own making into ordinary people's lives, like some wasps lay eggs in a caterpillar. Pops learned of the Thanador when he was fighting the Russians. It's said the Thanador can predict the future . . . He's like an oracle and it's said all stories come from him . . . If we go back they'll kill us and this way we may get out through the passes into Pakistan. The Thanador must also know how to stop my father's stories. *Inshallah*, darling . . .'

Malone reached over into the back where the provisions were and stroked Toto's neck. Fatima was going to follow her Yellow Brick Road to the end, and at least the goose could be released on Lake Chaqmaqtin. Malone would be sad to see him go.

The mountains at either side were spectacular now and snow-topped, reaching up into the sky, and as they ascended he felt his ears pop. The people were busy in the wheat fields and stopped and waved at them. Then he saw the track ahead was to cross the churning blue-and-white waters of the main river and he felt the fear of the previous night returning.

The driver poised on the edge of the fast stream for a second and then they were easing slowly across, the flow piling up at one side, but the powerful engine pulled them through and into a wood of white blossoming trees which bordered several small lakes.

The valley was becoming narrower and scree had fallen onto the road here and there, while at the side were forgotten vehicles and a burned-out, armoured car. A shepherd boy with an ancient rifle over his shoulder and a biblical leather sling in his hand was watching a flock of fat-tailed sheep and raised his hand, his teenage face already adult. The hanging tassels and beads on the inside of the windscreen bounced around and the music from the stereo and the shafts of sunlight that struck the bone-coloured rocks all seemed to resonate deep within Malone, as if this was his frontier too.

They were on a straighter, better bit of road when the driver accelerated, looking into his array of mirrors.

'There is a car behind,' he said in Dari. 'They coming very fast and I think they are trying to catch us.'

Malone turned but there was only dust and the barren sweep of the hills.

FOURTEEN

Kim woke happy on the morning they were going to leave the village. The boy, as she still called him, was already up and about and she found her Western clothes had been washed and pressed and left on a bedroll. There was green tea and nan and yoghurt and honey and she ate greedily, taking in her surroundings for the last time. If the fighters were true to their word, today she was going to be free. The operation had been a success and the young leader was already walking around, trying not to show pain, but she had seen it in his eyes as she changed the dressings. Instead, he faked a mixture of gratitude and hatred because women were not meant to be doctors. Kim took a deep breath. Free! She had thought she knew what that small word meant in the past but now she realized she had been fooling herself. She stepped outside again and stared at the peach-coloured dawn and all the way over to Pakistan and China. It felt special to be in her jeans and old cagoule. It was a good day.

Down in the valley there was a silver mist that looked as if you could walk on it, through the mountains, as in a children's story book.

She turned and was startled to see the boy in jeans and a jacket. But she took a step back at the reappearance of the young leader limping towards her on the arm of one of his men. He was dressed in the clothes she had last seen on Noah and which were slightly too small for their new owner. Despite herself, she felt a pang of disappointment. It was like seeing Native Americans dressed in Western clothes.

The women then came up one by one and she was surprised by how emotional they were in saying goodbye to her.

They didn't speak but gripped her forearms very hard.

The young leader came and stared into her face, again with an expression somewhere between thank you and hell, and nodded.

'We proceed now,' was all he said, in English, and as she passed the 'black' mulberry tree the man who mostly lived in it reached out and touched her hair.

Kim's last memory of the village was of the bleating of goats and the shrill cry of the eagles. She managed not to glance back as they went down a steep slope and up onto another ridge and down again to where the vehicle she had come in stood. They let her sit in the front and carefully taped UN to the other side of the large driving-mirror in large white letters. The boy then started the engine and nodded to her and they were off down the mountain.

She was so thankful she nearly started to cry.

Kim caught herself promising to be a better person when she got home, not to be so tough on herself and Malone. But she was determined to leave those illusions behind. Why had she always chosen make-believe over the real thing? Why had she refused to acknowledge her mother and father arguing through the thin walls of their house?

The way along a mainly dry riverbed into the mist was one of the most beautiful journeys she had ever made.

This valley was green and there were banks of flowers, yellow ones she did not know but deep-blue gentians she did, and hoopoes flew and swooped everywhere, and then the low cloud closed around them and they hung for a while, suspended in a different reality, while the boy who loved her was doing his best to miss the scraggy pine trees.

The cloud cleared and they were on an impossible incline with another stream, a waterfall spurting across the track, sending spray over the grass and causing a rainbow. She cried out in sheer joy and even the young leader in the back laughed.

'Yes, there are fairies in these mountains,' the boy was saying in English. 'There are fairies all over . . . I have seen them.' He stared at her for a second and then Kim realized he saw her in quite a different way from how anyone had seen her before.

'Free,' she said to herself.

In another half an hour, down a path that seemed only meant for a donkey, they were on farm tracks again and then, miraculously, a large highway.

Almost immediately a line of pinkish, sand-coloured American trucks passed them. A soldier waved to her as if from another world. The face was such an American face, broad, of German descent, a little overweight. It was not a face like those that had been around her in the village and she strove to think what the difference really was. Perhaps a certain wildness had been lost along the way. Another boy waved from the top of a Humvee, his hands on the large machine gun. Kim waved back and smiled.

'Good, good,' said the young leader in the back.

They pulled off the road at a tea house, the type of place where no convoy would ever stop. Men were urinating in a wooden latrine at the side of black-earth cotton fields. An empty drainage ditch ran beside the road and there was a burned-out truck and a large pile of wood. There were two other cars. Kim got out as did the boy, who went to the latrine, and the tall young man came towards her. She thought he was going to properly thank her at last but he took a phone from his pocket. He spoke in English.

'You stay here with these fighters who are going to attack the returning American convoy. You're then to take some of them north, eventually to Kunduz where you will be released, *inshallah*. I'm giving you my phone for that time. Do not show this to Muhammad, please. Now, go with Allah's blessing, peace be upon him.'

She stared into his eyes but they did not betray anything now, not love or hate, and he turned on his heel and was gone. Perhaps it was the morphine tablet she had given him.

Kim slid the mobile quickly into her jeans pocket.

The phone tight against her hip felt like freedom. The trouble was it also was one step closer to calling Malone. Most of her wanted to talk to him straight away. But a part of her, the part that had happened in the village, didn't even want to see him again, and could not explain what had taken place.

She should slip away and try and call the authorities now, she supposed, but that was thinking the old way. And for all she knew the young leader who had given her the phone might have it linked to another and know immediately who she was contacting and a bullet would be put in the back of her head, or they would just hit her with a hoe, like they did the goats; like she had to do with the goats, through her tears. Kim had begun to understand the world that lay behind the eyes of the young leader.

Her boy came back to the car, smiling, and they went and sat down in the shade together, tired. He smelt of the perfume his mother made from the wild blooms on the mountain. But then he was ordered to drive the car up the road and went reluctantly.

Kim took a breath of morning air tinged with diesel from a starting truck. She liked the smell of diesel. It reminded her of her mother and father's Winnebago camping holidays in the Rockies. What would they think of her? But how easy it was to change sides, or at least to fit in with the other side's politics and religion in order to survive because, when all is done and all the sermons preached, the enemy are no different from you, their hearts beat to the same rhythm and the same God has numbered all the hairs on their heads. Kim realized she wouldn't have thought of this before she took the road to Kandahar.

A man, one of the fighters who had come out of the tea house, grabbed her wrist. He had an eye-patch like a pirate and appeared to be in charge.

His own watch had stopped. Several of the other men huddled around her chattering in Dari.

'Dear me, we have only ten minutes,' the fighter said and let go of her.

'I thought they were coming back at eleven?' said another.

'No, they're coming back in ten minutes. This is a good watch.'

'We must take our positions.'

'We haven't agreed the firing positions.'

'There's a bomb.'

'The detonation wires are behind that truck. Do you have the car battery? Do not look at me like that, Mustapha. Do you have the battery?'

Mustapha and several others walked away arguing and the boy came over to her and smiled. He must have run from where he had driven the 4 x 4 to another stopping place up the road.

'Things do not always go to plan,' said the man with the eye-patch.

She shook her head and smiled.

The man with the eye-patch, who had a kindly face, then added, 'The young leader we brought here . . . wanted you to stand out front but I think you must keep behind the truck or the pile of wood. If the infidel fire back you must stay lower than a mouse and perfectly still or they will shoot you. But I'll get you away. You are my guest. Do not worry. The young leader doesn't have daughters as I do.'

FIFTEEN

Malone wondered how long the car was going to endure the punishment, as they bounced along the ochre-coloured tracks.

The road became more even and almost straight at a long, high-walled village called Kirkuz, where there were signs of a small airstrip, which had once been used by the Russians, who had tried, without much success, to make a proper highway and then given up. Here the valley itself with its shimmering poplars and terraces was exquisite. They stopped at a Christian-run dispensary to collect medical supplies for the people at Sarhad, which the driver had promised to take, no matter what.

Malone scanned the road behind them. The fields were green by the river and he wanted more than anything to get out of the cramped vehicle and just be able to be with his thoughts for a while, but there was not time. He began to wonder about Kim and where she was and what he was going to say to her.

When they started off again and he looked around, a red pickup was there in the distance, between the poplars and piles of white stones, bouncing up and down as they were, as if in pursuit.

They then began to ascend on rockier tracks, past a caravan of bellowing Bactrian camels, their long dark-brown hair matted with dust, up into the mountains, leaving the flatter valley behind. The peaks at either side of them were covered in snow. Near where Amin Beg sat in the back was the Kalashnikov, partly covered with a bagful of nan.

The heavy car was thrown around the sharp bends which started Toto honking as they went higher and higher and a hundred feet below them the Wakhan River flowed narrow and deep and the colour of ultramarine. On the bank he saw a group of women washing and boys fishing. The driver looked too and Malone thought they were about to head down the slope and into the water. They travelled on like this at breakneck speed for several miles and he could no longer see the red pickup anywhere.

The driver then skidded to a halt around one bend, just after a fall of small boulders which he had swerved to miss, nearly going over the edge.

'What on earth are you doing?' asked Fatima.

'You help me,' the driver said to Malone.

'Have we lost them?' asked Aziz.

'No,' said the driver.

Malone got out and the sun hit him with a blast on the face and prickled his arms. The driver motioned to him to carry the larger of the rocks that had fallen nearer to the edge until it did not seem possible for a car to get past. Yet their wheel tracks in the dust made it appear they had negotiated the obstacle. Below them was a scree-filled slope which ended in the fast-flowing river.

They got back in the car and Malone saw Amin Beg was smiling.

'What do we do now?'

'We wait,' said the driver.

'Wait?' said Malone.

'Waiting. With patience that Allah, peace be upon him, will grant us in his holy month.'

There was a little laugh from Amin Beg.

'I think it would be better if we went on a little. At least a little bit more,' said Aziz, who looked very uncomfortable. 'What if they have guns?'

'They most certainly will have weapons. Guns and possibly knives. And a saw for heads and carefully selected stones for stoning,' remarked Amin Beg casually.

The driver nodded and lit a cigarette.

'I should think they have all those. And grenades. Even the rocket-propelled grenades to fire at moving vehicles. I think I saw a launcher poking through the window.'

Aziz had turned around and was peering out of the back.

'Should we not be taking up a defensive position with the gun? With your rifle?'

Amin raised his eyebrows.

'Were you a soldier?'

'I . . . I was in a mujahedin training camp . . .'

Amin Beg appeared interested.

'You are wanting to be a hero then? So it's sad then that my rifle doesn't do its work.'

'Your rifle? It doesn't work?'

Amin Beg gave his maniac smile.

'My rifle has been sitting in my brother's house for many years. He grew to like the company of human beings. He will not shoot people, my rifle. I talked to him often. I say you are a rifle. You are meant to be warlike and my rifle says no, Amin Beg, I am different. He wants to be of use, like bread, which is why I put him with the nan. I've tried, most often, to shoot the men who look at my younger wife with lust and cunning and the rifle always misses them. The rifle takes pity on them and thinks they should be given a second chance. Pity! Pity is the enemy of any jihad against our fellow human beings! They must have told you often of this in the training camps of the Taliban and Al-Qaeda, of the peaceful rifles that refuse to be part of the jihad and shoot rocks and grass instead. The Prophet, peace be upon him, knew of this, which is why his sword, Zulfikar, had two blades, in case one of them yearned for a cup of tea and a long sit down in a vale of orange and blue flowers. As honourable men we may be in a constant state of murderous frenzy with our beards foaming with infidel children's blood but we cannot always take it for granted that our weapons will do what we ask of them. Rifles are often very like women in this.'

Amin Beg stared wistfully around as he said this. Aziz looked horrified, angry and confused. But Amin Beg continued.

'Imagine, an idiot like me was once about to start teaching in the university in Kabul . . . How rich the life of a complete idiot is . . . I was fond of the ancient Greek moral philosophers but there was a distinct lack of interest, if not danger, in that path when first the Russians and then the Taliban came to town. Look, here is the car of your enemies! I bet their beards are foaming with blood, Aziz! They are coming faster and faster. It is not so safe to drive fast on this road unless you can see the future. Can they see the future, Aziz? Can you write it down like Fatima's poor father? Does it not look amusing to you?'

The driver started the engine and slowly, unbearably slowly, they pulled away.

'Are you afraid yet, Aziz?'

The red pickup had disappeared in a bend but its engine was clearly audible. Their driver accelerated and they all watched as the pickup came into view. Malone caught sight of the men inside and thought he recognized one of them from the television. He glimpsed what may have been a gun and the surprise on the face of the red pickup's driver when he saw the rock fall and tried to drive around it, but at too great a speed.

The heavy vehicle held to the track for an instant and then the edge of the road itself started to slip away and the driver was forced to turn the wheel towards the scree to prevent them rolling over and the pickup tobogganed down the incline and splashed into the river, making a bow wave like a roller coaster before being swept immediately away by the torrent with a man frantically trying to get out of a side window, until the pickup became wedged against a boulder on a rocky beach.

The bearded man, his headscarf unravelled, scrambled out and waved his fist at them furiously.

Amin Beg sighed.

'Sadly, I conclude, those poor souls did not see the future. Either moral or physical.'

'This is madness!' said Aziz.

'Those men should have asked their car if he wanted to be part of all this,' said the driver, joining in the joke. 'It clearly did not. It desired a swim.'

'You are mad too,' said Aziz.

'Yes,' said Amin Beg with a chuckle. 'But our good fortune is to be not the ones who are angry and wetted. It's so much better not to have a brain. I sometimes thank Allah for sending me that Russian cannon shell.' He fingered the scar on his forehead. 'I never want mine back. I fit in so well without it.'

'Do not tease him any more,' said Fatima, laughing, and Toto the goose began to honk.

The sun was not as strong and the light had turned to grey when they pulled off the road and stopped by a collection of mud-walled houses. The air was thin and frosty. A man came out wearing an embroidered waistcoat and a small white hat and welcomed them inside for a cup of tea and freshly made nan. Fatima and Toto stayed in the car.

A girl was stroking a long-legged cat and she took Malone's hand and led him outside and pointed up at a mountain that was at the end of a valley at right angles to the road. The river thundered in a dark gorge behind the settlement. Above them a line of cloud cleared and the mountain was exposed, as regular as a cut jewel, with glaciers tumbling down its sides to a high wall of moraine that was, in itself, an impossible barrier.

The girl's father came out and gazed at the mountain with a big smile.

'Baba Tangi! I have climbed her. She is difficult. There are many mountains where you are going. They are all diamonds and emeralds and rubies to me. Once the Italians and the Germans used to climb here before the war and for a while we were rich.'

The speaker was a slight man with calm, oriental features but Malone suspected he was strong enough to climb Baba Tangi on his own. Malone envied him more than a little.

Malone took a drink of tea.

'They will come again,' he said.

The man seemed pleased at this. He was wearing a Rolex with a cracked glass on his wrist that had probably belonged to a dead climber. He spoke to Fatima in the car. 'Your father climbed the mountain when I was a boy. He and my uncle saw a *chhalawa*, a demon that runs at great speed and appears as an innocent child.'

No one disputed this.

The rest of the family and a savage-looking dog came out of the house and the driver said, 'We must go if we are to be in Sarhad-e Broghil before nightfall.'

A line of little girls in bright-red dresses and red headscarves waved to them, one clutching the long-legged cat.

To Malone they were gatekeepers. He had a feeling that the land beyond was going to be special.

'Here we are,' said the driver after another hour, as they came into a small settlement of scattered houses and compounds. 'This is as far as any car can go. There are no roads from here. This is the end. That is what "*sarhad*" means, the end.' Malone fell in love with Sarhad-e Broghil as soon as he saw the red mountain rising up from the lakelike riverbed ahead of them.

Fatima was excited too. 'It's as my father described it when he told me bedtime stories of djinns and witches and ogres with the heads of bats and women who, when they talked to you, brought

up coins of pure gold from their mouths, one after the other . . .
and there were pigs who hunted for rubies . . .'

The mountains spread out around them in a welcoming way.
The valley was no longer narrow. At the back of the green fields of
the village the land rose steeply to the clouds, the Pamirs and
China.

'I think we have two days before the men catch up with us,' said
Amin Beg seriously. 'I will take Fatima over on a horse and then
you can follow on foot with Aziz and a donkey. We will only get
two horses and they do not like snow and I can smell the snow is
coming. And you have to be fit to do the first pass on foot, no
offence meant, Fatima. Our enemies may not follow us further as
they will fear the passes will be blocked.'

The driver nodded. Almost immediately the car was unloaded
a man jumped into it and, after exchanging a few words with the
driver, roared over the grassy verge and onto the track back to
Ishkashim, sending a pair of nightjars swooping up and down
from a sign which said, in English, that a public hot-spring bath
house had been built by the Aga Khan Foundation.

There was a slight smell of sulphur but this was complemented
by the scent of new-mown hay and that of flowers beneath the
stands of acacia trees. The air in the valley was very still and flocks
of birds flew and wheeled, hunted by grey-winged hawks. A line
of yaks was being herded by two little girls dressed in an impossible shade of carmine red.

A pair of camels were crossing the immense plain, half a mile
away, fully loaded, through the main channel of the river, towards
the Broghil Glacier and Pakistan. Malone turned completely
around and everywhere there were snow-covered peaks, higher

and more remote than any he had seen before. Malone had read there were mountains here that had never been climbed by any man, there were secret valleys. Yet these mountains seemed to hum at him, seemed friendly. As if they were in the hands of a merciful God.

'I bet nothing has changed since my father brought my mother Leila here and she pressed blue gentians in her diary,' said Fatima, hands on hips. The temperature was dropping and it reminded Malone of a balmy summer's evening in the Rockies.

They went inside the first guest house, with an old sign that said *Arbob Toshi Boy's*, and put their backpacks in a Pamir room with the raised sleeping area around a central well and stove. The smiling owner, who had a thin brown face as folded as the mountains, brought them tea and Fatima carried their silver tray with nan and honey outside, while Amin Beg and the driver were still teasing Aziz about the rifle on the guest-house steps.

They drank and ate and then Malone walked with Fatima round the side of the one-storey mud building and over a drainage ditch, steaming with water from hot springs, to a rock which was their pillow as they looked out over the river plain and at the mountains of Pakistan.

'We could try and cross. It's your adopted country,' he began. He was surprised how much she seemed to be enjoying herself.

Fatima shook her head at him. 'Those not from the valley are not allowed over this border and many people have been shot. You must know that, Malone. Not unless I could get through to my father.'

'He sounds quite a man.'

She kissed Malone on the cheek.

'Well, he was head of the ISI. He controlled a lot of people and does still. I suppose that is one of the reasons he doesn't want to be controlled by these prophecies. And, of course, the stories themselves are so . . .' She shuddered.

Malone was dipping a piece of the nan into the thick, dark narcotic honey.

Fatima watched him scoop up some more honey and it ran down his chin. She sat silent for a moment, letting the sun's rays warm her face as it prepared to go down over the mountains. Below them a man was gathering up a small herd of sheep.

'I wonder . . . I wonder if he planned all these things,' she said.

'What?'

'How the Dorothy video got around so quickly. He was so cross about my trip.'

Malone laughed.

'He could have, I suppose. Only why would he put you in such danger? And he can't have planned anything since . . . What just happened to us back on the trail . . . Osama Bin Laden himself couldn't have planned that. I've never been in a country where the uncertain happens as a matter of certainty.'

Fatima stared at him, serious.

'I am sure he would not intentionally do anything to hurt me. But my father told me once he could make anything happen. A sensible person might think that his claims to write down the future after he has been writing the story of the British retreat at Gandamak to be megalomania . . . Except I have known things he has written down come true for me . . . Usually stories are just stories. The wind of reality blows through them all in the end and we are left standing naked and alone. But not with Pops.

'Recently, he asked me, in utter dread, how he, Hamza, had foreseen the greatest event of modern times, the pivotal moment, the turning of the tide back to the East after the Twin Towers fell, and failed to see the danger he was putting my mother in that night by merely taking her to a party at a friend's house instead of sitting under our catalpa tree and placing the white-and-purple blossoms behind her ears? He says when he writes prophetically it is with the same dread as he had one day in his village, before his bones were broken. That day a snake charmer refused to put alms in a blind holy man's bowl and threw dry dung at the holy man's back. But the blind holy man turned. At once the man's cobras fell dead and the snake charmer clutched at his neck and choked as a cobra slithered out of his mouth and he died too. One never can tell when one will meet with things that are outside the wisdom of man.'

'No,' said Malone.

Fatima then turned around and began to rummage in the pack.

'Look, Malone. I'm sure you believe me. But here is my father's writing about the retreat to Gandamak and you will see how it changes. He was going to destroy this but I saved it . . .' She gave him a plastic envelope and he took out handwritten pages, very carefully penned in green ink with an italic nib. It was a copper-plate hand from an old-fashioned education.

Through the ice and snow the column wound its way towards a ridge they could see in the far distance. One of the sergeants, a Highlander in a kilt, began to swear to himself. 'It's all to fucking fuck if you ask me.' Beside him, Captain Souter knew that he was surrounded and that there was no option but to make a last stand on this abominable ridge . . . The snow was coming down quickly and Captain Souter looked up and tried to catch the flakes in his mouth, as he had done as a child in the garden of his house in Leicestershire, but could not bear to look on the miniature portrait of his golden-haired wife. It took him back for a moment to green meadows and a blue sky and the browns of the thatch and the great oak tree by the lake . . . The regimental colours, which he had wrapped around him, were stiff with frost. The Pathans were laughing at them. He shouted again. 'Officer of the watch!'

But there was no answer. Were all the others dead and would he be dead soon? Elphinstone had surrendered and gone away with several others to parley with Akbar Khan but no one had come back. Poor, stupid old Elphy could not organize a piss-up in a brewery.

Out of the mist the Afghans ran forwards, many waving their cleaver-shaped knives, blood on their beards, trying to hack their way into the square, and on Gandamak Ridge as Captain Souter prepared for the last assault on his position, his hand seemingly frozen on his sword, he realized he was standing on the body of a child, a little boy, who gave a slight cry when he moved his boot. But the lad was stone cold and the sound only air escaping from his mouth. Captain Souter heard the firing all around him and his mind registered dully through the exhaustion that he was not dead. They must surely be rescued? To be defeated here would be a shame that they would never shake off, the beginning of the end of Empire . . . He smelled smoke and then saw on the ridge two funeral pyres of burning bodies . . . A sergeant screamed an order and there was a volley and the bayonets flashed through the powdery haze. Captain Souter was hit, staggered and then the square broke and he was fighting with his sword and no man around him was standing and the whole hill erupted in a shout of Afghan victory . . . It was not meant to be like this, surely?

Malone stopped reading as Amin Beg came around the corner. Fatima quickly put the papers away.

'Malone, oh my midnight cowboy . . . I have a satellite phone for you from the two men who are making a list of the birds around here for the Aga Khan Foundation. Your goose Toto is with them, striding around on his yellow feet. They are very excited by it and say there are many up at Lake Chaqmaqtin only six or so days from here. Do you want to make your call to your people now? The birdmen are gone tomorrow.'

Malone nodded and got up as the sun dipped over the horizon. He took the sat phone and held it up to try and pick up the satellite.

He remembered being in Nuristan and doing this once when the Cessna he was flying had burst a tyre on landing due to the altitude and cracked a propeller. Malone never got through on the phone then and they had to make do and mend and he took off expecting to fall out of the sky at any moment. He had really prayed, as all pilots do. He had been scared. This was not the safe, secure flying his father and uncle had taught him. Yet when he pulled the plane off that piece of dirt road, skimmed a bush on the ridge with his wheels and saw the Hindu Kush spread out before him like the whole of sweet creation, he would not have minded in that instant if the prop had failed, if he had fallen to earth, a grateful Icarus, to be eaten by the vultures and the wolves. To have had all the wild world within himself, even for an instant, was worth it. With Fatima he had that again now.

213

He recalled a stupid beer-coaster poem he had written after his father's death:

> *Murder me, Lord, when my time is up,*
> *With my head two miles towards the friendly stars . . .*

The word 'Thomson' showed in the sat-phone display and he knew he had the satellite.

Malone dialled Kim's number. It was still out.

He tried the Fort.

He heard an indistinct voice, breaking up.

'Hello, this is Malone . . .'

The voice on the other end reassembled itself.

'God, Malone! We've been trying to get you. You must . . .' The speaker sounded very concerned.

The word 'Thomson' then vanished from the display.

He tried holding the device up again but there was nothing. No voice, no signal, nothing.

Nearby two women had started putting firewood on their roof for a winter that was just around the corner. He realized this meant the snow must come up beyond the top of the doors. They stared down at him and one of them, with a red sash around a brown coat, nodded and said a few words to the other, as if they read his mind and understood what he was going to try and explain to Kim. Malone did not even know if she was all right and she had no idea where he was. He already pictured her lovely face contorted in anger and then she would weep, and Noah would be there for her, good old Noah.

Malone gave the phone back to Amin Beg and sat down again.

'My friends who count the birds say the last of the bar-headed geese are going from Chaqmaqtin now so if your goose is to join them and have his freedom he must be fast. We all must hurry when it comes to freedom.'

Neither of them said anything more as Amin Beg walked down the grassy meadows and onto the river plain. The greens and yellows of the little fields were exquisite and the farmers were still hard at work, the evening sun making their faces look blood red. A group were laughing and singing. It was going to be a good harvest. Malone turned around and saw the mountains and the towering clouds behind them. In the distance the bells tinkled on a herd of yaks. As Fatima put her warm hand on his he would have given anything to stay in that enchanted valley.

She pulled him to her and he could hear the steady, powerful beating of her heart. Looking out across the jagged peaks above the river to the ascending pinks and yellows of the sunset, he felt the rhythm of the special place. He thought they were going to kiss.

'You are very dear to me, Malone,' she said simply, pulling away again.

He swallowed.

'I love you,' he said, gazing into her blue-green eyes.

But she shook her head.

'Nothing is for ever, Malone, I know you'll have to go back to your wife ... and your religion and America ... It's all right. *Inshallah*, darling! Perhaps you should stay here and let me go on. Who's to know what problems are ahead?'

Malone felt cold.

'Don't say that. Please don't say that. I don't care.'

'Well, you should. I'm sure that Amin Beg, or his friends here, will show you how to slip past the men who are coming after me. You can get a ride back to Ishkashim and then to Faizabad. To your life before you met me, Malone. And . . .'

'And . . .?'

He heard the women laugh on the roof.

She stared at him, as if trying to assess how serious he was.

'I have to stay. After all that has happened,' he said at last.

She smiled and kissed his hand.

'If you still love your Kim you must go back to her, Malone.'

He hesitated.

'I saw the expression on your face when you were trying to make that call.'

The sun had gone behind the mountains now.

'No. I don't want to hurt her but I have to tell her. Being here. To be with you. It has changed everything.'

Fatima smiled at him.

'You don't have to do anything you don't want to, Malone.'

He held her to him. In the sky above the first stars were coming out and the snow seemed to glow from the mountain tops. She then broke away again and they went inside the caravanserai.

Malone thought they would be alone in the big Pamir room of the guest house. But as soon as they sat down on the cushions a cross-eyed boy appeared and watched them closely, smiling all the time. The old man, Arbob Toshi Boy, then came in and shifted blankets behind which was hidden a television. He turned it on. It showed a badly lit soap opera from Iranian television that was being re-transmitted by the Tajikistan state network. A couple stared endlessly into each other's heavily made-up eyes and he

216

saw Fatima glance towards him. But then she turned and asked the old man, 'Do you know where I will find the Thanador?'

The old man's face was serious. 'I do not advise it but if your mind is set you must go up to Lake Chaqmaqtin and towards the mountains to the south. You have to go just beneath the glacier that overlooks the lake. There you will find him. If that's what you want, child.'

Then Amin Beg came into the room and threw out his bedroll and so did Aziz, as there were nomads in one of the other rooms and birdwatchers in another. The birdwatchers then brought the goose back and Fatima played with the creature, as if she was seeing him for the first time. Malone loved the way she laughed. He wanted her now, he wanted her more than he had ever wanted anyone. She was in love with him too, he could feel it. She came over and sat by him and brought him a cup of green tea and another cup, which by a sleight-of-hand rummaging in her pack, was a gin and tonic. He saw how she felt. Her eyes were wide and almost brimming with a tear, despite all her playfulness.

'Don't look so serious, Malone. We are off to see the Wizard . . .! And then we can be alone. I want your shadow and mine to be as one in the future. Though I do not know how my father will react when I tell him about you. He may even have you murdered if he learns you are the only other man to have cut my toenails . . . We will have our time, Malone, and our world. Drink this tea and stretch out . . . Drink deep . . .'

Sixteen

A wave of fear swept over Kim as a car went past and yet she tried to hold onto the familiar shape and sound.

The rest of the men ran back from the tea house, rifles in their hands now, their eyes both wild and scared. Mustapha whispered something in the man with the eye-patch's ear and he addressed them all.

'A wicked person has stolen the battery because their car will not start! Because their car will not start and they go to a wedding! I have been in touch with the commander and he says we must do this attack. It has already been announced. The columns of the infidel must not be allowed access to this road. Anwar is trying to get the battery from an old car at the back but I think it is dead. Come on, we must hurry and take the positions. I will fire the RPG.'

With that he went forward to a ditch at the edge of the road. The man with the eye-patch was a thin man of about forty and, after the rest of them ran behind the woodpile and the battery was brought up for the roadside bomb, she watched him carefully load the rocket into the front of the old Soviet RPG. The launcher was partially made of wood and looked like a child's toy. The man put his hands on his breast and said a prayer. He took out a picture from his pocket and kissed it many times before putting it back and picking up the RPG.

As they waited the day grew hotter.

Kim thought the column was going to come out of the haze at any moment. Her mouth was very dry. She wanted a drink of water and remembered that her pack was in the car. In the distance she heard the hum of engines and saw the lit head-lights of a military convoy. She hardly dared breathe. She wondered if the same boys who waved to her were going to be there.

A man to her left was screwing one lead to another battery and chafing the terminals with a child's penknife. He made a shrug-ging gesture as if this was the best he could do. She heard him saying the wires ran underground, along one of the lines of cotton bushes, and near to the one-eyed man with the RPG. The boy's arm was around her and in a moment the trucks would be level.

They were passing.

The man pressed the wire against the terminal and nothing happened. He did so again. In front of the woodpile she glimpsed a civilian car and then a sheet of earth and flame and the woodpile was on top of them.

She looked up through the smoke to see the man by the road stagger up and fire his RPG at one of the vehicles and then they were all running and she was running with them.

One man was laughing. It was like being back in a schoolyard game.

They were running down the drainage ditch twenty-five yards from the road but it seemed as if they were being swept down a tunnel of silence. She couldn't hear a thing. There was a sweet smell in her nostrils and then the man with the eye-patch and the RPG overtook them, running for his life, bleeding, half his clothes blown off, but smiling and shouting, and she was conscious of tracer bullets zipping over her head. She turned around, just for a second, and saw the convoy had come to a halt with one of the trucks on its side and another burning. A heavy machine gun then opened fire as the American troops were engaged from another direction.

'We've killed many infidel!'

'I am not thinking so,' said the man with the eye-patch, truthfully, as they scrambled out of the ditch and got into the 4 x 4 they came in and another car.

'What do you say?'

'One truck did not go over the charge and I hit the wheels of the other.'

'I think the commander will not want to hear that.'

'Then we shall tell him there are many infidel dead,' said the man with the eye-patch. 'If he came out and tried it for himself he would find it not so easy.' The man looked at her and grinned in an embarrassed way. She hoped the American boys she had seen had not been injured, that it was only like a game of cowboys and Indians she had played as a child.

Kim was in the 4 x 4 with the boy and two other fighters and they rejoined the highway and had to slow several times as groups of speeding Humvees and green Afghan army pickup trucks went past them. But no one stopped them until they came to an Afghan police post further down the road.

'Did you see anything? An attack?' a middle-aged policeman asked in English after examining her work permit. He was fat and had a gold tooth. He narrowed his eyes when he looked at her.

'No . . . We would have given help. I'm a doctor. I'm going to the dispensary in Kunduz.'

Kim was surprised at her own words. How she so quickly elaborated the lie. The policeman nodded sympathetically, and waved them on their way.

The boy smiled at her and winked.

They travelled on for twenty minutes with cotton fields at both sides of the road. In one field were five camels, standing together. An ambulance sped past them on the other side of the road. The boy turned on the music and then switched it off again when a phone went off in the back and the man spoke so quickly and excitedly she couldn't follow the Dari.

'It's the commander,' said the boy. 'He's pleased with us. He is pleased with the operation and that we got the young leader out of our area. But it is not over for us. We have to pick up two oil tankers. The drivers have sold them to our local commander and we are going to distribute fuel among the villages near Kunduz. Then I can free you. I promise.'

They were nearly ten miles away from Kunduz when they drew into the side of the road and let the fighters in the back out to board two dark-red, rusting gas trucks, with huge cabs and long, narrow fuel tanks. The trucks belched smoke from their exhausts

222

as they pulled onto the tarmac and began their journey north. The boy smiled at her.

'I can get away with you?' he said. 'I have passport . . . I put new photo in passport and go to America . . . It good in America.'

She looked at his handsome, open face. She felt so sorry for him.

Slowly, they followed the two trucks and he reached over and held her hand and she let him.

They had not gone a mile before she saw a small armoured car at the side of the road and the NATO and the German flag. A man had tried to dash in front of the tanker but they did not stop. The soldier waved angrily at them.

'It's the German checkpoint. We do not obey them. They can only fire if we shoot at them,' the boy laughed. 'They get very angry.' She turned and saw a man talking into a radio.

They reached a mud-walled village as the sun was going down. There was a stand of trees and the two trucks fitted exactly into its shadow by a collection of huts as a mullah called people to prayer and the fast was broken, with men tearing at nan outside their houses and children milling around.

A girl ran up and handed Kim a date as she got out of the car.

She walked away from the houses with the boy and he kept asking her about America and her plans and she did not know what to tell him. There was a strong smell of gasoline.

'There isn't enough wood for cooking. They are too poor to pay for fuel. Everyone is too poor. That is why I want to go to America with you. You are beautiful. America is beautiful.'

She stared at him.

'You fight for the Taliban.'

He considered her words for a moment. He shrugged.

'Only Allah is perfect. There are better things than fighting. Finer things, and I am loving you, Kimberly.'

She did not say a word but stepped away from him, all his happy youth and strength, all his gentle formality. She began to walk into a nearby cotton field. He followed and they watched the orange sunset and the men who had clambered onto the trucks unloading the fuel that was being siphoned into anything the villagers could carry. She saw women bring out pots and pans and even an old metal bath. It was like a carnival with an old man dancing in a peach-coloured turban. She laughed and so did the boy. The children played around the tanker that was being unloaded and the harsh taste of gasoline burned in the back of her throat. A man called out to them and the boy, Muhammad, went over to talk to him. She liked to think of him as 'the boy' rather than Muhammad. Kim then took the phone out of her pocket, the one given to her by the Taliban leader, and tried to call Malone. But she thought the Roshan network said that the number was unobtainable.

Kim sat down on the dusty ground for perhaps twenty minutes and watched the mêlée around the tankers. The second one was being unloaded now and the villagers would probably all have fuel for the winter. She looked over at the far mountains. She liked these people. She liked them as she always had liked the people in the mountains where her family went on holiday (but always taking their religion as protection against the wilderness, against the frontier).

The boy came running back to her.

'You have a phone? My friend say you make call on a phone? He say you calling the Americans?'

She shook her head.

'The young commander gave it to me . . . He said I could use it when I reached Kunduz. I'm calling my husband.'

'Your husband?'

'Yes . . .'

'Give me the phone.'

'The call will not connect.'

He snatched the phone from her and then took it to bits and threw the pieces on the ground.

'It is very dangerous,' he began. 'We must get away.'

He looked worried but nothing happened and they ate food brought from the village and drank tea.

They got up to go back to the car and the sky was nearly dark with flecks of crimson in the sunset when there was a dull roar far away and then a whistling noise which grew louder. It was like the whistle of an old-fashioned steam train.

Kim had almost reached the car when the furthest tanker exploded in a ball of fire that blew them off their feet and into a drainage ditch, swallows of metal zipping past them. The flame scorched over them and then the second tanker exploded and she felt the shirt on her back burning and he was putting it out. Her eyebrows and eyelashes were singed . . . There was the pungent smell of burning hair and flesh. For a second she lay still and then she stuck her head out and saw only the smoking metal skeletons of the tankers. The line of trees had been incinerated, as had the wooden village. The village was gone and the people in it. And as she looked around her there were intimations of clothes and dark shadows in the sand which had once been children.

She could not speak.

'Come away, come away,' he was saying.

Kim was staring at hell.

Hell was a place she had been scared of all her life and here it was, human, and totally preventable. Did she bring it upon them with that single try at a call? Had the group been betrayed by the tall young man who had given her the phone?

'The phone . . .'

'Come away.' He pulled her.

'I have to go to them. I have to help. I am a doctor. At least I'm a doctor. I can help.'

In the distance, their ears ringing from the explosion, they did not hear the roar of a plane and then all the dust began to kick up in the fields as if it were raining hard. Bullets were hitting what was left of the trucks and the village and the people but it was like fierce summer rain on a ploughed-up corn field.

That was the ridiculous image she clung to. She had looked into hell and it was raining hard! Just like it had the day she met Malone in the campsite with a downpour running off her chin.

She thought of the child inside her and was glad she had got back to the loving part of her soul, to be able to see the beauty and the splendour of the world even in hell. That's some kind of paradise, she supposed.

Kim felt the cool rain on her face and then, quite suddenly, nothing more.

SEVENTEEN

Fatima said, 'Do not follow me, my love . . . I seek . . .' He then heard a fast horse galloping away in the cold pink light of dawn.

Malone woke, troubled from the dream. He had slept more deeply than he had for many nights. Then by his teacup he found the little eye-dropper bottle she used to give the laudanum to Toto. Fatima was no longer next to him but he was reassured by Toto's presence. The goose rushed across the room with its neck parallel to the floor and attacked Malone's toes, which stuck out from under the blanket. But something was very wrong.

Light was streaming in through the window and when Malone looked at his watch the time was seven o' clock.

They were due to go hours before and he threw back the covers and began pulling on his trousers and then his shirt. Malone's entire brain felt heavy and aching. She had left him without saying a word and he turned and bumped his head on the low beam of the Pamir room as he stood up.

He searched around for a message but there wasn't any, only a tiny scrap of torn paper. Malone looked accusingly at the goose.

Aziz was still on a gold-and-green bedroll with the covers pulled around him.

'She has gone, Malone. On the only horse.'

'Gone . . . When?'

'I was asleep. We are to follow with Amin Beg, who will act as our donkey man and guide. Do you think the men who want to kill Fatima are far behind us?'

'Did she leave a message for me?'

'I don't think so.' Aziz looked at Malone sympathetically. 'Often Fatima does things on the spur of the moment. Amin Beg will be coming soon and we have his rifle. I'm sure it is better than he says. A rifle is a rifle. Don't worry, I'm not going to be brave with it.' The words came awkwardly and Malone suspected he was not being told the whole truth.

Amin Beg then came in whistling.

'Why did she go? Why did she leave me here? Did she leave a message?'

Amin Beg shrugged. 'Didn't she tell you? There was only one horse. She is a good rider and will get over the pass before the snow comes. I'm not so sure she wants you to follow her. Perhaps this part of the journey is for her alone. But I'm a stupid man. I do not know things.'

'You know many things, Amin Beg.' Malone was looking at the empty opium dropper.

'It is dangerous to know shit these days,' replied Amin Beg.

Despite the panic he felt, Malone laughed.

'Should I follow her? Do you think she wants me to?'

Amin Beg sighed. 'Only you know the answer. But do not take up your time with questions. I did that for much of my life. Allah does not always tell us his plans and why should he?'

The goose then pattered across the carpets with his yellow feet and attacked Malone's toes again and he bumped his head twice more. A boy brought Malone some clean shalwar kameez and not thinking of the cold he took off his trousers and shirt and put them on, with an old quilted coat on top, loaned by the guest house.

An hour later Malone, Aziz and Amin Beg were on their way and the sun was hot on their backs as they followed the trail up into the mountains. On foot they made a good pace at first but, once they started to climb, even though his pack was on the donkey, Aziz began to walk more slowly and complain.

'It's my boots.'

'No, it is your soul that is slothful and lazy.' Amin Beg looked at the fat young man with the contempt of one who is fully at home in the mountains.

Amin Beg's pacifist rifle was wedged under a tent and a cooking stove on the donkey's back with sacks of potatoes and rice and Toto, who had his wings bound and one side of a saddlebag to himself. Following a dose of the serenity drops Fatima had left he did not seem unduly concerned.

For a while Malone trudged out in front, following the horse tracks and occasionally looking back to Aziz who was falling further and further behind and having an argument with Amin Beg.

Drainage ditches, the same perhaps for millennia, raised into foot-wide aqueducts, ran past him, sparkling with frost.

The track ahead was covered in cloud.

Malone glimpsed a first snowflake and then another and another as below him Aziz was making a determined effort to catch up.

Glancing back Malone thought he saw a car coming into the village. At this range he could not be sure. He ran down the path and grabbed Aziz who was already out of breath.

'Come on. I think the cousins may be just behind us. We have got to get over that pass. It is going to snow.'

'I can hardly move my feet.'

Malone felt it too. His entire legs suddenly were as heavy as lead. Amin Beg and the donkey had caught them up.

'Keeping going,' he said in Dari.

Amin Beg then broke out into a horrible dirge, before laughing and showing his very white teeth. The snow was falling fast and next he raised his arms and did a little pirouette. Malone looked up and a line of hairy, wide-horned yaks was descending towards them out of the low cloud on a track little more than a foot wide, dizzyingly vertical and increasingly covered in snow. On the path immediately in front of him loomed a huge black-and-white animal ridden by a boy that seemed to come from directly above, as if walking down a windowpane.

The yak herder was hailed by another coming up from the village with two animals, and was shaking his head and pointing to the pass.

Malone pressed himself against the side of the gulley as a horn brushed against his thigh.

Three more steaming yaks passed Malone and Amin Beg, climbing upwards in their slow, deliberate way, on the ancient spice route.

After the creatures had all melted into the whiteness, Malone again went back for Aziz and took him by the arm.

'It's not so bad. It will get flatter in a moment.'

But the slope didn't get flatter. It became ridiculously difficult. Was this why she had left him behind?

The path then vanished altogether and underneath the new snow were loose rocks and mud which clung to his boots that were already hurting him. His feet felt heavier than they had ever done before and they had swollen so he could feel the insides of the cheap boots he had bought in Pakistan. He laced them tighter but one of the lace holes had come away.

He picked a point twenty or thirty yards ahead and made for it and then did the same thing again and again. He used to love walking in the mountains but it was never like this and despite the snow it was getting colder.

He looked around again and Aziz was lagging far behind now and had sat down on a rock and the donkey and Amin Beg had stopped too. Amin Beg took out a little tin of the green snuff he seemed addicted to and put it under his tongue. The donkey's wine-coloured saddlebags made out of pieces of carpet glowed against the white snow and mist.

Malone turned and continued upwards. There was nothing else to do but keep going forward. He laughed to himself. That was a philosophy that had stood him in good stead once but no longer. The world did not really work like that, especially in Afghanistan.

He thought of Fatima's lovely face and prayed she had not left him for good. He did not want to go back to how he was before he met her.

Slowly, the path began to level out and for an instant the snow and mist swirled away and he could see the valley and the sun glinting silver over the river plain to Pakistan.

But then the weather swept back again.

Malone's shalwar kameez were drenched now and water was seeping into his cheap boots.

But he had always liked snow.

He and his father had played in the snow, sliding down a hill at the back of their house in Rock Creek on an old sledge.

Malone felt light-headed and he guessed that must be altitude sickness kicking in. The donkey and the other two had not appeared yet and he could not go on without Amin Beg's guidance. He knew the mountains as only one who had grown up in them can. There were no tracks or indication in the snow exactly where the path lay and in this mist he might easily find himself falling thousands of feet to the river below.

Malone was on the side of the red mountain he had seen from Sarhad and he sat down on a rock and waited.

He heard a raven make its guttural call very close by and then out of the mist below came the two ghostly figures, covered in snow as he was, and the donkey. He could see their breath turning to steam but he could not hear their voices. The snow muffled everything.

Amin Beg hurried up to Malone.

'The idiots, the cousins, who want to kill Fatima ... they're following us. The boy who came up behind us with the yaks tells me. Aziz is too slow and fat. He is worse than my grandmother who's dead. They'll catch us.'

Malone got up quickly and went over to Aziz and said in English, 'We have to hurry.'

The boy's face was red with effort. Malone saw a vein pulsing in his temples. His eyes looked dim and muddy.

'I don't think I can go on, Malone. I'll try to go back . . . I could hide . . . I was taught how to . . .'

Malone shook his head.

'Either they'd find you and kill you or you'd die in the snow.'

'My head aches. My feet will not move.'

There was a snorting sound from Amin Beg that Malone did not expect.

'If this fat waster was my son, I would whip him,' said Amin Beg. 'But he would probably only collapse in tears. His mother should have thrown him into the fire at birth. He is useless and lazy and shows the shit and corruption of our country. This is what we have turned into. Fat lambs' tails.'

Aziz began to cry and Amin Beg hit him in the face with his wooden braided donkey whip.

Malone did not have the strength to stop him.

'Get on, or you will feel my foot in your backside as well! You have enough butter on your body to climb a thousand passes. A girl of five can walk better than you. You spit on the grave of the Prophet, peace be unto his name, by your continued wretched existence.'

But Amin Beg's tirade had the desired effect.

Aziz wheeled forwards and made small chugging steps through the snow which was now a foot deep on the plateau-like top of the Daliz Pass and then Amin Beg pointed with his whip and skipped off into the mist in a direction that Malone would not have chosen. Malone kept his own pace slow so that Aziz was able to keep up. The boy was whimpering and his teeth were chattering.

'You see, Aziz. You can perform miracles.'

'I am dying, Malone. If ever I get home I will not move from being in front of the television. I will eat so many pizzas I will become too fat to walk.'

The mist cleared momentarily ahead of them and Malone stood quite still. The pass was a lonely place bereft of any closeness. The air was thin here and each breath made you think you were just in transit through this life. He was sure now he had reached a frontier, an invisible barrier after which the earth does not become more wild, a land both sacred and fatal and possessed of a terrible beauty. He took a gasping breath of the thinning air. Why are the dangerous things so beautiful? He was at sixteen thousand lip-numbing feet, and the jagged black peaks around him had turned to white. There were endless black-ridged mountains and a stream which plunged down into the cobalt-blue river. Gullies soared, dappled with snow on the other side, melding into ice fields and low cloud. Everywhere was magnificence and nowhere was there comfort or shelter. Whatever had gone before was dwarfed by the land they were stepping into. Malone felt instinctively frightened. It was as if they were walking with their donkey into the first circle of hell.

It had started to snow more heavily and the wind was blowing hard from the north. The three of them were together now and the donkey was slightly in front of Malone.

'Fuck!'

He instinctively ducked as there was the echoing crack of a rifle shot that smashed into the scree to their left.

Malone was thinking of Fatima as the bullet was fired. Of the childhood ritual she told him always took place with her bare-legged on a red-velvet boudoir chair . . .

He crouched down but there was no second shot, no continuous burst. He stumbled and began to slip and slide on the sharp scree.

Below him armed men were emerging from the mist and the ice-covered boulders. One moment there were just the tops of shale sticking out of the white and then the stones moved and became men. He saw their black turbans and camouflage jackets and them fanning out to the left and right where the narrow path met a small stream. They carried Kalashnikovs and were certainly the Taliban. At first Malone was about to run but Amin Beg shook his head. They were easy targets against the white. They, and the goose, were absurdly ... sitting ducks. Malone stood up. More than that, if Fatima was ahead they must help her. He had a tectonic desire to see her again. Fuck them. Even if he was going to die he was not going to run.

The men were coming towards him. It was then he looked down at his boots and saw blood on the snow.

Toto honked from his saddlebag and with his shiny yellow beak gently nibbled at the soft hair on the donkey's mane, the two dark bars on the goose's head standing out in the half-light.

There was red blood, almost black, on the new snow. Had he been hit? Was this how it ended with Fatima? With flying? He did not feel a thing but his head was reeling and he slipped again. There was a pain in his side. Everything was happening so slowly.

Then Amin Beg let out a low cry.

'Oh, no! *Bismillah!*'

Malone turned and saw Aziz was now falling to the floor with the AK-47 from the donkey in his hands. The bullet that had smashed into the scree had first made a small, neat hole in the thick jacket Aziz had borrowed from Arbob Toshi Boy's guest house. But as the boy sank to his knees Malone realized that it had ripped a hole in his back the size of a baseball and blood was spurting out.

Amin Beg took off Aziz's headscarf and stuffed it against the wound.

They stood still, staring down at the boy.

'I did not do wrong?' said Aziz, his breath rattling now.

'No, you didn't do wrong. You're a hero. Isn't he a hero?' said Malone.

Amin Beg nodded.

Aziz tried to get up and said in English, 'I'm hero. I am a hero on the North-West Frontier. I am a hero!' Then he laughed. 'The thing is I never wanted to be a hero. It was just . . .'

Malone was holding the boy when he died, with a look of both happiness and confusion on his face. The men below were coming up fast. Malone and Amin Beg lifted Aziz with difficulty onto the laden donkey. Then a bearded man was on them and Malone pointed to the rifle, which the man gathered up.

'You did not need to shoot him, you defiler of sheep!' shouted Amin Beg, as if he knew the man.

'He went for his rifle,' said the Taliban fighter quietly, shouldering his own.

'He was a boy!'

'I have been shot at by boys. The bullets are the same.'

The conversation was at an end but the bearded man did not appear happy with himself and Amin Beg did not offer him any green snuff and they spoke too rapidly for Malone to understand. They trudged slowly down to where the others waited by a pile of rocks near a stream and Malone saw many more donkeys and one horse trying to find grazing under the snow.

The man who had shot Aziz had an orange, henna-dyed beard and went, as if nothing had happened, and squatted on his haunches with five other men, who were watching all around them. They were only dressed in camouflage jackets over their shalwar kameez but had yellow, high-lacing, NATO-issue boots and were pressed together for warmth.

They sat in the snow and wind exchanging food, even though it was Ramadan. Sharing a single cigarette they seemed totally at ease with the place and the weather, the war and each other. A few of them had the beards expected of the Taliban but others did not and they mostly did not look at Malone with hatred. These were big, well-muscled men fed on a diet of meat, not rice and mouldy potatoes. Only one was dressed differently and had a white skin, wrap-around sunglasses and a black cap on his head.

He stared at Malone but then looked away and accepted the cigarette that was being passed. These were men on an important mission who had been interrupted by the absurdities of an infidel with a live, bar-headed goose on his donkey. Malone distinctly heard the word 'goose' and then the term 'malang', which meant holy fool.

All the fighters had AK-47s of different ages and muzzle designs that had been made in far-flung outposts of another revolution, but all were clean and oiled. The armed men appeared completely indifferent to the death of Aziz, although Malone thought he sensed a weight of sorrow on their shoulders in the falling snow that was probably for the wider conflict. He had no doubt that, if ordered by their officer, they would kill him too.

He then saw the elfin figure of Fatima behind them and another who he guessed was the group's leader. She came running up towards Malone.

'I didn't want you to follow me . . . I left you a note. Did you not find it? No . . . Oh my God, no!'

Malone went to put his arms around her and she let him.

'Aziz was trying to defend us. I think he was glad to be brave at last.'

Fatima was weeping.

'What does it matter now he's dead?'

'It matters,' said Malone. He was looking at the fighters.

Fatima cried for a time and Amin Beg shook his head over the body and mumbled under his breath. 'Oh, Aziz, in the name of Allah, peace be upon him, what have you done now? Cowardice finds the hero in us all, eventually,' he said in English. 'I'm sorry Aziz is dead, Fatima. Malone, these men are a lashkar, a village militia, coming over the glacier from Pakistan with military explosives for their brothers in the Taliban. They tell me Fatima had told them of her pursuers and they thought we were the cousins, possibly with the border police. Poor Aziz. I should not have said such words to him.'

Malone doubted that this was a simple village lashkar. The men had the look of those who had been fighting all their lives.

Fatima stroked the boy's hair.

Amin Beg said softly, 'It was impossible for these men to know for sure who it was. Then the boy went for my rifle. I had tried to tell him it was an unreliable companion.'

The leader, in his late twenties, who had the bearing of an officer and probably had been in the Pakistan army, walked slowly forward. He looked magnificent, like the picture of Byron in oriental dress Malone remembered from the poet's collected works. The officer's headscarf was tied exactly, even in the wind. His padded shooting jacket was open to the elements and showed a cashmere sweater. An expensive pair of Leica binoculars hung around his neck. He was clean-shaven and, although his features were those of the frontier, his expression was aloof and educated. Yet Malone guessed the determination that lay behind, even if the man looked as if he was on a hunting trip.

'I am most terribly sorry,' he said, in perfect upper-class English, gesturing towards Aziz. 'But if the shepherd boy who passed us on a yak is correct, those who are following you will not be far behind. We must take our positions.'

He shouted to his men and several of them hid themselves among rocks further up the track while the rest helped pull the horse and donkeys, including the one bearing Aziz, behind a large boulder. Malone and Fatima crouched behind a scree pile between the officer and Amin Beg. They waited in the falling snow.

'Why are you helping us?' Malone asked.

The officer raised an eyebrow slightly.

'I'm helping Fatima Hamza. She'll take a letter to her father for me. A younger brother of mine is being held by the civil police in Karachi and I want him released. He's wrongly accused of smuggling rubies. Whoever heard of being charged with smuggling rubies! They expect my mother to pay a huge bribe.'

The snow came down and they watched the land in front of them become white as the sky. A raven crossed it and was gone.

The officer peered into the nothingness occasionally with his binoculars. Malone could no longer make out the three men who had positioned themselves behind a cairn slightly to the right of the track. They had all but disappeared.

'I know about the stupidity with the video. But such blood feuds as these cousins indulge in are not good for our cause.'

'And what is your cause?' asked Malone.

The officer's face lit up, in a brilliant though possibly ironic smile. 'I want my country to be left alone to make its own mistakes. At least we know that Mullah Omar loves us. That is a lot . . . Look . . .'

Malone froze as slowly, from left to right down the pass, four men came, leading horses. From somewhere they had found horses to hire. It was not possible at this range to tell if they were the ones from the television and the car. Just like him they were sliding around on the snow-covered scree and Malone guessed they were city boys too, unused to this country in which the officer's men thrived.

One of the cousins was singing and for a few moments the four stopped, arguing. They were about a hundred yards away and they began to step forward again and one of the men laughed as he slipped and Malone thought of the faces contorted with anger on the television screen and remembered too the death of their cousin, killed because she was mistaken for Fatima.

They appeared unsure of the path or even how to lead the horses, whose bridles jangled. On they came and Malone smelled the cigarette one of the cousins was smoking and saw another had injuries to his face from the car crash. All had beards and the man in front even had a new North Face anorak.

The snow was falling straight down and had covered any blood on the path. Malone looked at the officer whose face was cool and expressionless. The lead horse stopped and reared and whinnied. Malone saw that all four men had rifles slung over their shoulders. The man in front was having trouble controlling his horse, which whinnied more.

Then there was an answering cry of Fatima's horse behind the rock.

The other men coming down the path halted too.

As they did, the shooting started. Three of the cousins were hit simultaneously. One man tried to escape up the pass and the prolonged reedy note of a Kalashnikov on fully automatic cut him down.

Malone saw him fall, surprised, clutching at his shoulder.

Those who had shot the four remained hidden until they were sure of their kill. There was no romance at all in the ambush, no bravado.

The horses did not run away but stood and shivered as the snow muffled the echo. The flakes were already starting to cover the corpses.

It seemed an age before only one of the Taliban fighters came slowly out of his position and prodded each man in turn. The first three were dead. The fourth man who had tried to escape held up his hands and cried out and began to pray and was left where he was. Then he shouted, 'Do not kill me. Do not kill me, my brothers. I am a believer and I have money!'

The fighters ambled back down the slope. The officer stood up as the three men came over to him and he nodded and they went back to the others and the pack animals. The mist swirled away and the mountains and the Himalayan chain shone in the sunlight.

'We are so small, and yet . . . And yet Allah, peace be upon him, numbers every hair on our heads. It was their time,' said the officer wistfully in English, and Amin Beg nodded and said a prayer.

Aziz's body had been taken off the donkey and laid out on the snow by two of the fighters.

Malone saw Fatima wipe her tears and try to stop crying. She went to her horse and her hands were shaking as she reached into the saddlebag. She searched frantically and then found what she was looking for, a simple paper rose that Malone had bought for her in Baharak market. Fatima fastened the bag and rushed out from behind the rock clutching the flower.

The wounded man was brought down towards the officer.

'Please, my lord, let me live.'

The officer turned his head on one side.

'Why do you come after this woman? Why do you follow her to the ends of the earth?'

The man peered at Fatima with a confused look. Then he said, 'She is a harlot, lord. She is the daughter of Satan. She must be brought before the courts. She has brought shame on my family and caused the death of my young cousin. You must know this.'

The officer shook his head.

'From what I hear it's your stupidity and pride which has caused much sorrow.'

The wounded man suddenly lost his fear.

'She must be handed over to a court and then stoned. Who are you to say this is not to be? We must be respected. She has shamed my family.'

The officer yawned.

'For singing songs from a Hollywood movie?'

'She must be killed. This was agreed.'

The officer took a step forward.

'I am mujahedin. I am told by my superior to be merciless with those who stand in our way. To break their bones as a lesson. You are in my way. This woman is a help to me. I ask you to show her mercy. She intended the film to be private, so it is nothing to us.'

'Then you are a dog! My cousins and I were given money to do this by important people . . . You should not stand in our way . . .'

Malone heard the man use the Dari word '*sag*'.

The officer shrugged and gave a tight little smile.

'I may be a dog, old boy, but you have had your day. I have to crack on,' he said in English. He nodded to his men.

The wounded man and the bodies of the others were stripped in the snow and their faces and hands were wiped with something from a jar, honey. The smell was strong on the cold air. While this was being done another man tied the four cousins together, right leg to right leg with ten-foot lengths of hemp rope, the wounded man also, as he shook with fear. The fighters then smashed the faces of the dead men in with rifle butts as their relative screamed. The body of Aziz lay on the ground by them. Fatima was about to run to him but Malone caught hold of her. She appeared as much angry as upset and he had never seen her like this.

The four cousins were dragged to the side of the precipice and one of the corpses fell away, the first dead man pulling the others inexorably over, the wounded man scrabbling for a hold on the snow with his bare feet, trying to undo his bonds, blood pumping from the wound in his shoulder.

'No, please, mercy! I am on your side. You are not meant to kill me! It is written. It is written on the paper . . .'

It is written, thought Malone.

But the last body slid away and the wounded man accelerated over the edge with a howl onto the rocks a thousand feet below, tied to his cousins.

Fatima broke free of Malone and ran to her nephew.

She put the paper rose on Aziz's cold body.

Malone knew the fighters wanted to smear honey on the face of Aziz and strip him, smash his skull to release his spirit and throw him over too. They did this so the dead would not be identified. It was also from an older custom up here in the Wakhan that the dead would not know who they were and so could not come back to haunt the living. The animals would tear the corpses apart and in only weeks they would be a collection of bleached bones. Perhaps that was why Fatima's country was the way it was, there were so many pale ghosts wandering unsure of whom to take revenge upon, so taking revenge on everyone.

Malone watched as one of the fighters leaned over the chasm and peered down into the abyss below. Amin Beg swayed slightly as he said the Muslim prayer for burial from a small book that he had produced from his rags.

'I want my nephew's body. I demand my Aziz's body,' Fatima was shouting.

The officer nodded. Her fury was such that even he looked alarmed.

At his order, Aziz's body was put on their donkey and she retrieved the rose for now.

One of the fighters went over to peer at Toto and Fatima pushed him away with a surprising strength. The man meekly went.

'You must tell his people that he died a martyr,' said the officer in English, with his slight smile. 'It will comfort them.'

'I think you're all mad,' Fatima said, her lips pressed tightly together. 'I think we're all fucking mad.'

The snow had stopped a half-hour later and, after sharing cold tea and nan with them, the officer said goodbye to Malone and came over to Fatima. He did not say anything more but his hand lingered on her arm. There was a quality about the officer that Malone thought must have reminded her of her father, when he was a young man up here fighting the Russians. Malone was grateful to this officer and his fighters as well. Without them the men would have caught Fatima and put her to a slow death by stoning and him too. But he could not forget the image of the man being pulled over the edge by his cousins.

He watched the small column go, walking by the donkeys and horses. The officer was last. He had taken the horse of Fatima and those of the cousins as part of the bargain. He spoke to Amin Beg.

'You didn't see us, did you my friend?'

'I saw nothing, lord. My eyes grow dim with all the sorrow of the world.'

'May it long be so, or we may visit you and drink your tea. Up by your lake by the green ice glacier.'

Amin Beg nodded to him.

'And we can go on?' said Malone.

Amin Beg seemed uneasy at the question, as if he knew such a request could quickly bring the opposite. He had probably seen this from softly spoken men who commanded others with guns all his life.

'As you like,' said the officer in English, with a broader smile, and he urged the horse after his men, overtaking the last donkey and making for the top of the pass. Then he called back. 'Do not forget to deliver my message, Fatima Hamza. About my mother's rubies.'

Only when he was out of sight did Malone see her begin to shake and cry. She did not let herself be consoled, even by him. He sighed. He was just so glad to see her.

Eighteen

'We must keep going fast,' said Amin Beg.

For an hour Malone had to all but run as they seemed to fly along the tiny slippery paths with the chasm below. After descending for a while they began going up again and he felt an increasing dizziness and tripped as he rounded a corner and nearly plunged down a vertical scree slope into the river.

The mist had lifted and the snow stopped but the mountains to the south were glittering and cold and he had no idea how much what had happened at the pass had taken out of him. Malone felt as if he were about to collapse. He had not thought how far it was going to be, over the endless ridges and then dropping down and skirting a cliff to another higher one, often on his hands and knees.

Malone cursed his soft lifestyle.

The mountain people did this every day on a handful of rice and a rock-hard piece of nan. Malone felt ashamed and on the verge of tears and he tried not to picture the white face of Aziz on the snow, or look at his corpse strapped to the donkey.

The sun was hot and despite the snow the temperature see-sawed from one extreme to the other. Malone had taken off his woolly hat and his shalwar kameez were almost dry. There was no shade here above the tree line and he stopped for a moment to tie his black-and-white-chequered scarf around his head, in a turban. The sun was burning his hands.

'Malone, you must be careful with the sun.'

Fatima saw how the backs of his hands were red raw.

She put a black-and-white scarf on her head too. The side of Malone's face was blistered and sore.

'I'm not that good with sun,' he said, desperately tired.

'Don't worry, the cold will soon return. You didn't have to come with me, you know. I left you a note.'

'There was no note.'

'They might have killed us all back there. You didn't have to come, Malone.'

'I did,' he said, and they were then too exhausted to continue the difficult conversation. Occasionally, they hauled themselves to the top of a rise to find Amin Beg talking to the donkey about a man in such and such village as if he were on a country walk.

When Malone rested on a stone next to Amin Beg he could scarcely move and it was hard to drink from Fatima's water bottle. It was as if he was not able to swallow.

He looked back along the path and found it difficult to imagine that this was one of the routes of the old Silk Road, that Alexander's army had been here, that the old liar Herodotus' informants had trodden these paths, with tales of giant gold-digging ants that were probably marmots, who it was said had collected dust in their fur, a true golden fleece, and Marco Polo and Genghis Khan.

Timur Leng or Tamburlaine's cavalry might have come this way to India in the fourteenth century. Malone wondered how many souls, British, Persian, Greek or Afghan, had encouraged each other along these terrible passes.

Malone heard a cry above and saw a lammergeier vulture, called the bone-breaker because it dropped bones from a great height to smash them for the marrow, wheel out of the sun, casting its shadow on Fatima.

Malone recalled that meant a rise to power.

Fatima was following his gaze. 'My father used to quote a saying from up here, "I was distracted by my love until the vulture came down from the sky and pecked off my cock." They are always joking. A typical greeting is, "I am going to kill you," to which the reply is, "You are a kind-hearted man." '

He laughed. But he knew the land above the pass was a harsh place. Whole Soviet units had disappeared here among the Kyrgyz nomads, whose summer pastures lay ahead.

Fatima did her best to encourage him although he was burning up. He was barely able to talk.

'Come on,' she shouted, and her voice echoed off the mountains, as she somehow managed to skip along the path in front.

Malone had nearly fainted twice when they began at last to descend on an endless steep latticework of paths and every step hurt. He was going to take his boots off at one point but Fatima insisted that would be worse and instead she grasped his arm and helped him, down towards the trees and where a stream flowed into the main river. They were on a very steep bank below the snow line and had to run down the slippery earth to the riverbed where Amin Beg went to fill the water bottles in the blue stream.

She and Malone followed him to a *rabot* beside another little stream, where he took the bags off the donkey. Fatima stroked Toto's neck with the goose still in the saddlebag.

The body of Aziz was put in another smaller *rabot* to protect it from animals and the goose was taken into the larger shelter by Amin Beg. Fatima and Malone tumbled in after him and laid out the one sleeping bag and two blankets. They sat on the cold, hard ground looking at each other, shivering with the sudden chill and how close they had come today to being killed, and he realized how pleased he was just to be alive, for Fatima to be alive. Amin Beg was getting the gas stove out of the donkey's saddlebags and lit a wet match. Malone thought he saw a slight shake of the head and disapproval in the man's eyes and moved his bedroll away from Fatima's. The wind started to howl across the flood plain outside and he remembered eating a few spoonfuls of rice, but not much else. He wanted to hug her to him and tears came into his eyes when she briefly stretched her hand out in the night, and he shivered and listened to the gale.

Towards dawn the wind had such a piercing howl it woke him. It was like the tales of the banshee his father frightened him with as a child, the headless coachman come to carry off the sinner to hell. On the trail Fatima had told him another nomad phrase her father used to quote. 'The wind has taken away all my clothes.' On a night like this anyone might start to believe in the djinns and *devs* who crowded the mountains. Malone tried to focus on her fully clothed shape in the darkness, in her sleeping bag. He had never felt so close to another living soul.

In the first light of dawn Malone awoke and his eyelashes were frozen and, as he managed to open them, his face was next to

Fatima's and covered in a thin sheet of ice. He had rolled across the earth between them in the night and the ice had stuck their skin together. He felt the panic of being entombed and broke free. He had been just able to breathe through his nose but the thought of being trapped for ever with Fatima under a veil of ice left him gasping and unsure.

He sat up and she was awake too, the thin ice mask formed by her breath crackling. Her hands went to her face and her eyes were wide as the ice broke into a smile and then a laugh and then a cough. He hugged her to him. They then woke Amin Beg who coughed and spluttered and Malone smashed a sheet of ice which had formed over the door-opening. Only the donkey and Toto seemed unaffected by the deadly freeze. Malone's teeth chattered.

'It's lucky we woke,' Fatima said, and they did not say more.

Outside the dawn was still pink down the valley but mostly the sky was dark and heavy with snow. The ground around them was frozen stiff, as were the plants, but no snow had fallen there, though when he looked up the mountains were white. If he had brought a tent they would be dead of asphyxiation. He went over to the trees and relieved himself and his urine froze.

He ducked back into the smoke-blackened *rabot* and crawled inside and found a choking fire of fragrant roots on which a kettle was boiling and Amin Beg was pouring out a cup of green tea for him and offering him nan.

'*Salaam alaikum.*'

'*Wa alaikum as-salaam.*'

'Why were our faces frozen with ice?' said Fatima.

Amin Beg stared at the fire. 'There is a special wind that you heard. Some call it a djinn, but it is a wind, whether or not it is a

251

djinn as well. When it blows it can bring down the temperature to far below freezing. Many are frozen to death. It often used to be so in our fight against the Russians. I was here then, *bismillah*. We once raided a camp and went in firing and they were all already dead. Frozen. A man was still standing at his post, his blue eyes open . . . There is a legend that on one of the glaciers near Lake Chaqmaqtin a whole column of Khan Alexander's army froze in that wind beside a glacier and are now entombed inside it. You can see them through the ice with their swords and tunics. One moment there was sun and the next the ice wind started to blow. I didn't expect it to happen last night. It never happens when there's snow. We were lucky. Possibly it was the warmth of the animals that saved us and the will of Allah, peace be upon him.'

'So we are fortunate,' said Malone.

Amin Beg smiled and shook his head.

'But who brings the death wind? The people who live here will say the djinn here is unhappy with us. For the death we have brought on a donkey. We must perform the rituals and I know a place to bury the poor boy I neglected. An ancient place where he will be with many kings. He will be happy there. I'm eternally sorry I called him bad names and hit him with my whip. But it's always so with the dead. They are infuriating. They have the last laugh because you cannot take the whipping back,' he said, putting green snuff under his tongue.

Amin Beg grinned at Malone and he began to feel an unaccustomed panic at letting this strange place inside him. He longed to put up barriers again. He longed for the emptiness that this insane land always conspired to fill.

252

After they had eaten they went a short way to the pretty glade where the donkey was grazing and Amin Beg carried Aziz's body from the small *rabot*. Even with the dull sky overhead it was a beautiful scene, the stream winding in and out of willows and bushes and huge buttercups coming into flower. Aziz was laid out on the ground with his jacket covered in frost.

Amin Beg and Fatima stripped the clothes off his body and Aziz looked like a fat child that had fallen asleep playing and was being put to bed. They washed his body in a rose-scented Russian washing-up liquid Malone found in the saddlebags and he helped tie the corpse on the donkey. They climbed several hundred yards along a narrow path with a steep drop at one side. The way widened slightly and went around a corner so they were facing down the valley. There was a series of small caves, a few with stones still in place, others without.

'In these tombs is the dust of kings who fought the coming of the Khan and lost but were honoured by him for their bravery,' said Amin Beg. He selected an aperture and Malone helped him slide the boy inside, headfirst, but not before Fatima reached into her pocket and put the paper rose back on his body.

Amin Beg sealed the entrance with a stone that had fallen away and then he said prayers for the dead. Fatima had her eyes shut and Malone found he could not pray. He should have looked after the poor boy better. After the prayers were finished Amin Beg said, 'We must hurry now as the weather may change again.'

So they returned quickly and loaded the donkey, making sure Toto was secure in the saddlebag, and went up the hill that they had come down behind the camp. This time they turned east along a tributary of the Wakhan River, and Malone saw below him a bridge made of logs, hanging over a chasm, at the bottom of which the water was deep blue.

The bridge was at least twenty metres above the water.

A black-and-white bird, a dipper, flew in and out of the water-falls further upstream. Fatima suddenly ran ahead of him and although his boots cut into his feet at every step he tried to follow her.

She ran to the middle of the bridge which had no sides or rails and where each small tree trunk did not meet the next you could see the water below. Only a few rocks held the bridge in place at both ends and several large grey-blue ones in the middle, presumably to stop it blowing away. She put her arms out at her side. Her full mouth was open, her head back. The water surged and thundered below and he was worried that she was overcome with grief. But he was wrong.

'It feels as if you are flying! Here in the middle of the bridge!'

'Yes,' he said. She now had a smile that was perhaps too radiant.

The black-and-white bird below them flew into the foaming water and out again, miraculously. Fatima went closer to the edge.

'I am crossing over, Malone, from one life to the next. Don't you feel that, Malone? Don't you feel closer to this country? Don't you feel you are changing? That we are changing?'

'I do,' he said, still a little concerned.

As the donkey made its first reluctant steps onto the bridge she took Malone's hand and they walked off the wooden structure and onto a switchback path of scree. In front of them he could see that the sky was darkening again.

Fatima stopped breathless at times but at others her lithe body seemed to slide around the boulders and she took short bouncing steps like Amin Beg.

But for Malone it was as if a giant hand was pushing him back. He did not want it to be so, as they scrambled higher and higher; the snow-capped peaks and a great green valley cutting back into Pakistan to immense glaciers were of unsurpassed beauty and on a scale which simultaneously dwarfed men and magnified the soul. His body was fighting him every step of the way and the wilderness was causing all the passions and poisons of his soul to bubble to the surface.

At noon he did not eat and barely drank a mouthful. It was not just physically painful on his sore lips. It seemed ridiculous.

He just gazed at the barren mountains, at the twisted rock-strewn path ahead. You did not go a yard in these mountains without slowly but surely becoming part of them. This was the deadly frontier and he understood why the people here found it hard to live with and impossible to live without. His forehead was burned and a sore on his lip had spread to the side of his face.

'Come on, my love,' said Fatima. 'We must go on.'

His heart rose at what she had called him.

Soon it started to sleet and to blow and it turned to hail and then back to the blistering sunshine which sought out every milli-metre of an unprotected body like fire ants. He had never before had the complete sensation that nature was trying to kill him. They came to another river, this time with a wobbling louse-filled tree trunk across the first part, and then it was a question of leaping from boulder to boulder, or falling into the icy water which further down joined the main stream of the Wakhan River.

He watched Fatima totter on the flaking wood and jump between the rocks with Amin Beg who came back for Malone.

His head was starting to spin. They seemed to have climbed higher than yesterday – he could see they were up to the snow line – and he was sure that inside his boots his feet were covered in blood. Amin Beg was beside him.

'We have many like this one to cross,' he said, almost proudly.

Malone put his foot carefully on the log and edged along its rotten length. A yellow-and-black bird, a golden oriole, flew out of the bushes in front of him. At the other side of the stream were a bed of blue gentians and wild rhubarb. His head whirled again like a carousel out of control. He remembered that he had what was left of his money in his pocket and it wasn't in a plastic bag! He staggered and almost went into the river, his headscarf falling from his head and being swept away in seconds.

He steadied himself and leapt to the first boulder and then the next.

'Trust yourself! Trust in Allah! Do not think!' came the mocking cry and a laugh from Amin Beg behind, who was standing nonchalantly in the middle of the log, looking down the precipitous stream. Toto went across in the saddlebag, the current hissing around the donkey's legs. The goose had managed to get one strong wing free. The two black bars stood out on the back of its head in the sudden bursts of sunshine backed by dark cloud and he began to honk and look up at the blue sky.

Malone leapt again and again and only put one boot in the water as he reached the other side. For reasons he did not fathom he lay down in the gentians, pressed his face against the intensely blue flowers and started to cry. He heard his mother's voice. She was asking him, teasingly, how he could have left Kim.

Amin Beg pulled him to his feet.

'Do not give in! Do not give in to the spirits! Even if you see bears with the faces of birds and birds with the face of your school-teacher! I have seen such things. It is the mountain fairies. They play tricks on us, especially if you are not used to going so high, to the roof of the world!'

They all spent the night in another shepherd's refuge where Malone sat in a dark corner and refused food, watching Toto peck at his nan. He tried desperately to drink but when he did he had to run out behind the wood-roofed dwelling and had the added light-headed feeling of dysentery under a sky full of the most incredible stars. He squatted there looking up at them. He pulled up his pants. The rare beauty was such he felt he could die at that moment, as he once had in the Cessna with the cracked propeller. He had the illusion that he had glimpsed everything it was possible to, through the eyes of a kindly God.

'I don't feel I can go on,' he said to Fatima, when he went back inside.

'It is not far now.'

She was feeding the goose with more little pieces of nan. The bird seemed to know where he was and made occasional attempts to struggle out of the basket and get away. Malone respected the bird even more now he knew where he lived and Fatima stroked Toto's sleek head.

'I have been giving him hardly any of the relaxation remedy and soon he will be ready to go free. I only hope that all his friends have not already gone from the lake. We will be there soon, Malone. And then you can rest and watch Toto fly. We will be at the end of our journey.'

He was tempted to say, 'And then?' but he didn't. If he knew anything about such journeys and frontiers there would be another one up ahead, another impossible ridge or a glacier to cross. The three of them slept under his small mosquito net in case camel spiders fell from the roof and were woken by snow blowing through the door.

The next day they crossed several more rivers and entered a valley in which the mountains became wider and wider apart. Malone hoped that they had finally reached the Pamirs and as the path neared a bright, pink-coloured scree slope at one side he stopped and clambered up the slope for fifty metres or so and then, using a stick, wrote in the soft mud of a spring:

My love she dances over the rainbow
Into the furthest heavens.

He staggered down again, exhausted, and he could not see the letters, even at a distance.

He turned and the others were now dots, with a herd of yaks following. He limped after them.

Malone did not catch the herd and the rest of them until they reached the next stopping place, a nomad settlement called Kashch Goz, where a man in a fur hat and leather boots came up to him hissing, took him by the shoulders and shook him. He shook him and shook him and did not stop until Malone thought his head was going to come off.

Amin Beg pushed between them. The nomad had a brown face and his lower lip hung down and he drooled.

'Gumbaz does not like you writing on his mountain. He fears magic and that what is written will happen. The Russians used to

write meaningless slogans like *Forward to the next five-year plan*.
But long ago holy men wrote other things which are still happening,
he says. I will show you some of this tomorrow near the lake.
What were you writing?'

Malone collected himself. The nomad was horribly strong and
stank of dung.

'I was writing a love poem for Fatima. I will go and rub it out.'
He turned and started back down the track. But Amin Beg repeated
this to the nomad in Kyrgyz and the man laughed and hissed and
they all chased after Malone, including Fatima, and dragged him
to the guest hut, the caravanserai, where there were other nomads
laughing and making tea and eating nan with fermented yak's
butter, which smelt like wet dog.

'They like you,' said Amin Beg. 'They like a man who writes his
love in the mountains. Even if you have a wife. They respect
greed . . .'

Malone blinked and they brought him a bedroll coloured
shining emerald and gold. These were the colours, he was not
imagining them, and she was at his side.

'Please drink, you must drink, or you will die,' she said.

She was so beautiful, even in the harsh white light from the
window coming off the snow, and he felt he did not deserve her.
He reached out and touched the skin of her cheek. She put peanuts
between his blistered lips and he took a sip of the scalding green
tea, which burned his mouth. Her eyes seemed to grow larger and
he thought she was going to burst into tears. But then she turned
and rushed out of the small hut with its stove and bed mats, slam-
ming the door so hard that the dust fell from the roof and so did a
large camel spider which a boy with slanting eyes and a

silver-and-gold hat, like an upturned bowl on his round head, chased and caught and showed to Malone before making off with it.

Malone picked the tea up and put it down again.

He was not sure how he was going to move from here. In the far corner of the room Amin Beg and a group of nomads were watching Malone closely, as if he might die. Outside, through a hole in the door, he could see Fatima hold up her hands to the gently falling snow.

Malone knew he had all the signs of altitude sickness and possibly exposure and dysentery and he should go back over the last pass and to a lower level. He knew people died up here very quickly. They became weak from not eating and drinking or they had oedemas of the lungs or the brain, which were quick and always fatal. He worried about Fatima. She had not said anything but he guessed she probably held herself responsible for the death of Aziz and in a stranger way for the poor girl who had been mistaken for her and killed and even the cousins who had come after her. They had not deserved to die like that, though Malone could not feel as sorry for people who did not know Fatima but wanted to stone her because of a song and a dance. He bet she held herself culpable too, in a different way, for what had happened in the village when it was attacked by the planes. They had welcomed her and Malone but they were part of the world those planes were from and now many of the village children were dead.

An hour later the nomads loaded him onto a makeshift stretcher. He did not see Fatima anywhere and Amin Beg had disappeared too. The snow was still falling and he wondered if he had been put outside to die.

He was terrified and opened his mouth to cry out but no sound came.

Malone watched a girl in a wine-coloured dress with a white head-covering held up with a hat underneath, which made her look like a lady from a French medieval tapestry, milking a yak which turned and turned as the girl pulled on its teats and tried to comfort the animal. Only yards away a huge dog, the shape and colour of a wolf, was tearing the last remaining meat from the head of a yak calf. In front of him stretched the grassy plain of the Little Pamir but on all sides were the icy slopes of the mountains. The wind blew around the yurts made of thick animal hides.

Two men then came and took him inside one of the larger yurts and left him next to a fire and a boiling kettle. A woman took hold of his arm. Above her, in the wooden framework of the tent, was a hole that showed the slate-grey sky. Around the walls were the precious blankets and boxes of the family in every colour and on the floor carpets in red and deep blue. There was a red screen painted with strange patterns. Malone was given milky tea with fermented yak's milk and bread straight from a metal hotplate by the fire of dried dung and roots. The woman moved a pickled yak's tongue behind the screen where Malone could just see the brass horn of an old-fashioned gramophone. The woman had one of the raised headdresses and a broad oriental face which was as white as parchment with large, pale, staring eyes that had the permanent expression of a child pretending to be frightened and a long, slightly flattened nose. She unnerved Malone. Her elegant fingers were heavy with gold rings and her hands were slender and delicate and did not seem accustomed to the hard work they

261

must do up here every day. Her cheeks did not have the red tinge of the girl outside.

The woman was talking in Kyrgyz but then she spoke in Dari.

'Are you having trouble with your lady?'

'No . . . I am sick.' The woman laughed.

'Men pretend to be sick often. It is the way with men. They are not constant. It is an imbalance in their waters. Are you sure this lady is your friend? Why do you come here?'

Malone hesitated. He was not going to tell the woman his feelings.

'I am going up to Lake Chaqmaqtin. With Fatima. We are going to see the Thanador.'

The woman shook her head.

'He's a stupid man. Who told you to go there? To ask him what?'

Malone swallowed. The woman's eyes seemed to see straight through him.

'Fatima wants to understand her country . . . To understand Afghanistan . . .' The words sounded ludicrously unconvincing under the woman's smile. 'Not Afghanistan . . . but the frontier . . . What we really want to find out is how her father can free himself from writing such terrifying stories about the future . . . She figured the Thanador was the person who can tell her that.' The woman shook her head at more.

'I can read troubles. Who suggested you do this?'

'Her father. Fatima's father. He is an important man in Pakistan but he is plagued by these stories . . .'

The woman was shaking her head and laughing.

'You have not worked it out yet, Mr American. You still wish an answer? You have not learned yet? Nothing has happened to you?

Afghanistan! Ha! You'll be surprised by the correct question and the real answer, by and by.'

The woman then started a cackling laugh and did not stop and the wind blew and the fire blazed up and earth on the floor got into Malone's eyes. When he looked again the woman was gone but he could still hear the laughter in his head, bouncing off the sides of his skull as if they were the sides of the valleys he had walked up. Malone struggled outside.

His reader of troubles had vanished and the girl with the white headdress, pinned in place with a large steel safety pin, was still trying to milk the yak and the dog was chewing on the corpse of the calf.

The girl glanced up at Malone in a knowing manner and he watched men and women, dressed in several layers of thick woollen clothes, herding the yaks into a group with their shaggy, wolf-like dogs. They all turned and stared at him and smiled, as if they knew the answer the woman spoke of, and Malone felt in that moment an unfathomable terror. His breath became fast and he sat down on a stone.

Who the fuck had he been talking to?

Malone focused on a satellite dish by one of the yurts to try to keep a foot in his own world. But when he stood up he saw the stone was covered in writing, the writing of the ancients. The stories nomads wrote to be carried on the wind. The letters were not painted and would have long disappeared if they were. Nor were they burned and chipped into the rock. They had somehow become a part of the stone, just beneath a familiar surface.

Malone limped quickly back to the caravanserai. He wondered if his altitude sickness was getting worse.

Nineteen

Malone slept close by Fatima in the icy hut where nomads were coming and going all night. He watched over the turn of her lip and her breathing. Having drunk too much tea he had to get up, tiptoe carefully between sleepers on the carpet-covered platform, and painfully put his boots on. There was a ridge of mountains behind the camp and he walked by starlight to a stream and gazed up at the heavens and saw a meteor shoot across the sky.

The stars were so huge and bright you could see their colours.

When he had finished he was suddenly conscious of one of the dogs, its hair luminous in the moonlight, staring right at him, only ten yards away. It had long legs and Malone saw it crouch down and, instinctively, he knew it was a wolf and was going to attack.

The animal then ran back yelping over the river, cringing as it did so. Malone turned and saw a figure blend into the shadows and disappear towards the tents. He rushed back and nearly fell through the door and into the stove. Inside, no one stirred and he took his boots off and went and lay by Fatima, whose body was cold and breath shallow. In the night he heard the howl of the wolf and donkeys started to bray and dogs bark but it was the wolf's eerie song that sent the shivers up his back. Toto was awake but he only made a very low hissing noise. He obviously did not want to draw the wolf's interest.

Malone went fitfully to sleep.

Later, he was woken by a terrible growling near the rough timber door and he tried to wake Fatima. It sounded like the growling of an animal larger than a wolf, a creature from the shadow world of the frontier in Hamza's stories. The growling grew and grew and then, on the other side of Malone, Amin Beg sat up.

It was he who was growling!

He was still making the terrible noise and then gurgled and stopped. Slowly, he sank back down to sleep and no one else in the room woke, or if they did, they did not say a thing. Malone stayed awake the rest of the night, listening to more wolves and the ghostly animal cries until the dawn made everything solid again. Several times he said prayers, both for himself and for Fatima.

In the morning there was snow on the ground but it did not conceal the fact that one of the donkeys had been torn to pieces. An ear lay on the fresh snow.

Fatima tried to persuade him to get up but for a long time he could not move. It was as if everything in him had come to a stop.

'Please, Malone. It is not too far now. There is snow but the way is mostly along a valley.'

Gumbaz, the hissing nomad from the trail, came in, kicking his leather boots against the stove, anxious for them to leave.

'Come on, Malone. Please . . .' she pleaded. 'If there is a man who knows my father up at the lake then he may have another satellite phone. You'll be able to call your wife . . . I mean, you will be able to tell her you are safe. We can get you back.' Then in a lower voice she said, 'Or we can be together, dear Malone, if that is what you want.'

He felt a deep rush of happiness.

Malone looked at her and nodded but to himself. He willed himself up from the bedroll and in an hour they were on the road and heading up a wide valley to the lake. The hissing nomad hurried them along and they walked for several hours across the wide grassy plain, seeing no one. Fatima hung back with Malone, urging him on. He knew his face was now covered in sores and eruptions and his hands were blistered too, as if there was a great heat inside him that was trying to escape.

Amin Beg waited for them.

'The nomads at Kashch Goz seemed to want us to go,' Malone said.

Amin Beg nodded.

'You were dreaming last night, Amin Beg,' Fatima added.

'No, I was not.'

'You woke, growling in the night,' said Malone.

'He had turned into a beast,' said Fatima.

'I had indigestion,' said Amin Beg, embarrassed.

Malone was relieved that their donkey was unharmed.

'Is that why they hurried us out of the village – because everyone thought we were turning into beasts?'

Malone had meant the question as a joke but the wind almost immediately started to blow. The river flowed over swampy hummocks of grass to the south. They were heading east in a wide valley and beyond that were the pink-and-white peaks of China.

'No, it was not because of that,' said Amin Beg, picking up a piece of fermented yak's milk that had been dropped on the trail and putting it into the pocket of his wool jacket which was bound up with string. 'It is because you talked with the grey woman and you went with her into the tent and she made you see those who are not there.'

Malone shook his head.

'I only went into a tent . . .' He thought of the woman's strange white skin. He remembered the marks on the rocks and the nomads in heavy clothes herding yaks.

'The village is frightened you brought her. She is a known demon and let us hope she is satisfied with the donkey's blood.'

Malone was suddenly angry with Amin Beg.

'This is nonsense. She was real. She gave me real nan and curd. When I went out in the night I saw a wolf and then someone in the darkness scared it away.'

Amin Beg shrugged and patted the donkey.

'For all you know she may have been the wolf,' said Fatima, to his surprise.

'Or whatever the wolf was afraid of, in the darkness,' said Amin Beg. 'Or merely the darkness. Ayee! When you cannot imagine what is there, it is better not to think at all. That is my considered opinion.'

At about two o'clock they reached the path to Lake Chaqmaqtin up the side of a ridge in front of them and Malone was staggering twenty steps forward at a time and stopping. Amin Beg wondered whether to go ahead for a horse or another donkey but Malone shook his head. It was better that he was walking. If he was sitting on a horse what was boiling within him would have more time and space to work. They waited for Malone as he slowly climbed the path.

'Look, there is the lake. There is the lake where we can release Toto.'

The land was green down by the lake but the snow still covered the path they were heading up and he could see no settlement, only a stream bed and a glacier from which blew an icy wind. He paused and leaned on Fatima.

'Thank you,' he said.

Fatima gave him a hug.

'I think there're geese on the lake. I can see birds flying down there.'

Malone shaded his eyes. There were spots on the shimmering turquoise water, which was more than two miles away.

'We . . . We ought to let him loose as soon as possible. We must waste no time,' Malone said, and began to walk faster up the hill after the donkey. Fatima did nothing to dissuade him. He did not want to say goodbye to Toto, or send him on a journey that took him over the Himalayas to India. But he did not want to stand in his way to freedom.

'Yes, my love,' she said.

But it took another dragging hour even to get onto the ridge from which they could see a grey ring of yurts and a newly built flat-roofed, lime-walled caravanserai. The settlement was perfectly camouflaged and behind it a path ran up to a pure white glacier, which had a greenish tinge underneath. Down the valley and over the river which ran into the lake there was a rainbow of sorts that vanished as the sun scudded behind the cloud.

'Well, here's your Emerald City,' said Malone, gesturing up towards the glacier, as people came out of their yurts to greet them, men, some with long wispy beards and in small jewelled hats and waistcoats, the women with the raised headdresses, white and pinkish red. They were all tall, with high cheekbones and slanted eyes. Yet they did not look Chinese.

Up by the glacier there was a larger, elongated yurt on its own.

He guessed that was where the Thanador lived, the Keeper of Nothingness. They went to the caravanserai, which was being used as a school. It was a simple stone hut with a carpeted sleeping platform and stove inside. Four boys recited the Koran under the kindly gaze of a mullah, who nodded and smiled.

'Come back before the sun goes down,' he said. 'It can be dangerous to lose your way.'

So they unloaded the donkey except for the goose and, with Malone going very slowly, they went down, past hills full of marmots, which Amin Beg called windack, to the reed-framed lake. There were several pairs of geese on the water that began to fly as soon as they approached, the primeval creak of their wings against the air sounding like a boat's rigging tightening in a stiff breeze.

Two of the bar-headed geese began circling upward and upward, one leapfrogging over the flight path of the other, seemingly for ever, until they were dots in the blue sky, and they were on their way south. Amin Beg looked up and smiled.

'In a day they will be eating fat Bengali snails in the rice paddies of India,' he said.

With those words and he knew it was an illusion, Malone almost felt himself again, trudging down by the shore, as he took the goose from the donkey's saddlebag and let him walk around by the water. Toto pecked at a couple of reeds but showed no sign of wanting to go out on the icy lake, or to join his kin at the other side. Instead, Toto nuzzled up to Fatima and sat down hard on his tail feathers like a human.

'He doesn't want to leave us,' she said.

'You have given him too much opium.'

Fatima laughed.

'He's truly an Afghan goose,' said Amin Beg.

'He was meant to go free. He was meant to fly and find a mate,' Malone found himself saying testily.

'That's the trouble with setting people free,' said Fatima. 'They may not want to leave.'

She bent down and stroked the goose and so did Malone. He then took his boots off and even Amin Beg looked away from his blood-caked feet. He went and paddled in the shallows in water so cold it felt hot. Toto showed no inclination to join him, but did a little dance from one bright-yellow webbed foot to the other. Malone struggled to put his boots back on.

'I had no idea he wouldn't go,' said Fatima, shaking her head. The goose got back into the saddlebag on its own.

'He is in love with you,' said Malone.

But then there was a calling of other birds from the lake.

Malone gazed up high over the glacier ahead and two more bar-headed geese were beginning their ascent to the freezing jet stream which would either transport them to another land, or kill them.

He got Toto to the edge of the lake and opened the saddlebag and slid the bird out.

Malone then flapped his arms and the goose twisted its head on one side, and then the other, and honked. Malone had to stop, out of breath, and try to focus. His gaze passed around the snow-covered mountains and ended up in what must be China.

'Come on, Toto, follow me, flap those nice big wings.'

Malone staggered up and down the shoreline several times and the goose watched him and then waddled back to the saddlebag and got in. Amin Beg was sitting down on his haunches and the nomads and the mullah and his pupils, who had followed, all laughed.

Malone went up to Toto and dragged him out. The goose looked around for a second or two and then ran and burrowed back into his bag. Malone berated him in English. 'You're a flyer, man! You're a fully paid-up sky pilot. You had a little accident but you have to get back up there. You've got to get up there to get the girl, man. To be free! Do you hear me, Toto? It's time. Time to do the real flying, the scary flying . . . the serious stuff.'

Toto then climbed out of the bag and surveyed his yellow feet. He began to flap his wings a bit. The little crowd cheered. But then he stopped and stretched his neck along the ground and looked at Fatima.

'Come on, Toto. You can do this.'

The goose was flapping his wings harder and stepped into the water and paddled around. He seemed unsure at first but then started to steam up and down.

Malone glanced up at the sky. He took a deep breath.

'Look! Malone!'

Malone turned and the goose had extended his wings and begun to slap the surface with his feet and power over the water.

There was another cheer from the mullah and his pupils.

'Go, you fucker, go. Give it more throttle. Give it more gas!' shouted Malone. Slowly, Toto hauled himself into the air and after a glide began to flap upwards again and then the flight became instinctive and efficient. The goose headed very rapidly for the far side of the lake and others of his own kind. Malone shaded his eyes and saw several geese take off and fly into the air with Toto, as another pair were starting to make their ascent that would take them south over the mountains.

'Go, Toto, go!'

Malone watched as the goose came flying down towards them again and at the last moment his new friends peeled off, frightened of the possibility of guns, and he began another slow circuit with them of all of Lake Chaqmaqtin. He was coming back one more time and this time had just one other goose with him.

'He has found a wife,' said the mullah.

But then, behind them was a rifle shot and Toto and his new friend faltered and then veered sharply to the left and flew quickly back to the other side of the lake, from where they began an ascent of the mountains.

'Don't shoot,' said Fatima, to a new and more muscular group of nomads. 'Do not shoot or I will kill you,' and Malone knew she meant it. Amin Beg's Kalashnikov was on the donkey. The man nodded and shrugged and shouldered his rifle. Malone waited for the goose to fall and Fatima grabbed his arm tight.

But it was the rifle shots which had set the goose free.

Malone followed the ascent of the geese, leapfrogging over each other, the crook on the neck of one parallel with the shoulder of the other, circling ever higher and higher until he lost them behind a mountain. Then for a few brief seconds one of the specks circled back, as if for a last goodbye, and was gone. Malone started to cry. He sat down on a tussock of grass and cried. His tears ran down his sore encrusted face to the earth and she had her arm around him. And now Fatima was crying too, sobbing so her whole body shook.

'I do not like goodbyes, Malone. Remember that.'

'Don't worry. He'll be back next year with his friend.'

She held him tight.

They returned to the yurts and sat at the caravanserai staring at the lake. He had never seen her look so serious. She wiped her tears with the back of her hand. The children clustered around Malone, probably curious as to why a man should cry about a goose.

Eventually Fatima looked up and smiled at Malone.

'We had to let Toto go, Malone. He is going home . . . Now I think it is time to go up and see the Thanador. Please come if you want to . . .'

Malone nodded. He winced as he got on the donkey and it plodded along the path by the stream to the glacier. He was able to see the different blues and greens more clearly as he dismounted. There were caves and one could walk underneath the ice. The green went from very light to the deep almost dark colour of emeralds and there was only a small mound of moraine where the glacier ended. Malone took a few painful steps in the glacier's direction but Amin Beg stopped him.

'Do not go further. It is not only very dangerous but also sacred to the nomads in the yurts.'

Malone came away. The young nomads he had seen by the lake, where one of them had shot at the geese, had come with them. They had donkeys and he was wondering if they intended to cross the ice field. He pointed but they all shook their heads and laughed. Further up the glacier he heard the ice cracking and moving. Fatima was beside him, her face beautiful in the soft light. Amin Beg stood by her.

'This is where your father found out about the Thanador, the Keeper of Nothingness. It is from nothingness all stories originate, around the camp fires, all the djinns and *devs* and castles and great khans . . . All the ladies in gilded slippers. You have to appreciate this metaphysical nothing to invent such lands and principalities. Why cannot we understand we are trapped in our stories?'

Malone thought he was beginning to see.

Amin Beg led him towards the single large yurt and pulled back the door flap and they stepped inside. A mother and two beautiful girls had baked bread for them, served with green tea and curds and honey. The two girls had pink headdresses and pink-and-gold coats over their wine-coloured skirts. Like their mother they had heavy necklaces of silver coins and bangles around their ankles and necks. They were light-skinned with huge, brown-green eyes and slanted cheek-bones and moved with a practised grace. When they laughed they raised the back of their hands to their red lips.

The fire flared and the light was going when a figure came around a screen by a gold-painted travelling case at the other side of the yurt. Behind the screen Malone guessed there was another separate chamber to the yurt. The man's face was in shadow. He was sitting on a chair covered in a piece of silk. Malone did not remember seeing a chair before in one of the tents. He made out an old man with a long beard.

The wind howled outside and Malone pondered the exact duties and powers of a Keeper of Nothingness.

There was a chill in the room and a particular pool of darkness surrounding the old man.

'Are you the Thanador?' asked Malone.

The fire seemed to be dying back again and then a greenish glow enveloped the figure but there was no answer. The two girls and their mother withdrew behind the screen and Malone and Fatima and Amin Beg were looking straight at the man sitting on the chair.

'Welcome,' he said in a voice that came from everywhere. 'Welcome, you have got to the end of your journey, Fatima Hamza.'

'I want to ask a question.'

'What is it?'

'Are the prophecies of my father true? What he puts down after he has been trying to write about the retreat of the British at Gandamak? Is it true that he predicted 9/11 and the rest?'

'Yes it is, my child. Quite true.'

'But he didn't plan the attack on the Twin Towers?'

'No, my child. He did not.'

The answering voice did not come from the seated man. The man shifted on the chair. The voice was very low and reverberated in the cold space. The green light around the figure's face intensified.

'How will he stop this writing of catastrophes?'

The voice laughed.

'All things come to an end.'

Fatima's voice rose. 'But what he has recently predicted. The floods and the fire . . . And the terrible whiteness that my father saw. He even told me that I was to die . . .'

The Thanador paused.

'The floods and the fire and the war of the whiteness will come to pass . . . A terrible, blinding flash. Of that I'm sure. But you must approach me closer, my child. You and your companion, Amin Beg. But not the American. The American is to stay by the fire. Walk behind the screen, my child. Walk behind the screen.'

Malone felt very afraid and Fatima was gripping his hand hard.

'Don't worry, Malone,' she said.

She looked tenderly into his face.

Her lips brushed his and he wanted too much to hold her. But Amin Beg took Malone's forearms and looked into his eyes.

Fatima and Amin Beg then stepped behind the screen and he sat back down on the floor, waiting and waiting. The fire burned down low. The air in the yurt was now intensely cold.

Malone got to his feet and the man in the chair raised his hand.

He sat down again and moments later the Thanador went behind the screen and was gone.

'Fatima?' Malone called out.

He heard the giggling of the two girls.

He got up and looked behind the screen but there were only the two girls and their mother and piles of blankets and boxes. There was no other chamber. There was only a mirror with his reflection in it, his face red and sore. He tried moving the mirror but there was nothing behind it except more boxes.

277

'Where are they! Where is the Thanador!' he demanded. At one point the hides which covered the yurt seemed loose. But he thought he had seen the start of another chamber. He had not known what he expected to find and had even had the crazy idea that her father, Hamza, was behind the screen, playing at being the Wizard of Oz.

To his astonishment he then heard a familiar voice from the room where he had just been. It was the voice of Basil.

'Is that you, Malone? Malone? Is that you?'

Malone went back to where the man he had presumed to be the Thanador had been sitting and pulled back the silk covering the chair. Underneath was the satellite phone he had tried to use in Sarhad.

Malone lifted the phone to his ear but the connection went dead on him. The girls laughed again and he thought he was losing his mind. He grabbed at the blue plastic device and went outside under the cold stars and redialled Basil's number. It rang and rang and he was just about to press 'cancel' and call the hospital when a British voice answered.

The voice on the other end was not Basil's.

It was the woman who he had last heard arguing over a stolen teapot, the elderly English lady with the medieval fringe, Miss Damaris Wace. He could picture the garden and the turquoise neck of the male peacock as he displayed by the pomegranate trees.

'Oh, God, that's Malone, isn't it? I'm minding his phone. Basil was trying to get another . . . I'm so sorry. I'm so very sorry to hear about Kim. Such bravery! I know there is nothing we can say in these circumstances and it must seem so unfair, but such bravery.

She was a saint! And we are so glad to hear that you are all right. I'll go and get Basil. He always knows the words to say in times like these. It's his job, I suppose, but most diplomats are completely useless, aren't they? I am so sorry, dear boy.'

She broke off and he heard the shriek of one of the peacocks.

'Malone?' Basil's voice came on the phone.

'Yes.'

'You know the news?'

'What news . . .?'

'I am so dreadfully sorry, old chap. Where are you?'

'Lake Chaqmaqtin.'

'My God. Listen to me and listen carefully, Malone. You're in dreadful danger. But first there's news that I must tell you.'

Malone swayed on his feet. He felt faint.

'What's happened, Basil?'

There was a pause.

'I'm not good at this, Malone . . . Well, Kim and that preacher, Noah, were ambushed the day they drove down to Kandahar. He . . . He was . . . beheaded and it was thought that Kim had been killed and her body dumped elsewhere. I think that's a Canadian Zone and they didn't have the men to search and night was falling. They went after some car tracks but they just seemed to disappear into scrub. Absolutely nothing was heard. Then weeks and weeks later a German patrol panicked when two petrol tankers were hijacked for village fuel by the Taliban up north of Baghlan. The Germans thought the tankers were to be used as bombs. The tankers were taken out in an airstrike and most of a village inciner-ated in a fireball. I shouldn't say this, but between you and me thousands of people probably died. There was to be a huge wedding. Kim survived the bombs only to be killed in the strafing run afterwards. The locals insisted she was going back to help. We had reports from the checkpoints that the Talibs used her as a ticket north. They say one of the big fish was being moved up to Faizabad to start more operations there. One of the last things Kim did was try and call you. Of course, the Taliban may have set her up somehow. Made sure she was in the line of fire. I'm still attempting to find out. We've done exactly the same sort of shitty thing.'

Malone was crying now.

'Was she with someone when she died?'

Basil cleared his throat.

'Yes, it does seem so. A young Talib. Her body was taken to Bagram and will be flown back to the States if you do not object. But I have more news as bad if not worse. Is Fatima or any of those with her able to hear this?'

Malone could see no one in the darkness now.

'No, she's not here. She's vanished.'

Basil paused. 'You must get out of there, Malone. Whoever she is, she's not Fatima Hamza . . . Fatima Hamza and her father were shot in Karachi more than two months ago. The bodies were found last night stuffed in a freezer.'

'What?'

'You must not trust anyone that has been travelling with you. Even the cousins who denounced her on the television . . . they were in the pay of the Taliban, or those who claimed to be. I'm so sorry but I think you were being used . . .'

Malone was shaking his head.

'No . . . We let the goose go earlier . . . She was in tears.' Malone paused. 'Are you saying she works for the Taliban, Basil?'

Basil sighed. 'If she did that would be the simple explanation. What is true is that trouble has broken out wherever you have been and one raid found mercury tilt switches at the Ishkashim hotel where you stayed. And cyanide. The manager shot himself before he was questioned. Such things are details. It is the plans she passed on that trouble us. And, perhaps, handbooks for psychological indoctrination techniques ... As for who she is working for, we have no fucking idea. Your Dorothy is very, very dangerous. Don't worry, we will ... And the Dead Officers' Club was blown apart by a car bomb the other day.'

Malone tried taking deep breaths.

'But her father ... Her father writes about Gandamak and then begins to predict the future ... He was in New York and predicted 9/11. He is quite a kindly man who has this routine when he writes. He had a very nice wife who was an actress. He was devoted to her and brought her baskets of flowers!'

There was a pause.

'This Hamza was never in New York and his wife died years ago.'

'In a hail of bullets in Clifton?'

'No, she choked to death on a canapé at a party. Apparently she was very fond of her food. The girl you met was not Fatima Hamza. The real Fatima Hamza is quite plain and probably had not heard of *The Wizard of Oz*. She was about to undergo an arranged marriage ... I am so sorry. About Kim ...'

Malone was shaking his head.

'But Hamza ... He was not too big and wrote under a catalpa tree in a green-velvet smoking jacket ... His wife was a film star who was kind and beautiful and gave water to the kraits that lived in the settee in his garden ...'

There was a silence on the other end.

'No, Malone. None of these things are true. The truth is none of us were looking for a woman who was being pursued by the Taliban because she had impersonated Dorothy in *The Wizard of Oz* and was travelling with an American and a goose. What seemed absurd was an extremely sophisticated operation. She had perfect cover . . .'

But Malone was able to take no more. He flung the satellite phone far into the twilight.

Malone howled until no more sound would come from his lips and walked up towards the cold of the glacier. He heard steps trying to follow him and he screamed abuse and they stopped.

Malone felt disgust for himself. Disgust for everything. He thought of the business with her toenails. He walked all around the yurt but there was no trace of a back door.

Then he saw the tracks. The tracks that led to the glacier.

He looked up and saw there were lights on the glacier, red lights against the snow. If she had gone up there, surely she meant him to follow. Why was she up there?

His boots scrunched into the hard snow but they had no purchase on the ice, which stretched like a darkening river in front of him. He had to hold his hands out both sides like a plane to balance.

He tripped and fell into the shallow little stream that ran from the base of the glacier. Malone then turned over and stared up at the Milky Way. None of those stars was ever going to look the same to him again. Not ever. And he did not want to fly to them any more. He did not even want to do the safe flying. He had never taken things as seriously as he should and you have to be serious to truly fly.

Kim knew that. She was serious unto the end.

Malone climbed onto the gentle slope of ice and inched his way up the glacier, peering down into one crevasse, into a great realm of emerald, like the Emerald City in Fatima's favourite story.

He put on his head torch.

There was a slight dip in the glacier and he made his way around a scattering of rocks and strange pinnacles of ice that stood there like old men preparing to greet him. There was still light enough on the spectral ice, like looking at the land from the sea. He climbed quickly past another deep crevasse and sat in the shade of a pinnacle and stared at the faraway lake.

Two geese honked above him, starting their impossible journey together to India.

Love makes you ignore every hardship, he supposed, so why had he not been better to Kim? Had Fatima really deceived him with everything, had none of her elaborate stories been true?

It was almost funny.

That was the secret of this fucking frontier. It was not that the Afghans were any better fighters. They just told the best tales.

Yet he was now mixed up with the fictional Hamza. He closed his eyes and saw the 9/11 planes again exploding against the buildings, the fire reminding him of the marigold flowers Kim liked so much. He could smell them.

Malone felt it hard even to let go of the barefoot, broken-boned orphan. His story had explained so much. It was like walking out of the movie *The Wizard of Oz*, and letting go of Dorothy and the others.

A black vulture soared high above. *Inshallah*, darling.

He pressed his nose against the ice and felt as if he was falling, like all those men from the towers, all those fathers who thought they controlled the world. He then closed his eyes and in a deceptive flush of warmth nearly went to sleep.

He got up again, picturing the face of Fatima, but this time he lost his footing and went skidding back down the steep slope of ice.

Malone remembered nothing more.

TWENTY

One afternoon Malone found his mother in bed with a friend of his father. Her left leg was outside the sheet. The man had looked alarmed but his mother had smiled and lit a cigarette. The most awful thing was they were not making love. They were both eating chicken sandwiches in bed like they were married, as if deception was the most normal thing in the world. So Malone had fled to the little graveyard and was pushing down the stones when the caretaker and policeman got him. But he did not care. He felt all the emptiness of the world was inside him.

There was shouting.

A strong light was shone into his eyes and it was the voice of the mullah and the chattering of nomads. Together they managed to haul him onto the back of a large and very gentle yak which rocked its way down to the caravanserai, where Malone was propped in a corner.

He stared straight in front of him and his lips were moving but no sound came out. It was probably her father's fault, he began to think. But then he remembered that the dapper little man who wrote about Gandamak and translated *The Dostan of Amir Hamza* only existed in the stories of the girl who called herself Fatima.

'Malone, you have to drink this tea,' the mullah said.

Everyone in the room was watching Malone under the single Chinese electric light bulb connected to a Chinese battery charged by a Chinese solar panel. The nomads were allowed freely through a border no one else crossed for reasons too old to know. Also there was a terrible minefield.

The mullah poured the hot liquid between Malone's blistered lips and he coughed but did not take more. Malone thought of how many men and women must have met for a few weeks on the Silk Road, from different lands and cultures and races, and loved outside politics and time. But this had been far more.

It had not been safe flying.

It had been . . . Malone gasped. He knew how his father felt.

The mullah and the nomads spent all night sitting there, comforting him and trying to get him to drink or eat the *mish mish*, the sugared peanuts and the raisins. The light went out at eight and there were fifteen nomads in the caravanserai. Almost all of them did not sleep either and he could sense their sympathetic attention in the dark. Malone was shaking, he was burning from inside.

He knew he had to get a hold of himself or die. The nomads knew it too, although they would say he was fighting with a *dev* or a demon, who possessed him and was eating his liver, where all emotion resided. But he did not want to fight any more. In the morning the door opened and there was a yellow light on the newly fallen snow.

Malone was still staring straight in front of him.

The mullah came into the hut. 'She has gone, Malone. So has her friend.'

'It's snowed,' another of the nomads said in English and stood at the cold stove, smiling around at the weathered faces which regarded Malone steadily and suspiciously and with a degree of fear. 'They did not go over the glacier,' said the man by the stove. 'That was others. They went back to Sarhad.'

Malone sat for several days in the caravanserai with the nomad girls bringing him food he did not eat. He thought about Kim. He tried to picture her and her smile, but the flaking walls of the building kept coming between them. The face, the creamy skin swam into focus and then away again, as if she was teasing him in a way she never did in her life. He did not want to see her in front of him to ask forgiveness, he just wanted her face to be there one more time; he would not even care if she told him off or wanted to go to Alaska. On the trail here he had been thinking what he was going to say to her a million times, not only that he had found another but that he was turning into himself again, up here on a barren mountain, scorched and weakened by his own passion and the frontier.

But the truth was he kept glancing around for Fatima. Her image floated back to him in a moment. He heard her voice.

It was on the third night that he noticed Vosik, the Tajik mullah, do a whirling dance at the other side of the room. A nomad boy started to sing. It was not the dirge sung by Amin Beg that Malone had heard on the trail but almost a tune, it sounded a little like the blues. Vosik sang a line of the song and waved at Malone to reply.

The mullah who he had seen teaching the children in the day, and had let him sit there unmoving, then sang another line.

Suddenly Malone began to sing. Tears came into his eyes. And the words were:

Somewhere, over the rainbow, way up high,
There's a land that I heard of, once in a lullaby . . .

He looked nervously about him and everyone smiled.

The next morning he tried unsuccessfully to eat but was fed sugar-laced green tea. To his surprise, most of the snow had gone and a warm wind was blowing down the valley. 'Do not be deceived,' said the mullah. 'Winter is coming here. It is always like this. You get these warm days and snow again and then suddenly, one day, the snow never goes away. The frost is around the heart of the land.'

Malone spoke in Dari.

'I am going back to Sarhad.'

'You're in no fit state. Your legs will not take the journey. You are sick and if it snows again you will never get over the pass and there's no one to go with you. You will die in the snow.'

Malone shook his head.

'And how are you going to get there? Are you going to fly?' said the mullah.

Malone nodded to the mullah.

'Yes, that's exactly what I'm going to do. I am going to start really flying. I have been on the ground too long. I am not going to stay down here with those who are scared. I'm going to fly! And not just the careful kind.'

If Toto the goose was making the flight to India, he was going back to Sarhad. That was where the nomads said Fatima was going.

The next morning Malone rose early and loaded his donkey with the pack. The mullah bade him goodbye. The schoolchildren and the mullah and all of the nomads were in a line, waving to him. Two of the girls were crying. Malone nodded and turned and with the donkey walked very shakily towards the west where night still hung over the white expanse of snow. With every step he felt the rocks under his boots that were hurting him, but he was trying not to limp.

Malone's head spun as he went down the incline.

He inhaled a long breath of the clear cold air. He had no idea how he was going to get to Sarhad but he was not going to step one pace back. He was sure now that must be the way she had gone.

He had not walked so very far when he had the impression that she was walking lightly beside him with Amin Beg and her father Hamza and her film-star mother. Her father was as handsome as he had imagined and Amin Beg was joking with him.

'You are so sly, Hamza, as to convince the entire world of your own foolish tales . . .' Malone shook his head, he knew the apparitions were not real, a product of his altitude sickness. But he did not want the friendly phantoms to go.

Hamza patted Malone on the shoulder. He was dressed in an immaculate set of tweed plus fours, as if for shooting. 'I do like you, Malone, and so does my wife. Perhaps I have been silly with these stories, you know. And you know we cannot forecast the next cup of tea and certainly not the cricket. But there has been a seismic shift in our old world and I must take heed. I must stop playing the policeman and look to a new beginning. What is special about this wild place is that there is nothing here. Nothing! We are in the middle of an ancient road. We are still at the beginning of all stories. We are forced to confront the terrible splendour of ourselves. The terrible splendour of creation! Now that is something, my dear boy. That is something!'

TWENTY-ONE

Malone had not expected to make it to Kashch Goz, yet somehow before nightfall he dragged himself among the yurts and barking dogs. Every now and again he imagined he saw Fatima and her family and Amin Beg with him, out of the corner of his eye. But then he turned and they were gone.

It was even harder the next dawn to rouse himself and get ready, surrounded by nomads begging Malone to stay and not to die, but he was then caught in an absurd argument with Gumbaz, the hissing nomad in the brown fur hat. If he understood things correctly, the hissing nomad claimed that the donkey that Malone had was his Kyrgyz donkey, and must be changed for a Waki donkey. But this was not going to be possible as the passes were about to be blocked with snow until spring and all donkeys would die and the chain of donkeys between peoples be broken.

Snow had begun to fall as they argued in front of the caravan-serai and the hissing nomad pointed at the flakes and nodded. He pulled the donkey away from Malone.

'OK, then, take your fucking donkey.'

Malone unloaded his pack from the animal and lifted off the saddlebag with his food. He took tape and string out of his pack and with a frame made out of pieces of two sticks, tied the pack and saddlebag to it. He hoisted the frame on his back. It felt like a ton weight and he began to stagger.

Gumbaz, the hissing nomad, still danced in front of him.

'You will stay. There is snow on the pass. You are fool.'

'I am a fool. It is widely known.'

Malone supposed the hissing nomad meant to charge him money.

'You are a biggest fool! You have lost your woman and your goose.'

'I have to get to Fatima.'

'She has not come this way.'

'She has.'

The man smirked at the name and hissed but then quickly backed away. An old woman had come and stood beside them and the hissing nomad hurried back to his yurt without another sound.

The old woman put her hand up to Malone's cheek and smiled.

Her hand was surprisingly soft and warm and then he walked off down the slope and for a while the weather was kind to him.

He tried not to think how many nights in the open were ahead, or of the freezing ice wind. When he turned and took one last glance back before starting on the high path which skirted the mountains there was a dot on the horizon and he was sure the old woman was still watching him. He hoped she wished him well.

The pack was now incredibly heavy and for a moment as he shuffled onto the scree path he wondered about leaving most of his stuff. Two eagles shrieked directly overhead.

Malone steadied himself against a rock and when he closed his eyes he saw a white rushing mist, like from a busted steam pipe. His mouth felt dry and his head was beginning to hurt and all around him the snow was falling and he was concentrating hard.

After a few hours he stopped and put his pack down, completely exhausted and with two-thirds of the day's march still to go. He was sure he was going the right way, travelling west. He reached into his rucksack and opened his water bottle and drank, but he had only half a canteen.

Try as he might he could not force anything else down his throat and so he got shakily to his feet and put his head down. He plodded for several hours before he came to a stream. Normally, he would have gone further up the stream to make sure that there was no rotting corpse of a yak or a mountain goat but every step hurt and each was measured against the limited reserves of his body.

He recalled his father saying that a mujahedin fighter had told him that men who are at their limit had two weeks left before they died.

Malone laughed.

Well, he was at his limit three weeks ago. He drank as much of the water as he could. Still, the very act of swallowing seemed alien to him. He put several sugared peanuts into his sore mouth and managed to chew them and with a great effort swallow. They made him feel sick and in a few more hundred yards he had to stop and run to a rock and pull his pants down. When he looked round, the ground was bloody. He scratched snow over his mess and then walked on, the snow getting deeper.

He had no sleeping bag and had wanted to take one of the padded bedcovers with him on the donkey at Kashch Goz but it had become forgotten in the argument with the hissing nomad. He could not find the *rabot* he recalled, even though the alignment of hills appeared to be the same.

There was only a wall and a shallow cave, which he crawled into and listened to the wind, and the pattering of a large animal which came and went outside in the starlight.

Malone reached out his hand and picked up a sharp stone. He hurled the stone and whatever it was outside padded away on the frosty scree and did not come back.

At the stop for his second night, a *rabot* he stumbled on just off the track and not one he had used on the journey here, he managed to light a fire with dung and brush that filled the stone shelter with smoke and gave off no heat at all. He sat and shivered again almost until dawn.

When Malone woke there was a warm wind blowing and the sky was red and he was surprised to see the snow had gone. He started on the track only to be caught up by two nomads riding yaks and pursued by dogs. He could not understand what they were saying but they gestured for him to turn around and pointed to the sky and made a booming sound. They then hurried on and their dogs ran after them.

'I'm going to get there. I am going to get home,' he said to himself.

The day continued to be warm with low grey clouds, and as he carefully crossed streams he saw birds he did not know the names of picking at the trees. They were brown and white and pink and like a huge robin. He plucked a rose from a tree and tried to put it in his pocket safely to give to Fatima.

'But she's not fucking Fatima!' he shouted to himself.

Malone reached a boulder on a ridge which overlooked the gorge, where the Oxus was in full flow. It was the kind of boulder that tribesmen shot around in stories of the North-West Frontier, like Hamza's endless tape-loop story of the British retreat to Gandamak.

But then Malone's legs went and he dropped to the ground like a stone and for several minutes the sky was filled with bright bees and points of silver light.

He had trouble getting his breath. He just wanted to lie there. To stop it all and lie there, but a voice was telling him to get up. That it was all right. That he was going to make it to the end of his journey.

He struggled to his feet.

'You're going to make it, Malone,' said the female voice. It was Hamza's beautiful wife, Leila, walking beside him, dressed as a 1960s film star in a huge hat. 'We must find a porter to carry your fucking luggage.'

Malone was not in any way sure how he survived the next night, or it may have been three nights. The path changed and the snow came and went but he was heading always west into the setting sun. He did manage to eat small pieces of the nan and the sugared peanuts and raisins but not the fermented yak's milk. He winced. The cramps in his stomach were unbearable and made it almost impossible to sleep. Once he had a spasm in his right leg and for a while by the side of the track thought it was all over. He had not filled his water bottle up at the last spring and his mind was wandering. But the voice had him going again.

'Don't worry, Malone. You are going to get there. It's not far now. You are going to get there.' The voice was happy and now American and he was sure it was Kim, although he saw no figure on the trail. He could see her face now and he was not going to let her down. But then he was not sure at all. Her voice was different.

The day before the Daliz Pass he spent in the black hole of the shepherd's *rabot* by the river, thinking of poor Aziz who they had buried nearby on the mountain. As he looked into the darkness he saw pictures of the journey, of the airstrike, of the Taliban, just as clearly as if they were projected on a screen. Aziz smiled at him and said everything was all right now and he was not scared any more. Without warning thunder started to roll down the valley.

Malone had never before associated thunder with snow but the air was a degree or two warmer. Then, through the door he saw the valley outside lit up in stark black-and-white and after that came an explosion so loud it seemed the mountains were going to crash down on top of him. He crawled to the opening and watched as immense threads of lightning snaked down onto the peaks. When he thought the storm had reached its climax there was another brighter flash and an even greater explosion that reverberated through the earth of the riverbed. There was a smell like struck flint in the air. He eased himself further into the entrance just in time to see the lightning strike a stubby tree towards the river. It burst into flame. There was another strike close by. He went back to where he had been sleeping, by an unsuccessful yak-dung fire. Malone sat there in the darkness shaking like a child.

He could not even weep.

He prayed for his phantoms to join him but there was only the darkness.

On the final day he stumbled weakly outside and the mountains were covered in new snow. He only took a half-step at a time and managed, inch by inch almost, to get onto the corkscrew path that led to the high trail, which would take him up thousands of feet to the pass. He laughed. It was absurd.

He was never going to get there. He was going to die. The nomads were going to find him next spring, picked clean by the vultures, and dump his bones over the side into the river. He never should have agreed to fly Fatima up to Bamiyan. He never should have got involved with that stupid video, and from the very start she was using him . . . But he loved her, how he loved her.

He no longer heard the woman's voice.

All around him were blackened bushes from lightning strikes and places where the shale had slid into the valley below.

He was rounding one bend and there was a cracking noise and the mountain ahead of him began to move and he grabbed onto a thorny bush as the ground beneath Malone crumbled away and he found himself covered with rock and soil that swept down from above with a roaring sound into the valley. There was mud in his mouth and his eyes but he kept still and waited until he was sure the avalanche was over.

Slowly and painfully he disengaged himself from the debris and the mud and wiped it from his face.

Inches from where he was standing the land now fell vertically three hundred feet into the river and the path was gone for a hundred yards. He picked a leaf of the wild rhubarb and wiped his face some more.

'That was a close one,' he said to himself.

Malone then began the painstaking business of retracing his steps and climbing up and around. He had to climb higher and higher on all fours. To get back on the right path took him an hour and he was utterly exhausted.

He stopped and looked at the swirling snow and mist of the mountains. However much it hurt, even if it killed him, Malone realized he loved all this too.

'You're going to make it, Malone. I am with you. Only a bit further now . . .'

The voice had come back!

He reached the high trail and found two sticks and for the next hours he toiled on the traverses and across the rivers and tree-trunk bridges.

The snow was coming down in larger flakes and the path became wilder and then he recognized a stream bed. It was the one where he had met the Taliban.

It all seemed so much bigger, alone.

He turned and saw the awesome black mountains across the river in Pakistan. And all around the snow came down thicker and thicker. He attempted to take a drink from his canteen and eat a few of the peanuts, trying to imagine they were the most delicious steak he had ever tasted.

The trail was all white in front of him now and he was taking a guess with the path. He could easily be walking straight over a precipice but the voice came again.

'Don't give up on yourself, Malone. You're going the right way. For once you are going the right way.'

One of the sticks gave under him.

He threw the other away and staggered, his chin stuck out in front of him. Was this was how it ended, all in white? He had to get the pack off his back. My God, it weighed so much.

Malone took another step that he was sure was going to be his last and then stood perfectly still. There was not a noise around him, everything blanketed by the snow. But he realized something.

He was walking on the level!

He was walking on the flat. He was on the top of the pass! He was on the top of the Daliz Pass and there was no scree under his boots.

Malone inched forward and he recognized the slope of the path ahead between two hills where a raven was picking at carrion. He stumbled forward and then was half sliding down a narrow gully where the snow had fallen on top of scree. The cloud began to lift and the snow became finer and he suddenly saw the incredible valley and the fields of Sarhad below, so neat and so green it was like a dream of paradise.

He halted right there and breathed in and out. He marvelled how far he could see and tears began to course down his cheeks.

Wind picked up the dust across the alluvial plain towards the Pakistan border and it looked like an army of djinns had turned out to greet him.

'Thank you, oh thank you!' he said to whoever had been helping him, speaking those soft words of encouragement in his ear.

Yet it seemed to take Malone the rest of his life to trudge the final painful miles down the slope and into the village. Children were coming home from the school with a big black painted star on its side and everything was being readied for winter, the women returning from the few stands of trees with panniers of logs, brushwood and yak dung they had collected. He gulped in the safe odour of farming.

The smaller children were in new, bright, silver-buttoned waist-coats that marked the end of Ramadan and there were trays of brightly coloured sweets outside several houses. A herdsman pointed at Malone and then ran quickly to the border-police post. The children were dancing around Malone along the track and saying, 'Ameristani! Ameristani!' Malone looked out far across the river plain.

He saw a figure out in the middle of the alluvial plain gazing up at the towering sky.

Malone limped to her fast as his legs would move, as the stones of the river were tinged with the soft pinks and yellows of the evening sun. He thought his feet were going to fall off but he did not care any more. If he reached her and kissed her that would be enough. And then he did.

'Malone!' He knew it was Fatima's voice this time.

Fatima kissed him and kissed him and then kissed him again. She kissed every inch of his sore and blistered face. He had come

to her. He had come from the roof of the world through the mountains of death for her. In the immense valley the sun was setting.

'Oh, Malone, I love you!'

She laughed and they both walked back to the village ringed
with the snow-topped mountains. Malone had come for her and
this was now going to be their home . . . Hamza and his wife were
shaking his hand and Amin Beg was there too, a mischievous look
on his face, and Aziz . . .

But when he woke Fatima was not there and he was in the guest
house. A boy brought him tea and nan and the narcotic honey
which tasted of brandy and a simple note, in green ink, which
contained one word, *Home*.

The boy who brought the tray said the Aga Khan Foundation
birdwatchers, who had photographed a large-billed reed-warbler,
Acrocephalus orinus, possibly the rarest bird in the world, were
coming with a satellite phone. They were happy. The only reason
they might not arrive and help him was if they had already gone
to Pakistan in search of birdwatching fame. Fatima had not travelled this way with Amin Beg, or if she had she had avoided the
village. No one knew for certain about the note. A large party of
Taliban had marched into the village the day they had left and
chased away the border police.

He would have given anything for a few more minutes with
her.

Malone shrugged. Winter was coming and the single-word
message was more than he expected.

Home.

He wondered when the note had been left? He laughed because
that was the start of another story. He wondered wherever she

was, whoever she was, if she was telling his story now. And then he began to croak.

' "We're off to see the Wizard, the wonderful Wizard of Oz."'

The song took all the air out of his lungs. He was gasping for air and he was carried outside where he propped himself against a stone and realized he had done all this for a handful of small kisses.

Those who fussed around him were anxious and Arbob Toshi Boy was shaking his white-haired head. Malone hoped for the birdwatchers and their phone, he waited for Basil to come and cluck over him.

The truth was he had been doing some serious flying and when he blinked he saw Fatima, Hamza, Leila, Amin Beg and Aziz propped against another stone as men were winnowing the chaff from the harvest in the background. 'Fucking *inshallah*, darling . . .' There were men in British army red coats and white pith helmets and young Captain Souter looking longingly at a miniature painting of his sweetheart. There were tribesmen with long rifles and the sad-eyed Akbar Khan standing by Lord Elphinstone in front of a crowd of shirtsleeved bankers from the Twin Towers. Behind them were the endless armies who had fought over the Silk Road from Tamburlaine to Alexander to the Russians. His father was there too, talking about flying, with his mother looking on adoringly, as Judy Garland danced into view with the Cowardly Lion and the Tin Man and the Scarecrow.

Yet here, most important of all, was Fatima, telling him she loved him and making everyone gin and tonics. A pain was growing in his chest. He had busted something back on the trail and they were talking of oedemas. Wherever he had flown he was not coming back that easily but he did not care. He blinked again and the family of stories vanished. But he knew they were going to return, eternally.

The wind blew dust across the white stones of the river plain. Was it the birdwatchers making their way on a camel, or a djinn? Was he going to be rescued? It was on the edge of evening now and the mountains were crowned with gold. He wondered if somewhere Fatima was telling his story and he was taking his place alongside Hamza and the rest.

A shadow fell across his face.

Malone looked up and the barman from the Dead Officers' Club was standing there with a silver tray on which there was a gin and tonic and a pile of small change. The barman smiled and winked.

'You cannot buy a drink in this club unless you're dead. That's the rule. That's the rule, and we keep to the rules. Where is a club without rules? This is Afghanistan, Monsieur!'

And so it is written.